# ANGEL OF DEATH

*By James Anderson*

# ANGEL OF DEATH

## JAMES ANDERSON

A CRIME CLUB BOOK
**Doubleday**
NEW YORK   LONDON   TORONTO   SYDNEY   AUCKLAND

A Crime Club Book
Published by Doubleday, a division of
Bantam Doubleday Dell Publishing Group, Inc.
666 Fifth Avenue, New York, New York 10103

**Doubleday** and the portrayal of a man
with a gun are trademarks of
Doubleday, a division of Bantam Doubleday Dell
Publishing Group, Inc.

Library of Congress Cataloging-in-Publication Data

Anderson, James, 1936–
Angel of death.

"A Crime Club book."
I. Title.
PR6051.N393A78   1989   823'.914   88–30904
ISBN 0-385-24983-7

# ANGEL OF DEATH

# 1

"Let's just say that I'd like to snatch that woolly wig off Mr. Justice Harmon's woolly head and stuff it down his throat."

Detective Chief Superintendent Alec Webster of Scotland Yard was white-faced as he spoke. His words brought a sudden hush to the small group of reporters who had surrounded him on the steps of the Central Criminal Court in London.

After a few seconds one of them said, "Do you really want us to print that, Mr. Webster?"

"Every word."

"Think again, Alec." The speaker was Bill Parker, a senior crime reporter, whom Webster had known for years.

"Want something a little tamer, do you?"

"Yes—for your own sake."

"OK. You asked for a statement. Here it is: I and my colleagues spent nearly two years bringing Johnny Corelli to justice. Now, after a trial lasting almost a fortnight and costing heaven knows how many thousand pounds, he's walked away a free man. I consider that the jury's decision is the worst I've known during twenty-five years in the Metropolitan Police. And I think the judge's summing-up was a disgrace to the British legal profession. Good afternoon, gentlemen."

The next day it was splashed all over the front pages. YARD MAN SLAMS TRIAL JUDGE was a fairly typical headline. Webster read the reports in three papers over his usual breakfast of black coffee and cigarettes. Then he found that, in addition, one of the gossip columnists had picked up his original remark about the wig and the woolly head. Well, he couldn't complain at that: he'd told them to print it.

He sat back and thought. He didn't regret any part of the more formal statement. He'd say the same again. But there could be no pretending the matter was over. Senior police officers just couldn't go round saying things like that about Her Majesty's judges. He'd better get his oar in first. He went to the phone, rang the Yard and left a message to be given to the Assistant Commissioner's secretary when she arrived: Detective Chief Superintendent Webster would be glad of an appointment with the AC at the earliest possible time.

After ringing off, he finished dressing, made his bed, locked the flat, took the lift to the basement garage, and drove to the Yard. When he arrived he found himself the centre of attention. From his colleagues, and especially from his subordinates on the Corelli case, there was general approval for what he'd said; though it was plain that nobody doubted he was in deep trouble. As was his way, he listened to all the comments impassively. He told nobody of the decision he had already made.

He was informed that the AC would see him at 10 A.M. When the time came, he went in feeling calmer than he would ever have imagined he could in these circumstances. "Good morning, sir," he said. "I appreciate your seeing me so promptly."

The AC studied him without speaking for a few seconds. He saw a lean, wiry man, not especially tall, but having an air of quiet power. The face, square-featured, had the hardness of experience around the mouth and around the deep-set grey eyes; though with his unlined skin and thick black hair it didn't seem possible that Webster had been a policeman for twenty-five years.

"I was going to ask you to come, Webster," he said.

"Indeed, sir?"

"Catch any TV or radio news last night?"

"No, I was out all evening."

"So I assumed. I tried several times to ring you. But you must have seen a paper this morning."

"Three, sir. That's what I wanted to talk to you about."

"To tell me you've been misquoted?"

"No; the reports are quite accurate."

"I see. This is a serious matter, you know, Webster."

"That's why I'm here. I've come to hand in my resignation."

"Resignation!" The AC looked startled. "Oh, I don't think there's any need to go as far as that."

"I think there is, sir. I'd prefer to resign than be sacked."

"There's no question of your being sacked."

"Just officially reprimanded, is that it? I know that's the least you can do to me. In addition, I'd be expected to apologize publicly. But I won't accept a reprimand—or apologize. I stand by everything I said—except that bit in the gossip column about the wig. That was silly—but I didn't think they were going to print it. I quite realize, though, that you can't possibly over-look something like this. So all I can do is quit."

The AC said, "I don't want to lose you, Alec. I want you to reconsider.

You will have to make some sort of retraction, of course, but it doesn't have to be too abject."

"I'm sorry, sir, but I can't do it. Frankly, I've been sickened by the whole business. Corelli's one of the biggest villains in London. He's got a finger in every dirty racket imaginable. Every man in the force knows it. So does most of the legal profession, including Corelli's own counsel—and the judge. Yet Harmon lets him get off. He casts doubts on perfectly reliable witnesses, just because one or two of them were nervous, got flustered and contradicted themselves under cross-examination on minor matters. It was Harmon's own treatment of them as much as anything else which made them nervous. You can't really blame the jury so much: they knew nothing about Corelli's background. But even then you'd think they'd have had enough sense to *see* that the man was a crook and the witnesses telling the truth. But no. And so two years' work is down the drain. Corelli's already in Majorca or somewhere, sunning himself and laughing his head off at us—the pigs. In a few months he'll be up to his armpits in the rackets again. Well, I can't start trying to gather evidence and get witnesses all over again. I've had enough. The whole system stinks, and I'm getting out of it."

This, for Webster, was a remarkably long speech, and it seemed rather to take the Assistant Commissioner aback. He said, "I've got a lot of sympathy for you, Alec. I'm sure everybody here has. But we've all had to put up with this sort of thing in our time. We've all arrested villains we've known were guilty, only to see them walk out of court scot-free. It's a most frustrating experience. But it's no reason to throw up a most outstanding career at the age of—how old?"

"Forty-six."

"At the age of forty-six, with further promotion certainly still ahead of you."

"It's a reason for me, sir. I agree when you say we've all experienced it. I have, often. You learn to accept it occasionally—with petty crooks—first offenders. But we shouldn't have to experience it when we're dealing with big-time professional criminals. It's monstrous that it should be so difficult to get a guilty verdict. The rules should be changed. At the very least, if a defendant's had more than a certain number of past convictions, we should be allowed to bring it up in court. Well, I'm news just at the moment. Perhaps my resignation will draw people's attention to the state of affairs."

"Is *that* why you want to quit?"

"No. But maybe that'll be a worthwhile spin-off."

"Look—don't make up your mind immediately. Take a few days off—get away. I'll stall things—"

"Sorry. I have made up my mind. Nothing's going to make me change it now."

The AC looked at him keenly. He'd known Alec Webster long enough to recognize the expression on his face and the tone in his voice. And he knew it would be a waste of time to argue further. He gave a sigh. "I'm very sorry," he said. "Very sorry indeed. You'll be greatly missed."

"But what will you do?" asked Jim Lomax, Webster's best friend in—or out of—the force.

Webster shrugged. "Anything that pays well. I want to get in on the act."

"No ideas at all?"

"None. Got any suggestions?"

Lomax considered. "There are usually openings for security officers going somewhere."

Webster chucked his cigarette stub into the grate. "I can't see why any firm should want an ex-plain-clothes copper for a job like that. External security in any large organization these days means electronics and guard dogs. Internal security is mainly a matter of foiling book-cookers—and the best man for that is an accountant, or at least some ex–Fraud Squad chap. I'd only be of use to a company if, say, one of the typists was dipping her fingers in the petty cash and they didn't know which one. That isn't really my idea of crime-fighting."

"Yet I just can't see you in any other line."

"No more can I."

"You might go private."

"And spend my time shadowing errant wives to illicit rendezvous? No thanks. Oh, don't worry about me. I can manage on my pension well enough. My expenses aren't high."

"Don't tell me you'd be content doing nothing, Alec."

"Perhaps not. Maybe I'll go abroad. There ought to be an opening for my talents somewhere in this great big wonderful world."

"Well, you're certainly lucky that you haven't got any ties in—" He stopped abruptly.

"No wife, you mean, or family?"

"Sorry, Alec. I wasn't thinking."

"Forget it. It's quite true—it probably will be an advantage now."

"Well, your resignation got a lot of publicity. And the AC made it quite clear you were leaving of your own accord, not getting the push. So perhaps you'll get some offers in the post."

"Perhaps," said Webster.

During the next few days Webster did receive a number of invitations for job interviews in the general field he and Lomax had discussed. In addition, there was an offer from a ghost writer of assistance in the preparation of his memoirs; the chance to manage a casino in Brighton; and two thinly veiled proposals of marriage. None of these, however, had a strong appeal. He began to get bored, and started seriously to consider trying his luck overseas.

Then one morning he was alone in his flat when the phone rang. He answered it. "Ex–Detective Chief Superintendent Alec Webster?" asked a highly cultured male voice.

"Speaking."

"Oh, good morning, Mr. Webster. My name is Smithson. I'm speaking on behalf of Mr. George Roussos."

Webster felt his eyebrows going up. *"The* George Roussos? The shipping millionaire?"

"That's correct. Shipping among many other things, of course."

"Of course. Well, well. And what can I do for you, Mr. Smithson?"

"As you may know, Mr. Roussos is in this country at the moment, and he heard with great interest of your remarks at the Old Bailey and your subsequent resignation—with the statement that accompanied it. He would like very much to see you."

"Indeed? May I ask what for?"

"He has a proposition to put to you."

"What sort of proposition?"

"I'm not authorized to divulge any details over the telephone, but I can assure you, Mr. Webster"—he lowered his voice slightly—"that it will be a potentially quite lucrative proposition. Mr. Roussos's propositions always are."

"For him, you mean?"

"No, of course not—" For a second there was the slightest edge of irritation to Mr. Smithson's voice. Then he stopped and said smoothly, "Naturally, his propositions are usually lucrative to him as well; but in this instance, I assure you, he has no eye to personal profit at all."

"You intrigue me," said Webster.

"Good. Can I tell Mr. Roussos then that you are prepared to meet him?"

"I don't see why not. Where and when?"

"I suggest Mr. Roussos's suite here at Claridges. Shall we say this afternoon, around three?"

"Yes, that'll be quite convenient."

"Very well, Mr. Webster. We'll look forward to seeing you then. Goodbye."

Mr. Smithson rang off. Webster put the receiver down and stood staring thoughtfully at the wall for ten seconds. Then he picked up the phone book, looked up the number of Claridges Hotel, dialled it, and asked for Mr. George Roussos's suite.

It seemed to be the same voice that he had just been speaking to which answered. "Mr. Smithson?" Webster asked.

"Yes."

"Alec Webster. You rang me a couple of minutes ago."

"I did. Is something wrong? Can't you come?"

"Oh, I can come. It's not that. I was just checking the call was genuine. I'll be with you at three."

He hung up, lit a cigarette and tried to remember as much as he could about George Roussos.

The one thing everybody knew about the man, of course, was that he was immensely wealthy. He was a Greek, born in the slums of Athens. He had made his first fortune from shipping. To the public he was probably most famous as the owner of a luxurious ocean-going yacht, the *Angel,* on which he entertained lavishly during long Mediterranean and Caribbean cruises. These had become notorious for wild behaviour. He had been married twice, first to an American woman, who had died some years ago, and by whom, Webster seemed to recall, he had a daughter; and about a year previously to an Englishwoman, whose name Webster could not remember. He was certainly among the richest men in the world.

And he wanted to see an out-of-work, middle-aged, ex-policeman. It was an intriguing prospect.

# 2

"Mr. Webster? Do come in. I'm Smithson."

He was just as Webster had pictured him: tall, willowy, elegant; hair for Webster's liking just a little too long. He stood aside, and Webster went into the beautifully appointed sitting-room of George Roussos's suite at Claridges. "Mr. Roussos will be here in a few minutes," Smithson went on.

Webster looked at his watch. "I am a little early."

"Do sit down. Can I get you a drink?"

"Thanks. I'll have a Scotch and water, please." He sank down into a deep armchair and looked around him. "Is Mr. Roussos staying in London long?"

"Just till the end of the week." Smithson brought Webster his drink. "He doesn't stay anywhere very long these days."

"Do you travel with him?"

"Oh, no, I'm based in London. He keeps replicas of me in most of the world's capitals, Mr. Webster. Only the language or the accent changes."

As a piece of self-perception it surprised Webster, and he felt a touch of respect—not for Smithson, but for a man who employed someone with the superficial appearance of a shallow, socially gifted young twit, yet who actually was nothing of the sort. Webster smiled. He said, "You told me you couldn't divulge the details of this proposition over the phone; can you do so now I'm here? Just to prepare me for when Mr. Roussos arrives?"

"No, I'm sorry. I would gladly, but I just don't know. Mr. Roussos simply instructed me to phone you and invite you to call. I was to indicate that it could turn out to be well worth your while."

"I see." Webster sipped his Scotch thoughtfully. "What sort of man is he to work for?" he asked.

"Not easy. But fair, generous—and never dull."

The door was thrown vigorously open from the outside, and Smithson said, "Oh, here is Mr. Roussos."

Webster stood up and turned to face the man who was sweeping (this was the only word that seemed to fit) across the room towards him, beaming and with his right arm outstretched.

"Ah, the great detective!"

George Roussos was about fifty-five and built like an all-in wrestler. He wasn't more than average height, but gave the impression of being half as broad as he was tall. He had very dark eyes, a square face and short-cropped grey hair. He was wearing check, flared trousers and a bright blue, open-necked, short-sleeved shirt that revealed muscular and hairy arms. The hand which gripped Webster's was stubby-fingered and like a vice. "Nice to see you," Roussos said loudly. "Jerry been looking after you?"

"Yes, very well, thank you."

"Good—good. OK, Jerry, clear out now. Go and comb your hair for half an hour."

"Very well, sir. Good-bye, Mr. Webster." Smithson made a silent exit.

Roussos said, "What you drinking?"

"Scotch and water."

"Let me top it up." He made to take Webster's glass.

"No, really, thanks, this is fine."

"Aw, come on, that's a miserable little drop o' juice." He stretched out and his fingers touched Webster's glass. Webster drew it nearer to his chest and his hand tightened on it.

He said quietly, "No thank you, Mr. Roussos. This is all I want."

Roussos looked at him keenly. Then he said, "OK, OK," and turned away. Webster felt he'd won a tiny but somehow significant victory.

Roussos picked up a tumbler and filled it about a third full of Scotch. Then he ambled across the room, kicked off his shoes, took a swig from the glass, and dropped onto the settee, swinging his feet up on to it and putting the glass on the floor. Webster sat down again.

Roussos said, "I read what you said about that beak." He threw back his head and gave a loud guffaw. "I liked that. I don't like beaks, Alec. A beak sent me to the pen for a month once. Know what for?"

"No."

"Knocking off three oranges. I was twelve at the time and in two days I hadn't eaten nothing but a couple of crusts of bread. I suppose I should've been grateful. At least they fed us inside—after a fashion. Now I own one of the biggest orange groves in Greece." He was silent for a moment, then gave another big laugh. "Stuff his woolly wig down his woolly throat. I like that."

Webster didn't correct the quotation. He just said, "I withdrew that part and apologized publicly, you know."

"I know, I know, you had to do that. Didn't make it unsaid, though, did it?"

"I suppose not."

"That bloke Corelli was really guilty, was he? Or did you frame him?"

"I don't frame people, Mr. Roussos."

"Never?"

"Never."

"Ever wanted to?"

"Frequently. But I've never succumbed."

"Why not? Because you thought it'd be wrong—or didn't you have no nerve?"

"Bit of each, I expect."

Roussos nodded vigorously. "Good—I like that. That's an honest answer. And was what you said in the papers true, too—why you're chucking in the job?"

"Yes."

Roussos downed some whisky. "An honest cop," he mused.

Webster found himself puzzled by Roussos's style of speech. It couldn't be described as broken English. On the contrary, Roussos was perfectly fluent and idiomatic in the language, and though his grammar was a little shaky, he clearly had a pretty wide vocabulary. Yet his slang was a strange mixture, and his accent like nothing Webster had ever heard before. However, this wasn't a thing to concern himself with now. He said, "Mr. Roussos, why did you want to see me?"

Roussos flapped a hand. "Don't rush me, Alec. You ain't in no hurry. You're out of work, ain't you? Help yourself to another slug, if you want it, and let's talk a bit. Don't you like having the exclusive attention of the seventeenth richest man in the world?"

"Yes, of course. I was thinking your time would be valuable."

"No you weren't: you're all uptight, wondering what the hell I want you for. That's right, ain't it?"

Webster smiled. "Yes, I suppose so. Sorry."

"What you saying sorry for? I wouldn't think much of you if you weren't in a hurry to know. OK, Alec, I'll tell you. I gotta job for you, if you want it —and you'll be a fool if you don't."

"Well, I guessed that much. What sort of job?"

"One that could be dangerous. That worry you?"

"Depends how dangerous. Tell me more."

"Well, it ain't permanent. It'll last three, six, maybe twelve months at the most—I can't say. But it'll pay well."

"How well?"

"Twice your screw at Scotland Yard. Want me to go on?"

"I'd be a fool to say no at this stage."

"OK, but this is private—between the two of us. Understood?"

"If I'm going to take on a dangerous job, I reserve the right to tell one other person—another police officer—the bare outline of what I'm going to be doing."

"I guess that'll be all right. Well, in short, I want a bodyguard for my daughter."

"You don't want me," Webster said.

"Why not?"

"I'm not qualified. I'm not a sharpshooter. I'm no karate or judo expert. And I'm forty-six years old. Oh, I'm fit enough and I reckon I could handle myself in a rough house. I know how to use a gun. But I'm a detective. I solve—or try to solve—crimes, after they've been committed. I work with my brains. You want a younger man—and one's who's been specially trained in bodyguard duty. An ex–American secret service agent, for example—the kind you see around the President. What's more—"

"Aw, shut up! Listen, will you? Don't tell me what I want. In the first place, no one's threatened to bump her off. What I'm expecting is a kidnapping attempt. Now, to kidnap her, they'll have to get close to her. And as I figure it, it won't be a question of a couple of toughs grabbing her in the street and shoving her into a car. The guys who are planning the snatch are smart—and professionals. They're going to be subtle: to try and con her—or me. So what I want is someone who can spot a crook or any sort of fishy set-up; someone to outwit them. A man who's spent twenty-five years catching crooks will be better at that than a man who's simply been taught how to kill people or knock them out quickly. Besides, I've already got her watched permanently by guys who are quite capable of preventing any straightforward grab. I want a brain. OK?"

"Well, if you put it like that, I suppose—"

"Right. Second, I want someone Irene'll listen to, take orders from. She's the most dam' stubborn girl you can imagine, so the man I take on's gotta have a bit of authority about him. You have. Third, I want a man who knows the faces of as many London crooks as possible. I'll explain why in a minute. So how about it? Will you take on the job?"

"Don't you want to know a bit more about me first?"

"I know all I need to know about you. You were born in Cornwall in 1930, went to grammar school. Did your National Service in the Army. Served in Malaya. Joined the police in 1951, got into plain clothes in less than two years, and not stopped climbing since. You been married once. Your wife left you. No kids. Parents dead. One married sister you spend holidays with sometimes. You live alone in a little apartment in Westminster. You like watching cricket when you get the chance, but you got no hobbies. You been what's known as dedicated. But right now you ain't got a thing to be dedicated to."

Webster said dryly, "You've been busy."

"No. All I had to do was say, 'I want to know all about Webster,' and two days later it was put in my hand."

"What made you pick on me?"

"I saw your picture and I read what you said; I liked both."

"Thanks."

"Well, what about it? Signing up?"

Webster lit a cigarette. "Yes, all right," he said.

"Ain't you going to thank me for offering you the job?"

"No. I reckon you want me more than I want the job. You've warned me that it's dangerous work, that I'll be taking on smart professional villains, and that your daughter's a difficult proposition. I think *you* ought to do the thanking."

Roussos gave his loud laugh again. "I like a man who talks back. OK—to details. You better ask me all you want to know."

Webster said, "I'll have that top-up now, if you don't mind."

"Help yourself."

Webster stood up and helped himself. "Tell me about your daughter, Mr. Roussos. How old is she?"

"Twenty-three."

"Is she here with you in London now?"

"No; she's in Boston with her grandmother. My first wife was American. Irene lives with the old lady most of the time."

"But you don't expect this attempt to take place in the States, or obviously you'd go to an American detective to help you. What makes you think it's going to take place at all?"

"I had a tip-off letter."

"In London?"

"No—from London, but it was sent to me in Athens. Arrived just before I left for England. It was from a broad. Claims to be the girl friend of one of the gang. She don't want him to get mixed up in it—knew he could get life if he got nabbed. So she'd decided to tip me off, so that I'd be able to stop it happening. She said she'd phone me when I got to London. But she ain't yet."

Webster frowned. "I wonder why she went to the trouble of writing to you first. Why didn't she just call you up or write when you got here?"

"I guess she wanted to be sure of being able to get to me and decided to prepare the ground in advance. Or perhaps she wanted to tell her man there and then that she'd already tipped me off—'fore he got any further involved. And maybe he wasn't very pleased, and that's why she ain't been in touch again."

"She didn't give a name, of course?"

"No."

"Sounds to me it could have been a hoax, Mr. Roussos."

"I don't think so. She knew too many details about our plans—things nobody could know unless they'd done a fair bit o' research. And laid out some dough in bribes."

"May I see the letter?"

"Didn't bring it with me. Didn't want to risk losing it. And I figured that if this gang found out the dame had sent it, they might try and get it back. I can get it sent on."

"When are you expecting your daughter to arrive here?"

"Irene's not coming here."

"But you said the job was being supposedly planned by a London mob."

"Yeah, but not *in* London. That's one of the things makes me think the tip-off's genuine. If Irene *was* coming here, and the letter just said she'd be snatched while she was here, then I might go along with it being a hoax. But no. It's being planned for the Caribbean."

"The Caribbean!"

"My wife and me are taking a party of about a dozen people for a cruise on the *Angel,* starting next week. The yacht's berthed in Port of Spain, Trinidad. Irene and her grandmother are joining us there."

Rather dazedly, Webster said, "You want *me* to come along—on a Caribbean cruise?"

"You wouldn't be much use here in London, would you?"

"I'm sorry—I just didn't realize." Webster was trying to collect his thoughts. "I imagined you wanted me to organize protection while Irene was in this country."

"I know what you thought. I didn't want you to take on the job just to get a free cruise."

"Good Lord." Webster didn't know whether to be annoyed or amused.

"Don't you wanta come?"

"Yes, of course I do. But look, you think these villains are planning to go out from Britain to the West Indies especially in order to kidnap her?"

"I only know this broad was able to tell me when Irene's meeting us, that the old lady, Mrs. van Duren, is going to be with her, where they're coming from and when we're sailing. Now that says to me that they're serious and they got some definite plan prepared. Of course, it may be they know now the dame tipped me off and they've scrubbed the whole thing. But I ain't taking no chances."

"Had you made an effort to keep the details of this cruise especially private?"

"I told Haller—my skipper—not to talk about it more than he had to, and to tell the crew the same. The guests agreed to keep fairly quiet about it too. There's going to be some well-known people on board, and we don't want reporters swarming round whenever we put into port. What I mean is, the itinerary's not a state secret, but anyone who wanted to find out would have had to work on it."

"Do you think one of your guests is involved?"

"Could be. The letter suggests it vaguely."

"Anybody specific?"

"No; but it makes sense. Look at it like this: If some punks are planning to snatch Irene, they'll stand a far better chance of pulling it off if they've got a spy on board—someone who can keep them posted about our plans, and about Irene's personal routine, when she's planning to go ashore when we're berthed, who with, and so on. Right?"

"Yes."

"OK. It happens that on this cruise there are gonna be one or two people along that I don't really know all that good. Now: why, of all the cruises Irene's been on with me, should a snatch be planned for this one? It could be the mere fact that one particular person was gonna be on board, and could pass on this inside dope, which gave the crooks the idea for the snatch in the first place. Get me?"

"Yes, I follow. It's a good point."

"On the face of it, it seems crazy to think that any of 'em could be mixed up in anything like that. They're all high up socially—and pretty well off, I'd say. But you can't never tell. So I decided that if the crooks might be planting an undercover agent on board, I'd have one, too."

"So my brief really is to keep an eye on the other guests?"

"Well, part of it is."

"But if it's just a question of someone passing on information, they can do that by means of a letter or phone call whenever we put into port. They wouldn't have to give themselves away. There's not a lot I could do about it."

"I know. But I figured a guy like you might be able to spot a crook straight away, without him doing anything that'd look suspicious to anyone else."

"There's no special sign that marks them out, you know."

"But over the years you must have developed a sort of—of feeling for anyone not quite right."

"I wouldn't be sure of that. But tell me—did any of your guests try to wangle the invitation—fish for it?"

"Not so's you'd notice. But like I said, the crooks might have approached somebody who they already knew was going to be on board."

Webster nodded slowly. He was thinking. After a few seconds he said, "Very well. I'll do what you ask, but I'm not promising anything."

"I don't expect you to."

"You said watching the other passengers was part of my brief. What's the rest?"

"Oh, just to keep your eyes skinned for any face that's known to Scotland Yard. And though I said I didn't really want you as a bodyguard in the usual sense, if the crunch did come I'd expect you to pitch in and do your best to protect her."

"That goes without saying."

"Good. I guess when it comes down to it, what I want mainly is to have a pro around—on my side."

"I understand."

"Now—nobody must be allowed to find out what you really are. And I don't want Irene or her gran or my wife to know until it's really necessary. I didn't tell 'em about the letter and I don't want 'em worried."

"Then I'll have to have a cover."

"I've thought about that. We'll say you're an engineer. You've invented a new device, a stabilizer, say, and I'm thinking of installing it in my fleet. I've already told the wife that's why you were coming here today."

"But I don't know anything about marine engineering."

"That don't matter. None of the others will either. Haller don't talk much, but if he does show any interest, you just say you're legally bound not to talk about it with anyone. If you like, you can say I forbid it."

"Suppose someone recognizes my face? I've had a fair bit of publicity lately, you know."

"Yeah, but only in this country. Nobody who's gonna be on board has been in England during the last couple o' weeks except the wife and me. Claire won't recognize you from those pictures in the papers."

"Sure?"

"Well, we'll find out in a few minutes. She should be home any time now. Your name might strike a chord with her, though, so you'll have to have a new surname. I thought Williams. Suit you?"

"It's as good as any other."

"That's everything settled then."

"How long is this cruise scheduled to last?"

"About a month."

"You said you might want my services for as long as twelve."

"So I might. I'll pay you for a minimum of three months, anyway, whatever happens. But if these crooks try anything during the cruise, and make a hash of it, and you catch 'em, then at the end of the cruise you can go away and do what you like for the rest of the three months. But if nothing happens, or if they try, and blow it but get away, then I'll want you to stay near her for a few more months. From then on the situation's open. I don't wanta have to make up my mind yet about what to do after that."

"Fair enough. Can you tell me the itinerary?"

"North from Port of Spain along the Lesser Antilles—Tobago, Grenada, Barbados, Martinique, St. Kitts, etc., etc.; take our time, drop anchor whenever we feel like. There's scores of other little islands as well, where we might stop off. You can see the openings it might give the crooks. I don't suppose the cops in all those places are quite up to the standard of Scotland Yard."

"Did you think of cancelling the cruise?"

"Course I did. But what good would that do? I'd always have it on my mind that having got the idea, they'd be sure to try sometime. I want to get it over one way or the other."

"So really, you'd be glad if the attempt did take place?"

"I guess so, in a way." Roussos gave a deep chuckle. "Crazy, ain't it: a guy who wants someone to try and kidnap his daughter."

"Tell me about the crew of the *Angel.*"

"What can I tell you? There are about twenty-five, including the kitchen and cabin staff. As far as I know, they're all OK. They get big wages. It's a very nice job. Haller's been skipper for ten years. He was master of one of my tankers before that, but it got too much for him. He earns big money, too, and he'd be a fool to risk losing the job. Still, he might be tempted at the thought of a real fortune in ransom money. Anybody might."

"What it amounts to, then, is that outside your family, there's not going to be a soul on board you know you can trust?"

"Except you."

"Can you give me a run-down on the other passengers?"

"I could, but I won't. I want you to size 'em up yourself."

"But I could check if any of them has got a record."

"I'd rather you didn't. I don't want you prejudicing yourself against anyone in advance. I'd be very surprised if any of them did, anyway."

"You're the boss. About a dozen guests, you said?"

"I meant a dozen passengers altogether, including the family. There'll be you, me, my womenfolk, and seven others."

The door to the corridor opened and a woman came into the room. Webster got to his feet. Roussos stayed where he was, just raised a hand casually, and said: "Hi, sugar. Meet Alec Williams."

Webster's immediate reaction was that the endearment was highly unsuitable. Sugar suggested softness and sweetness, whereas Claire Roussos gave an impression of angular hardness. If George Roussos's shape could be likened to a somewhat misshapen cube, his wife was a narrow, elongated diamond. She was tall and thin and had a narrow face, with high cheekbones and a pointed jaw. She was dressed in a dark, closely fitting suit, which heightened the effect of sharp and jutting shoulders and hips. Her hands were long, with prominent knuckles and wrists. Her face was pale, her eyes a very light blue. It was difficult to judge her age. Forty-eight, forty-nine? With a slight shock, Webster realized that she must once have been very lovely. But now the skin had tightened over her bones, giving a haggard weariness to her appearance. It was an interesting face, but never again would it be described as beautiful.

Webster said, "Good afternoon, Mrs. Roussos."

She was eyeing him up and down appraisingly, as though she was trying to decide whether to buy him. At last she seemed to give moderate approval to what she saw, and held out her hand. "Mr. Williams—now let me see, you're—"

Her husband interrupted, "Alec's the inventor of that new stabilizer I was telling you about, honey. He wants me to equip the whole fleet with it. Thinks I'm made of money, I reckon."

"Well, no doubt you've been trying very hard to convince him that you are, George." She had a rather husky voice and spoke in the unmistakable accent of an upper-class Englishwoman.

Webster said, "I'm confident that in the long term my device would show a profit for Mr. Roussos."

"If he does buy it, Mr. Williams, you can be sure it will."

Roussos chuckled. "How much money you spend today, Claire?"

"Oh, I don't know exactly."

"I'm sure you do, honey. How much?"

She looked hard at him. "George, surely you don't want—"

"Yes, I do. Don't worry: I like you to spend my dough, you know that. So give."

"About nine thousand four hundred pounds." Her voice was cold.

"That's my girl."

"Happy now, George? I'm sure Mr. Williams is suitably impressed." She turned to Webster. "Are you staying for tea, Mr. Williams?"

"Thank you, but I'm afraid I can't."

"Don't be afraid, Mr. Williams. There's really no need. Will you excuse me now? I must go and change. George likes me to wear as many different outfits as possible each day, and I feel a wife has a duty to please her husband in all things, however hard she has to work at it. Good-bye. I hope we meet again."

Roussos said, "Alec's coming on the *Angel,* Claire. Remember I told you I might be asking him?"

A startled look flashed into Claire Roussos's eyes. It was gone in a second, but Webster would have sworn that the information was quite new to her. Nevertheless she said smoothly, "Of course. How stupid of me. *Au revoir,* then, Mr. Williams."

She crossed the room and went out through a door into the bedroom.

Roussos said simply, "She's terrific, my wife. I've never met anyone like her." He swung his feet onto the floor, stood up and spoke more quietly,

"She swallowed the story all right, and she didn't recognize you. So that's OK. Now, anything else you want to ask me?"

"I can't think of anything offhand, Mr. Roussos."

"Well, get in touch if anything occurs to you. We're flying out to Trinidad next Monday. I'll have Smithson let you know take-off time. He'll send a car to take you to the airport. And by the way, better call me George."

Seconds later Webster was in the corridor.

## 3

"You lucky devil!" said Lomax. "What a job to land! Bodyguard to a million-aire's daughter—on a Caribbean cruise—at twice your screw at the Yard! It's the sort of job every copper dreams about."

"I suppose so."

"So—what's the snag? Why aren't you turning somersaults?"

"Well, it's not going to be a sinecure, Jim."

"Do you take this threat seriously, then?"

"I don't know yet. But Roussos does, and though he's crude, he's no fool. And I think he knows more than he's saying."

"Such as?"

"I believe he may have definite grounds for suspecting one of his guests. I think the letter he received just confirmed a suspicion he already held. But he can't cancel this person's invitation, and anyway, being a fair-minded chap, and not absolutely sure, he won't tell me who his suspect is for fear of prejudicing me. He wants me to pick the villain out on my own accord. And that won't be easy."

"All the same, it's still not what you'd call a tough assignment, is it?"

"I'm not sure. I mean, there's nothing improbable about the girl being a target. Quite the contrary—they could demand a ransom of millions for her. And that sort of profit could attract the very smartest villains. They could risk a really big investment: plenty of muscle, guns, boats—helicopters, even."

Lomax rubbed his chin. "I see your point. OK, assuming the worst, got any ideas who might be behind it?"

"A few names sprang to mind, of course." Webster mentioned three. "But I've been asking round today: they're all in town at present, and there's not the slightest hint that any of them are planning to leave the country. You've heard no whispers of a really big job being planned, I suppose?"

"Nothing on this scale."

"The trouble is kidnapping's not a thing anyone specializes in. It's not like bank robbery, say, or protection, where you could make a list of the top twenty villains. Except for political groups, kidnapping's usually a one-off job."

"Which is to your advantage, surely: it means the villains won't be experts in the field."

"True, but I'm not an expert at fighting it, either. And remember this: whatever Roussos says about having men to guard her, *I'm* the hired professional—the ex-Yard man. Basically, her safety will be *my* responsibility. We'll be cruising among remote West Indian islands. Probably sometimes there won't be another policeman within hundreds of miles. I won't have the whole of the Met on call, if the worst does happen."

"I grant all that, but I still say you're worrying too much. Maybe a snatch was planned. But this girl tipped off Roussos. She was supposed to contact him in London. She hasn't done so. As Roussos said to you, that most likely means she told her boy friend what she'd done—and as a result they've cancelled the job. The girl friend's probably picked up a couple of cracked ribs or something, and the affair's over."

"Perhaps you're right. I hope you are. But I can't afford to assume you are. Which is why this trip is not going to be a holiday for me."

Claire Roussos said angrily, "You should have told me you intended to invite another stranger on the cruise."

"Sorry, honey. Didn't think you'd mind. He seems a decent enough guy, quiet and all that."

"That is not the point. We've already got too many outsiders. They won't mix. It could be awkward."

"Bull! Williams'll fit in."

"That's not what I mean."

"But I need to talk to the fellow—and at length. This gadget of his could be a big help. It's important to me."

"More important than being able to relax—talk freely?"

"Oh, the *Angel*'s big enough for that even with another half-dozen people on board."

"Well, I don't like it. I get nervous with too many strangers around."

"Seems to me you get nervous pretty well all the time these days, Claire." She glared. "What do you mean by that?"

"You're all on edge. And you're smoking too much."

"You mind your own bloody business. I'll smoke as much as I like. I've got a lot on my mind. I want this cruise to be a success. I'll be the one who gets the blame if things go wrong."

"Things won't go wrong."

"I'd feel a lot more confident of that if the blasted boat wasn't going to be full of strangers."

*"Full?* Oh, come on!"

"You know what I mean. If we'd stuck to the original plan and just had friends—"

"Whose friends? Some of your lot I don't know too good, remember."

"You know my lot, as you call them, a damn sight better than you know this Williams. You know practically nothing about him. And I don't trust him."

"Honey, he's not going to knock off the silver."

"That is not what I'm worried about."

"He's all right, Claire. I've had him checked out."

"You and your check-outs! How do you know they're reliable?"

"They've never let me down yet."

"There has to be a first time," Claire said.

"Now, Irene," Emily van Duren said firmly, "naturally your father wants you to spend some time with him at least once a year."

"But I don't see why I can't go stay with him and Claire for a couple of weeks later on. I hated the last cruise."

"Well, I can see through *that:* he obviously hopes that the close confines of a ship, with strangers present, will ensure at least the appearance of harmony between you."

"He shouldn't depend on that."

"Irene, I've always supported you in your dispute with your father, but you must keep up appearances."

"Oh, don't worry, Grandmother dear. I shan't scream or throw things. That doesn't mean I have to be the life and soul of the party, though, does it?"

"I shouldn't imagine he expects you to be that."

"I can't understand why you're so keen I should go—when you disapprove of Father so strongly."

"I disapprove of his life style: his drinking and his gambling and his friends—of both sexes. Nevertheless the Scripture is quite plain: 'Children obey your parents.' Your father wants you to go on the cruise; therefore I say that you ought to go. I'm not looking forward to it any more than you are, I assure you."

"Then why do you come? I'm sure it'll be too much for you—and terribly hot."

"I have no intention of letting you go alone. I can well imagine the sort of things that will be going on aboard the *Angel. Angel,* indeed! Even the name is irreverent."

"But your heart—"

"If it's the Lord's will to take me during this cruise, so be it. I know I don't have long in this world, anyway—"

"Oh, Grandmother, please—"

"—but if I die, I shall at least have died doing my duty."

"But I can take care of myself. You don't have to worry about my being seduced to a life of debauchery. Actually, if I wanted to be, I don't see how you could stop me, but in fact, I don't find the prospect at all attractive."

"I know all that. You're too much of your mother's daughter for that. It was Helen who took after George. Besides, I do not for a moment suppose that your father would deliberately lead you astray. I don't doubt he's genuinely fond of you."

"Well, then—"

"Let's say that my mere presence may, if nothing else, serve as a reminder that life aboard the *Angel* is not the norm. Moreover, perhaps working together we can act as a restraining influence on him—as your mother did."

"I wonder how she managed that," Irene said thoughtfully. "And I wonder if he liked it."

"He always seemed perfectly content. They both did. I must admit that it seemed to me, although I opposed it in the first place, a very happy marriage. There's no doubt that it changed him considerably for the better."

"Yet within a year or two of Mother's death he was back to his old ways."

"Perhaps that was a good thing."

"Grandmother! You shock me! What about his immortal soul?"

"Don't mock, Irene. I simply mean that if he hadn't reverted to type, I might never have succeeded in obtaining custody of you and Helen. I'll always be thankful for that—even though she did choose to go back to him as soon as she was old enough. That was no fault of mine. At least, I don't think it was. I—I wasn't too strict with you both, was I?"

"Of course you weren't. I've told you that hundreds of times. It was simply that she wanted different things from me."

"I hope you're not just being kind, my dear. You know, I still think so much about—"

"Don't please; you'll upset yourself."

"Yes, you're quite right. I mustn't dwell on the past."

"Precisely. And that's another reason I don't think you ought to come on the cruise. It'll bring everything back again."

"Perhaps. But I've made up my mind, so that's that. Besides, I must confess that my motives aren't wholly unselfish. I *am* curious."

"About Claire, you mean?"

"Yes, and about the effect she's had on him."

"Do you think she may have become a restraining influence, too?"

"Well, she didn't strike me as being that type on the two occasions we met."

"Nor me. In fact, she seemed altogether a strange sort of person for him to choose. I would have expected him to pick either a motherly, sympathetic type, who'd look after him and be a good listener; or alternatively some sexy little glamour-puss of about twenty. Claire's neither one thing nor the other."

"Well, I can't say I approve of your choice of words, but I know what you mean."

"On the other hand, she certainly seems to have had some influence on the guest-list. I mean, only one film actress, one racing motorist, and one best-selling author. And against that, a UN official, a woman scientist, an attorney, and a marine engineer."

"None of those professions is a guarantee of respectability."

"Ah, but don't forget the clergyman."

"As I said when we received the letter, I do not for one moment believe that George has invited a clergyman on the cruise. That is simply a joke at my expense—'a priest, solely for your benefit, Emily.' That's what he said: typical of his rather crude yet naïve sense of humour."

"Well, I hope it's not a joke and I hope he's a bishop."

"Why a bishop?"

"Because then I can make a note of what he really says to the actress."

"That is not very nice, Irene."

"Sorry. I must have inherited my father's sense of humour. But don't worry: that's the last joke you'll hear from me until this pestilential cruise is over."

The phone buzzed discreetly in Nathan Quine's Manhattan office. He gave a groan and lifted the receiver. "Yep?"

"A call from London, England, for you, sir. Mrs. Claire Roussos."

"Put her through."

There was a pause, then came the familiar, slightly husky, very English voice. "Nathan?"

"Claire, my sweet. How are you?"

"Pretty fit. And you?"

"Tired. Just aching to relax on the deck of the *Angel.*"

"Busy?"

"Not really. I have about twelve letters to dictate, a waiting-room full of clients to see, a meeting with the people who'll be running my political campaign, and then this evening I'm lecturing to a night school law class. Just an ordinary day."

"I'm sorry I asked. Well, I won't keep you a moment. I'm just ringing to confirm everything. You'll be arriving on Monday, as arranged?"

"That's right. Early evening."

"Good. I'm awfully glad you're going to be there, Nathan."

He detected a note of strain in her voice. "Getting a little edgy, my dear?"

"A bit. Basically I am responsible for this cruise. It's my first time as hostess, and I just wish it was only going to be for—well intimates; you know."

"I know."

"As it is, there are going to be far too many people on board whom I hardly know. The old lady disapproves of me, I'm sure. Irene is certain to be difficult. And now George has invited another virtual stranger along."

"Oh? Who's that?"

"A man called Williams. He's a marine engineer. George is thinking of fitting out the fleet with some gadget he's invented. Oh, he's all right, I think. It's just another 'X' factor."

"Now listen, Claire: don't worry. No one is going to blame you if things go wrong."

"Want to bet?"

"Well, no one who matters. And you know you can rely on me for moral support."

"I know that, Nathan, and I do appreciate it."

"Everybody else confirmed?"

"Practically. The Mullers are getting there late Monday night, Philippe and Karin Tuesday morning, and Hilary Orchard Tuesday afternoon. The only person I haven't heard from since we first arranged this do months ago is Lancelot Trent."

"Oh, no doubt he's still up to his neck in crocodiles deep in the South American jungle."

"I only hope he does turn up."

"Lance will show, all right—with some fantastic tale to recount. He always keeps appointments—makes quite a fetish of it."

"I feel better for talking to you, Nathan. How do you always manage to buoy a person up?"

"Professional training, my dear. Part of a lawyer's duty to boost the client's morale."

"Immediately before the judge passes sentence, you mean?"

"Oh, judges never pass sentence on *my* clients, Claire. They just say, 'You are discharged.' "

Claire chuckled. "Good to talk to you, Nathan. See you next week."

"Looking forward to it enormously."

"Wish I could say the same."

"Everything will be just fine."

"Hope so. 'Bye, Nathan."

"So long, Claire."

He hung up and sat back, rubbing his eyes. Strange for Claire to be so uptight; she was usually the most self-confident of people. Of course, it was true that this cruise would be less of a vacation for her than for the rest of them. My, but he was ready for a break himself. He stretched, yawned and pressed the button on his intercom.

"How many clients waiting, Marje?"

"Four, Mr. Quine."

"Who's the first?"

"Charlie Lewjoski."

"OK, roll him in. And tell the other punks to clear off. I can't see 'em today. In fact, better tell 'em I can't handle their cases at all. They'll each have to find another mouthpiece."

"They won't like it, Mr. Quine."

"Then they know what they can do, Marje."

Lancelot Trent, sitting on the bunk in the smelly cabin which he was having to share with the drunken first mate, fortunately now on duty, read through the rough outline he had made for the final chapter of *South American Way.*

It was good stuff, he knew it was: colourful, exciting—and funny. Surely this one would sell well—surely.

But he'd thought that about the last two. And they'd both been frightening flops. Frightening because he was a man in his fifties and writing racy travel books was his only skill; because if this book failed too, he'd been warned that his New York publishers wouldn't take another one. Nor would the book club people. Thank heavens only his agent knew how bad the sales in every country had been. People still thought he was a best-selling author. Everybody believed that everybody else was reading him. For the time being he could hold his head up. If only they knew . . .

So the book *had* to sell well. Then he could chuck the other business. He'd never liked it. But without the cash it brought in, he wouldn't have been able to finance his travels during the last few years. Without travel there would be no more books. And without books there would be no more travel. And he'd be finished. Might as well blow his brains out now and have done with it.

What had gone wrong, anyway? Why had the public stopped buying him? He reached for the draft he had already made of the earlier part of the book, and flicked through the pages. As he did so, despair clutched at him. It was as good as the last book—but it wasn't any *better.* That was the trouble. His books had grown so alike—so samey. When he'd started writing, they'd been original and fresh. But he'd been churning out the same sort of stuff for twenty-five years now, and people were bored. What was it his books lacked? Well, love interest, of course. He'd been told before now that he ought to recount a few amorous adventures. ("Never mind if they're true or not, old boy; who's going to know?") But he couldn't do that. No, that was a thing he could never write about. A man could only write one way. The cobbler should stick to his last. To try anything new at his time of life would be a recipe for disaster.

Thinking it over, though, even that last chapter wasn't up to much really. It wasn't *bad*. But it was a tame ending for the book—just sneaking out of the country like that. He needed a climax. Perhaps he could do something about it on the *Angel*. Re-arrange the chapters. That might help. He ought to be able to work on board a ship like that, with every luxury and no distraction. Bit of a change from this stinking old tub. Yes—he could make the book all right; he was sure of it. And then when it was published, and a big success, all his worries would be over.

All the same, he wished he did have a better climax for it.

## 4

The first thing that had struck Webster had been the brightness. Now, as he stood leaning on the rail of the upper sun deck of the *Angel,* berthed at the quayside in Port of Spain, it was almost painful to the eyes: the multitude of vividly coloured sails, shirts and dresses; the brilliant white hulls and funnels; the intense cloudless blue of the sky; all seeming almost to be given an inner light by the impossibly huge and hot sun.

At this particular moment, however, it was none of this which was engaging his attention. His eyes were fixed on the big, open, luggage-laden car which had just drawn up near the gangplank on the quayside; and on the two occupants of it. One was an old lady: small, white-haired, and wearing a determined expression and a light grey linen dress. The other was—could it be a young girl? Yes, it was; but he could be forgiven for having momentarily thought that he was looking at a particularly unattractive middle-aged woman, who had grown exceptionally careless of her appearance. She was plump, wore glasses with thick black rims that would have been suitable for an old man, and not a scrap of make-up. Her skin was pallid. Her brown hair hung straight and lank and had apparently been hacked carelessly off round the nape of her neck. She was wearing a long, shapeless black dress, which even to Webster's un-fashion-conscious eyes looked about five years out of date. And as she alighted from the car he could see she was shod in stout, low-heeled brown leather walking shoes and thick woollen stockings. Her face was fixed in a scowl.

So this was his charge: Irene Roussos, heiress. Webster's immediate reaction was that if she were his daughter, any kidnappers would have been welcome to her.

Irene assisted the old lady from the car. Then they began slowly climbing the gangplank. As they did so, Roussos appeared on the main deck and stood waiting for them.

"Hi, there," he called.

The old lady looked up. "Good afternoon, George." Irene kept her eyes downwards. There were no smiles or waves. When they arrived on deck, the old lady presented a stiff cheek for Roussos to kiss. Irene did not even do that, and Roussos had to work hard to reach her cheek with his. Then all three disappeared from Webster's sight. Two crewmen started down the gangplank to fetch the luggage from the car. Webster raised his eyebrows to nobody in particular, turned away from the rail and made his way down to the bar. In the welcome shade and coolness he sipped a lager and lime, smoked a cigarette and wondered just what he ought to do next.

It was late afternoon on the Monday following his interview at Claridges. He had accompanied the Roussoses from London in a private jet, and after landing at Trinidad, they had been driven straight to the *Angel*'s berth. Webster had unpacked and stowed his things away in his superbly appointed stateroom and had spent the next couple of hours getting a thorough knowledge of the layout of the ship. He would have liked to have had a look around Port of Spain, which he might never have another chance to see; but it was important to remember that he was on duty, not on vacation. It was possible that an exact knowledge of his surroundings might prove valuable before the voyage was over, and he preferred to obtain this before the other guests arrived and became suspicious of his snooping.

The *Angel*'s design was fairly conventional. The upper or bridge deck contained the wheelhouse and chart room, a small central sun deck and, aft of this, the Roussoses' private suite, consisting of sitting-room, bedroom and bathroom. On the main deck, below, was the big deck building. This housed a superbly equipped galley, aft; the dining saloon; Roussos's private study; a card room, a library-cum-writing room; and the main saloon. Forward of the deck building was the pool. The lower deck contained the guests' staterooms aft; the engines and radio room amidships; and the crew space forward. The staterooms could be reached by either of two flights of stairs—one inside the deck building, the other outside, near the stern. Corresponding stairs, leading to the crew's quarters and engine room, were situated to port and slightly forward of the deck building.

Webster met Captain Haller, an elderly, taciturn man of indeterminate nationality, who, it seemed, chose to mix as little as possible with Roussos and his guests. Fortunately, in view of Webster's supposed profession, Haller spoke little English.

The other passengers were scheduled to arrive during the next twenty-four hours, and Roussos was hoping to sail on the following afternoon.

Webster finished his drink, wandered out on deck—and immediately encountered his charge. Irene had made the one concession to her surroundings of removing her stockings and shoes and putting on a pair of sandals, and was sitting on a deckchair, moodily drinking a glass of orange juice. She looked up as Webster approached and her frown deepened.

"Who are you?" she asked.

"Alec Williams."

"Oh yes, the inventor. He told me you were on board. Sit down." She spoke with an educated New England accent.

Webster took the chair next to hers.

She carried on sipping her drink without looking at him for a few seconds before asking, "Are you famous or something?"

"Not especially."

"Then what do you have to offer?"

"A stabilizer. But I can't talk about it."

"I don't want to talk about the crumby thing. I mean, you're not on board because of that. If everybody who wanted to sell him something came on the cruise, we'd sink. No, only the rich, or the well-born, or the famous, normally get invited aboard the *Angel*. I was wondering which you were."

"None of those things."

"You haven't had your name in the papers lately?"

"Not that I know of," Webster said, after only a fractional pause.

"Sure? Because that's the best qualification: to have been written about in the gossip columns or talked about in society. He longs to be a full member of the international jet set. Do you know who his hero always was, before he died?"

"No."

"Aristotle Onassis. Father tried to ape him for years."

"Really?"

"Yes. Can't you see the superficial resemblances? Multimillionaire Greek ship owner, with smart second wife, some years younger than himself, daughter by first marriage, luxury yacht. Trouble is, he's no Ari, Claire's no Jackie, I'm no Tina, and the *Angel*'s no *Christina*. We're all sort of rather second-rate copies of the real thing. Even the guests he has on board are normally only minor-leaguers in the gossip column rankings."

All this was appallingly offensive—or would have been had Webster really been a guest of her father. He looked at her closely, to see if she were joking. But her face was set in an emotionless mask. Her voice and manner had been like those of a lecturer describing the habits of a type of primitive tribesman.

In a light tone, he said, "Ah well, perhaps he sees potential in me—and recognizes that one day I'll be world famous."

She gave a grunt. "Do you know who the others are going to be?"

"No; do you?"

"Yes, he wrote. Nobody you'd cross the road to meet. Some attorney who wants to be President, and a British explorer, and a French race driver and his Swedish girl friend, who's an actress, and a Swiss UN man and his scientist wife. Oh, and some sort of priest."

"Sounds quite an interesting crowd to me."

"Wait till you've met them!"

"Why didn't you invite some friends of your own, if you feel like that?"

"I wouldn't be friends with anyone who'd want to come."

"You sound like Groucho Marx."

"What do you mean?"

"He said, 'I wouldn't want to join any club which would have me as a member.'"

She didn't smile, just said seriously, "I know what he meant. It's so nauseating, too, when you think of all the people who'd really benefit from a cruise like this."

"If you feel like that, why on earth did you come?"

"One doesn't disobey a royal command—not in this family. Besides, it annoys him more to have me aboard than if I defied him."

With the same sense of slight surprise that he'd experienced when first realizing that Claire had once been good-looking, Webster saw that Irene could, if she wished, be so now. Her features were first-class, and her eyes in particular lovely. She was pasty-faced, but that would quickly pass. She was plump, but not excessively so, and it could have been a pretty plumpness.

"Is that why you make yourself look such a frightful mess?" he asked her suddenly, "to annoy him?"

He had the satisfaction of seeing her face momentarily register anger. Then it went blank again.

"You're very rude, aren't you, Mr. Williams?"

"You're not, I suppose?"

"I can afford to be. My father's the seventeenth richest man in the world, as I'm sure he's told you."

"And you hate him."

"No. I pity him. I resent things he's done. But I'm not all that interested in him."

"Do you always talk like this about him to people you've only known a few minutes?"

"Not always. But quite often."

"I'd say you hate him," Webster replied.

It was two hours later when the next passenger arrived. Webster had just changed into the new white tuxedo he'd had to purchase, and was alone on the main deck enjoying the dimmer light of evening, when a taxi came along the quayside and stopped. A man carrying a small suitcase got out, paid the driver then ran briskly up the gangplank. On reaching the deck he looked round, saw Webster and strode across to him, hand outstretched. "Nathan Quine," he said. He was short, stocky, with grizzled sandy hair and a pugnacious chin. He could have been anything between forty and fifty years old.

Webster thought, The attorney who wants to be President. Aloud he said, "Alec Williams."

"Glad to know you. George or Claire around?"

"Dressing for dinner, I believe."

"My tux is somewhere in the bottom of my cabin trunk. You wouldn't know if it's arrived, I suppose?"

"No, I wouldn't; sorry." He looked along the deck. "Here's Dimitri coming. He'll be able to tell you."

Dimitri was the chief steward, a small, sad-eyed man, who had been with Roussos in one capacity or another for about thirty years. It appeared that Quine's luggage had arrived and been unpacked. He'd been put in the stateroom next to Webster's.

"I'll show Mr. Quine the way down," Webster offered. He was glad of something to do, and besides, wanted to get to know all the other passengers as quickly as possible.

They went down to the accommodation deck. Webster said, "This is yours, I think," and opened a door.

Quine went in. "My, my," he said, "this is beautiful."

Webster followed him. The lay-out of the room was identical with his own, but the predominant colour here was grey, whereas in his own it was blue. "Your first voyage on the *Angel?*" he asked.

"Yes."

"Me too. It's going to be an experience."

"Stay a while if you've nothing to do," Quine said. "Put me wise to the set-up here. Who else has arrived?"

"Only the Roussos family, plus old Mrs. van Duren."

"Ah, I've heard of her. Quite a *femme formidable,* they tell me. Very religious."

"I wouldn't know. I haven't met her myself yet. She's been resting in her room since she arrived."

"You're not an old family friend, then?" Quine had removed his coat and shirt and had started washing his hands and face vigorously at the basin.

"No, I only met them recently in London. What about you?"

"I haven't known George long. Claire I've known for years. Her first husband was an old buddy of mine. He was English, of course, like you. Quite a big noise in his own field in London."

"Oh, what was his name?"

"Pete Ferris. Owned several night clubs and gaming joints."

"I've heard of him," Webster said. Ferris, he remembered, had had a good reputation in a sphere of activity that threw up its fair share of villains. "He died a few years back, didn't he?"

"About four. Great guy. Chuck me that towel, will you?"

Webster did so. He said, "Do you know who else is expected?"

"Well, there's Paul and Maria Muller."

"He's the UN official?"

"That's right. Swiss. We run across each other in New York from time to time. Maria was Maria Epstein, you know, the scientist. You've probably heard of her, too."

"I can't say I have."

"Tragic history. One of the most brilliant research chemists in Europe before the war, they tell me. Now she's making cosmetics."

"Is that so?"

"Yes, runs a little manufacturing firm near Hamburg. Has a house next to the works. Oh, you'll hear her whole story before the cruise is over, I'm sure. She told me the first time we met—said she was sure I'd be sympathetic, as both being Jewish we had much in common. Funny thing is, I'm not! But I didn't let on—it was worth hearing. Surprising marriage, though. No one thought Paul would ever give up his freedom. Great life he had: looks, charm, luxury apartment in Geneva, world travel on a diplomatic passport, all expenses paid, and a girl at every airport. And then one day he marries Maria, gives up his home in Switzerland, and moves in with her. Ah well, who can say where Cupid's dart will strike next, eh?"

One thing was already becoming clear: Quine was a gossip. And as such he was going to be a useful person to cultivate. "There's an actress coming, too, isn't there?" Webster asked.

"*An* actress? You'd better believe it: Karin Johnson, no less!"

"Karin Johnson? Is she very well known?"

Quine stopped short in the act of buttoning his dress shirt. "You're kidding?"

"No."

"She's *the* young actress of the moment. The hottest property to come out of Sweden since Ingrid Bergman. She got an Oscar nomination for *Yesterday's Woman*. That was her second Hollywood movie."

"I believe I have heard of her, now you remind me."

"He believes he's heard of Karin Johnson! What have you been doing with yourself for the last twelve months, pal? In a monastery? Or are you just not interested in movies?"

"I used to be at one time. But I've lost touch lately. Too busy. I just watch the old ones on television when I get a chance."

"I see. What is it that keeps you so busy?"

"I'm a marine engineer." Then before Quine could ask any questions, he said, "Karin Johnson's coming with a Frenchman, isn't she—a racing motorist?"

"Yes, Philippe Barrault. Le Mans winner. Not to mention top skier—

French international—mountain climber, tennis player, etcetera, etcetera. Life's unfair, you know. Who can compete with a guy like that? Karin and him are George's real catch for this cruise, of course. If we make the society pages it'll be they who'll put us there."

"Do you want to make the society pages?"

Quine carefully attached a clip-on bow tie. "I'm not sure. Difficult to say how good that sort of publicity is for the image."

"You have political ambitions, I believe."

Quine shrugged. "Well . . ."

"Eye on the White House?"

"White House? You've got to be kidding! No—I hope, with luck, to get into the Senate in a couple of years. That's the height of my ambition."

There was a knock on the door and Roussos entered. After somewhat formal preliminary greetings, Quine asked, "Is anyone else arriving tonight?"

"The Mullers."

"What about Karin Johnson—and Philippe?"

"Tomorrow morning. Lancelot Trent may be arriving tonight."

Webster said, "The travel writer?"

Roussos nodded. "That's him. Do you know him, Alec?"

"No, but I'll enjoy meeting him. I've read several of his books. He's quite a character by all accounts."

"Oh, he is," Quine said, putting on his tuxedo. "They call him the last of the mad Englishmen, you know."

"Yeah—how'd he get a nickname like that?" Roussos asked.

"Oh, he's supposed to have been to nearly every country in the world and done practically everything. He's walked across the Gobi Desert alone, lived with the Eskimos and wrestled a polar bear; been made the blood brother of a New Guinea cannibal chief—after just avoiding being eaten himself; fought a duel with a Spanish nobleman; been married to a Persian princess; won a horserace against Mongolian tribesmen; all of it wearing a monocle and an Old Etonian tie."

"I wonder how much of that's true," Roussos said.

Quine shrugged. "I wouldn't know."

Webster said, "There are photos that seem to back up most of his yarns."

"Well, he'll be an interesting guy to have along, anyway," Roussos said. "Now let's go get a drink before we eat."

# 5

The main saloon was about thirty feet long by twenty wide and was the social centre of the yacht. As Roussos, Quine and Webster entered through the forward door, a Steinway grand piano occupied the corner to their right. Next to it was a comprehensively equipped recessed bar, with tiled walls, separated from the room by two small, semi-circular counters, a space between them being just wide enough to pass through. The bar was now manned by a young, white-coated steward. Behind the bar was a tiny galley, which contained storage space for glasses and crockery, a sink with hot and cold taps, a refrigerator and an electric kettle. Glasses and cups could be washed here, and coffee prepared, saving the considerable walk to the main galley. A door from this small galley opened on to a short passage, which led from the main passageway to the port side of the deck.

The wall of the room opposite the bar was dominated by a big open fireplace surmounted by a large mirror. Deep settees and easy chairs were dotted about the room, together with small occasional tables. A quadrophonic stereo system and a huge television set connected to a video recorder, equipped with a large library of tapes, were at the far end. However, it was the colour scheme that really hit the eye. The floor was covered by deep, wall-to-wall carpeting of purist white. The walls were white and so were the curtains. But there was no lack of colour. Half a dozen abstract paintings in strong bright colours adorned the walls; gay cushions were on each chair; and there were many bowls of richly coloured flowers. It was a striking room, showing a highly original taste.

"What do you think of it?" Roussos asked.

"Charming," Quine said.

"Frances, my first wife, designed it years ago. I've never changed the colour scheme, just replaced things with replicas when they get old. Claire wants to re-do it. Suppose I'll let her. See that painting at the far end? How much?" He glanced from one to the other.

Quine said, "I really wouldn't have an idea."

"Nor me," said Webster.

"Eighty thousand bucks in New York. I forget the artist—you'll see the signature at the bottom. And the yellow thing on the side wall cost twenty-five thousand quid in London. They tell me they've both appreciated since I bought them. Not that it'd matter to me if they turned out to be valueless. Money just don't count with me these days. I said to Claire what I said to Frances, 'Get what you like. Just make sure it's the best. In the long run it pays.' This carpet cost three thousand bucks, you know."

"I've frequently told George that he ought to put a tag on everything, saying exactly what it cost."

It was Claire who spoke as she came into the room, accompanied by Mrs. van Duren and Irene.

Roussos gave a guffaw. "Trouble'd be, folks might start making us offers for things."

"I'd have thought you'd enjoy that, George. And think how you'd save your voice, not having to tell people the price of everything. Though, on second thoughts, you wouldn't want to save it, would you?"

"Not me, sugar. I like the sound of it. And my guests better like it, too, or they know what they can do."

Through these exchanges Irene was standing silent and poker-faced. She had still done nothing to either her face or hair and wore not a single jewel. She had deigned to change into an evening dress, but it was a drab, off-white affair that looked dated, a size too large for her—and even a little dirty. Webster saw Roussos frown as he caught sight of her. She was certainly a striking contrast to her stepmother, who had on a dark red gown and a brilliant ruby necklace.

Mrs. van Duren had come in on Claire's arm. In the other hand she was carrying a walking-stick, holding it as though, given the least excuse, she was prepared to use it on anyone standing within reach. Everything about her—her back, her mouth, the fingers with which she shook hands—seemed to Webster to be as hard and unbending as that stick.

She fixed small and very bright eyes on him as Roussos performed introductions, and said, "Williams, eh? Welsh?"

"No, ma'am—at least, not for several generations."

"What do you do? Anything? Or do you just loaf?"

"I'm a marine engineer."

"You don't look it."

"Oh? And what do marine engineers look like?"

"Engineers mostly look as if they're used to dealing with *things*—things they can control and whose actions they can predict. You look as if you're more accustomed to dealing with people—like a minister or a lawyer or a politician is. You weigh people up. Scientists and technical people usually don't. Think that's crazy, do you?"

"No, I think it's an interesting theory."

"That's a cowardly sort of word—'interesting.' You can call any crackpot

—or wicked—idea 'interesting.' Saves you having to say if you think it's true or not."

"I don't know whether I think it's true. But I promise you I'll work on it for a while. I'll try and watch people watching people, and then in a year or so I'll write and let you know whether I think it's a crackpot idea or not. How about that? By the way, does it apply to women, too?"

"Shouldn't think so. Women always weigh everybody up. Not that I've met many women engineers. What am I talking about? I haven't met any. Don't rely on my being around in a year's time though. I have a weak heart —or a cardiac condition, as everyone insists on calling it."

"I'm sorry."

"Oh, don't be. I've had a good run. Well, I must say you seem a cut above the general run of people George gets on this sin-ship."

"I get the impression you don't altogether approve of your son-in-law?" It wasn't the sort of thing one normally said to a woman within five minutes of meeting her, especially when the man in question was your host—and employer. But it seemed that a blunt unconventionality might be the most effective policy with Mrs. van Duren.

"He isn't my son-in-law any more. He's my granddaughter's father. That's why I'm here. Somebody has to look out for her moral welfare." Her face hardened. "There's been a lot of wickedness on this boat in the past, Mr. Williams. And I don't suppose it's over yet. One day punishment will be meted out—perhaps sooner than anyone expects."

A couple of minutes later Dimitri appeared in the doorway and intoned, "Dinner is served, madam."

Roussos clapped his hands. "Ah, great—chow. Let's go and dig in. Honey," he said to Claire, "you gotta eat more this trip. You're getting too skinny. I want to see some more meat on you." And passing behind her so that she could take his arm, he gave her a friendly slap, the sound of which seemed to echo round the room."

Claire gave a tight-lipped smile. "You're so considerate, George. I'm sure our guests find it quite touching."

Quine offered his arm to Irene, and it was left to Webster to escort Mrs. van Duren. They made their way aft, along the central passageway. On their right they passed first a short passage leading to the deck, off which opened the back door of the small galley; then Roussos's private study; and finally stairs up and down to the bridge and accommodation decks respectively. On their left were first the library; next the card room; and lastly a door leading to the starboard side of the deck.

At the end of the passageway was the imposing dining saloon. This was panelled in light wood, with engravings of the ships of the Roussos fleet around the walls. A big, highly polished table was in the centre of the room.

It was candle-lit and laid with silver and cut-glass tableware. They took their places. The table was really too big for the six of them, as it gave no chance to conduct a private conversation. If one's neighbour was to hear, it was necessary to speak loud enough for everybody else to do so too.

Roussos spent the first few minutes announcing what everything on the table had cost. But once the food was served he concentrated on it and fell silent. The menu was not at all elaborate or exotic, but for six people there was an enormously wide range of superbly cooked dishes: fish, roasts, steaks, chops, cold meats and salads with wines to match. Roussos ate voraciously. He started off with some highly flavoured Greek vegetable soup, which the others bypassed in favour of fruit juice or *hors d'oeuvres*. He followed this up with two enormous steaks, accompanied by french fried potatoes and green vegetables. He grinned at Webster. "I got a taste for chips on my first British ship. Hey, that rhymes. I'm a poet." He almost literally washed down his food with glass after glass of vintage claret from a private bottle. Afterwards there was a choice of a rich sticky gateau, ice cream, or fruit. Roussos had some of each, together with a half bottle of sweet sauterne.

With Roussos almost fully occupied in eating, and Irene not even trying to be sociable, conversation during the meal was largely left to Claire, Quine and Webster, with occasional interjections from Mrs. van Duren.

"Won any good cases lately, Nathan?" Claire asked.

"Of course. I win all my cases, Claire, my sweet; you know that. If I'm not sure I can win, I don't take them on."

"You haven't by any chance had an innocent client since I saw you last?"

"I doubt it, my dear. What would be the fun in that? Any fool can get an innocent man off."

Webster said, "You seriously mean that all the people you defend are guilty?"

"Ah, I didn't say that, buddy. Not being innocent's quite different from being guilty. To be guilty you have to be proven guilty. My clients don't start out innocent. But they do end up not guilty." He chuckled.

The Corelli case was still painfully fresh in Webster's mind, and he found himself getting irritated. "You're happy with that state of affairs, are you?" he asked.

"With my clients continuing to get off? You bet your sweet—sweet life I am."

"It doesn't worry you that because of you, dangerous criminals are walking around the streets?"

"It would worry me more if they were in the slammer after I'd defended them."

"What about the police, who spend months, perhaps years bringing a man to trial?"

"They shouldn't bring him to trial—or the DA shouldn't in the States, or the DPP in England shouldn't—unless they can prove him guilty. I'm all against these try-on cases. Somebody says, 'Let's put it to a jury and see what happens.' Well, when I'm defending, nothing happens."

"But if you didn't stand up in court, when you know your man's guilty, and swear that he's not—"

"I don't do that."

"Then what do you say?"

"I say, 'Members of the jury, the evidence against my client is woefully inadequate. He swears he was in Sacramento at the time this crime was committed in New York City. Witnesses have supported that claim and the prosecution has utterly failed to break his alibi. No jury in the world ought to convict a dog on this kind of evidence.' And that, my friend, is quite true. Let the cops break the alibi before the case comes to court and they'll get their convictions."

"How can you expect the police to break a false alibi when the villain probably laid out a couple of thousand setting it up?"

"You seem to feel strongly on the subject, Mr. Williams," Claire said.

"Well, I've got a cousin in the police. He tells me about his cases. I've come to realize just how unjust the whole business is."

"Well, don't look to lawyers to make it just," Quine said. "Look to government. I'm just an advocate—a sort of actor, if you like—just like the guy who's prosecuting is. I'm not concerned with justice. I'm concerned with winning. And that's how it has to be—or no one will ever get the best defence."

Claire was shaking her head in mock amazement. "This has been remarkable: a serious, ethical discussion on the *Angel*. Wonders will never cease. She won't ever be the same ship again. But please don't take it too far, or you'll frighten my husband."

Roussos just grinned.

After dinner they returned to the main saloon for coffee and liqueurs. It was while these were being served that Paul and Maria Muller arrived.

Paul Muller was almost too distinguished-looking. He was about fifty, faultlessly attired, with iron-grey hair, a small moustache and horn-rimmed glasses. He spoke perfect English in a deep voice. Maria Muller looked several years older than her husband. She was a square, stocky woman, dark-skinned, rather flat-featured and expressionless.

Claire greeted them with greater warmth than she had yet shown. "Darling," she said as she kissed Maria, "you're looking wonderful. It's lovely to see you. I've got absolutely heaps of things to tell you."

"How are you, Claire? You are looking very well."

"Oh, I'm fine, Maria." She turned to Muller. "Paul—handsome as ever. And I suppose just as charming."

"One tries, my dear. And it's not hard to be charming to you." He kissed her hand, then straightened up. "Roussos—how are you. Good to see you again. You remember my wife?"

Roussos shook hands with them both. He said, "Come and meet my daughter and her grandmother. And Alec Williams. You know Nathan Quine."

Muller's manner as the introductions were performed was of someone greeting for the first time people he had been longing all his life to know. His wife was much less effusive. She spoke very quietly, mostly in monosyllables. Then she stood back, listening to Paul making small-talk, her attitude like someone waiting to be interviewed for a job she didn't really care whether she obtained or not.

The Mullers, it seemed, had dined on the plane, and refused food. But Paul accepted a cognac and Maria a coffee. After about a quarter of an hour the party started to break up. Mrs. van Duren said she was tired and went to her room, Irene accompanying her. The Mullers made the same excuse and left a minute or so later, Claire going with them to show them to their stateroom. Roussos, Quine and Webster remained chatting. Ten minutes later Dimitri entered and announced the arrival of Lancelot Trent.

Trent was tall, thin and bald. He had a large hooked nose and a bristling military moustache, presumably a legacy of his days as a regular army officer. The famous monocle was screwed into his left eye. He was wearing grubby cotton trousers, held up (Webster peered closely—yes, the legend was true) by an Old Etonian tie. With them he wore an open-neck khaki shirt, and a bush jacket. He was carrying a duffel bag. He shook hands all round. "Terribly sorry to be late, my dear chap," he said to Roussos. "Fact is, I've just got off the most bally awful old Portugese tramp you can imagine. I got held up by a little misunderstanding with the rozzers in a certain banana republic. I didn't have enough of the spondulics for the air fare, and the beastly little tub was the only thing that gave me a dog's chance of getting here in time."

"Where's your luggage?" Roussos asked.

"Here." Trent waved the duffel bag.

"Is that all?"

"Every blooming thing. I'll have to buy some togs tomorrow morning—if you can lend me a few quid—just to tide me over until I can arrange to pick up some cash at a bank somewhere en route."

"Yes, of course."

"Thanks. By the way, is there a typewriter around I could have in my room?"

"Sure, you can have the one from my study. I won't be using it."

"Appreciate it."

"What do you want to eat?"

"Oh, any odd scraps from the pig bin. Could do with a Scotch and soda, though. What I really want is a hot bath."

When Trent was eventually settled with a couple of ham sandwiches and whisky, Webster asked, "What exactly was this trouble with the police you mentioned?"

"Long story. They've been having a spot of bother there with a gang of—well, what? Freedom fighters? Murdering terrorists? Resistance workers? Or just good old fashioned bandits? Take your choice. They're all the same to me. I've been living with these johnnies for a month or so. First outsider to contact them at all. They nearly shot me, as a matter of fact—actually had me tied to a tree when I mentioned I was the chum of a fellow they hold in pretty high esteem. No names, no pack drill. Well, after that they treated me like a longlost brother. Last week I said goodby-ee to them and toddled off down to the capital city. I booked in at a hotel and then cabled my New York agent to tell him what I'd been doing, and approximately when my book'll be ready. Few hours later, had a visit from the constabulary. They had a copy of the cable and accused me of being in cahoots with the rebels and plotting to overthrow the government. Gave me a rather unpleasant working over and locked me up. Next day, I got the inspector alone and convinced him— at the cost of the local equivalent of about a hundred and thirty quid—that I was as innocent as a moderately new-born babe. That accounts for my state of temporary stoniness, by the way. He let me go, but he advised me to get out of town before the secret police arrived. I hared it straight down to the docks. I just had enough to pay for my passage here. The rest, as they say, is history." Trent drained his glass.

Webster glanced at the other two listeners. Roussos looked as though he were hanging on Trent's every word. Quine appeared non-committal. Webster himself wasn't sure how to take the yarn. He'd spent a good part of his life listening to unlikely stories, and thought he'd become pretty adept at spotting the false ones. But on this occasion he couldn't do it—no doubt because he wasn't able to ask the kind of searching questions he'd normally put. Trent's whole persona—the dated schoolboy slang, the playing down of what, if genuine, must have been alarming experiences—gave the impression of being phoney. On the other hand, if Trent were a sham, he'd fooled thousands of readers for many years. Normally, of course, it wouldn't matter in the least either way. But Webster was on board the *Angel* for a purpose. Roussos thought one of his guests might be involved in the kidnapping plot. And if Lancelot Trent was a blatant and habitual liar, Webster couldn't afford to assume that he was merely a harmless braggart.

Paul Muller lowered himself luxuriously onto the bed.

"Magnificent," he said, speaking in German. "I have slept in the world's best hotels, and never have I had a more comfortable bed than this."

His wife, who was desultorily examining the stateroom's fittings, answered without turning. "The only drawback being the identity of your room mate."

"Oh, don't say that, Maria."

"Won't you find it monotonous to share with me and no one else for the whole cruise?"

"I think not. There will be many compensations during this voyage—the food, the wine, the sunshine. What about you? Will you find sharing with me distasteful?"

"Distasteful? No. There are twin beds. And as I remember from our honeymoon, you are clean and tidy in your habits. So long as you do not come to bed late and wake me, we should manage tolerably."

"You know, Maria, when we were first married I did hope that we might become—well, not intimate, but good companions; that we might develop a sort of sympathy. But we are, if anything, farther apart now than then. It is when we are more or less forced together in this way that it is brought home to me. We can never love each other, but can we not be friends?"

"How can that be? We have nothing in common."

"Oh yes, we do, Maria—something very important."

"I mean apart from that. Just reflect: I do not care what I eat or drink. I have no interest in music, no fondness for art, or literature . . ."

"I have often wondered: is there anything you do care for? Or any one?"

"Certainly no *one*—not now. Any *thing?* Only peace, and freedom—to do nothing, go nowhere, meet nobody unless I so choose. To live an unruffled life, without excitement or anxiety, without any emotion. That is all."

"All? You think that is a little thing to ask? I think what you seek is the most difficult thing on earth to obtain. Perhaps impossible *on* the earth; *under* it, may be."

"The grave, though, is inevitable."

"But perhaps it is not obtainable, even there." He broke into English. "But in that sleep of death, what dreams may come?"

She said sharply, "Don't say that!"

He looked surprised. "Why, don't tell me I have hit on a subject you feel strongly about."

"Death *is* the end—of everything; of all thought, all emotion. Do you understand?"

"If you say so, my dear," said Paul.

Webster had been hoping for a private word with his employer before retiring that night, but he didn't have to ask for it, as when they were leaving the main saloon with Quine and Trent, Roussos whispered to him, "Come along to my study in five minutes."

Roussos's study contained a large flat-topped desk; two office chairs and a couch, all upholstered in black hide; a safe; a filing cabinet; a drinks table; a bookcase, containing some standard works of reference—and very little else. The walls were panelled in a darker wood than the dining saloon, and the only things on them were a large world map and a clock. The desk carried a telephone, linked to the yacht's radio room; an elaborate intercom, which enabled Roussos to communicate with every room on the ship; a tape recorder; a daily calendar; a desk diary; pen rack and letter opener. For the desk of a busy man it looked unnaturally neat and unused.

Roussos noticed Webster glancing round after coming in and, as if in explanation of the general tidiness, said, "I'm gonna take it easy this trip. Usually I bring a secretary and get bogged down with work. This time I've left all my secretaries behind and I aim to spend as little time in here as I can."

"Good idea."

Roussos went to the drinks table, poured two Scotches and put them on the desk. Then he moved to the safe, turned the combination lock and opened it. He reached in, lifted something out and closed the safe again. When he turned round, Webster saw that the object in his hand was a slim black automatic. Roussos laid it on the desk. "You'd better carry this," he said. "Just in case."

Webster picked it up. It was a Beretta.

"Ever used one?" Roussos asked.

"Yes; not in anger, though: only on the range."

"I know some guys prefer a revolver. I can get hold of a Smith & Wesson .38 if you want it. But I thought this would be less bulky—it shouldn't show in your jacket pocket. Will it do?"

"One gun's much the same as another to me. I explained I'm no expert on firearms. British police don't normally carry them, as you know."

"Just as long as you know *how* to use it. It is loaded. There's more ammo in the safe if you should ever want it."

Webster checked that the safety catch was on and put the gun in his pocket. It fitted neatly and unobtrusively.

"I'm glad you called me in," he said. "I wanted to talk about security and find out if there was anything special you wanted me to do."

Roussos gave a sniff. "Don't think so. I don't reckon there's much danger while we're in Port of Spain, do you—at least not while Irene's on the yacht? The town's pretty well policed. The crooks would be crazy to try anything here when very soon we'll be off into the wild blue yonder where there isn't a cop for miles. I'm having the decks patrolled by a couple of armed sentries every night, by the way."

"Good. But I heard Irene say this evening that she's going to have a look round the town tomorrow morning. Do you want me to go with her?"

Roussos considered. "Well, as I told you back in London, I've got a couple of my toughest men detailed to stay close to her whenever she goes ashore. But it wouldn't do no harm if you went along too. It's daft not to take all the precautions we can. Maybe you could actually go *with* her—not just follow behind like they'll be doing. OK?"

"Certainly. I think you're very wise."

Roussos chuckled. "Not many people have called me that in my life: crafty, wily, yes. But not wise."

"You surprise me."

"Why? Whaddya know about me?"

"Well, I—"

"D'you ever read how I got started—worked my way up to all this?"

"I know you came from a very deprived background."

"A slum, Alec, call it a slum and have done with it. Know what my father was?"

"A labourer, wasn't he?"

"A drunken sot. And my mother was a slut. I ran away when I was twelve. I don't know if they ever bothered to look for me. I pretty well starved for six months. That was when I got thrown in the clink for stealing the oranges. I promised myself then that one day I'd be rich. I'd always been sort of gripped by the sea and at last I managed to get a job as a cabin boy. I loved it. Every minute of it. I was quick and pretty soon I was an able-bodied seaman. I used to question the older men and the bosuns all the time, and I learnt to be polite to the officers and the engineers, and I learnt about things like engines and navigation. I also knew I'd never get anywhere in the world if I could only speak Greek. I made up my mind to learn English. And I did, from scratch, without any books or proper teaching."

"That must have been tough going."

"It was. And I've never tried to pick up a word of any other lingo since. Know how I did it? I only sailed on British and American ships. That's why I speak English so funny: I just picked it up from the yankee or limey tars, and their tarts in the waterside bars. Not that I ever threw my money away on those broads. I just used to listen to 'em talk. And I never took more than a day or two off. Soon as I could after we put in anywhere, I'd sign up again. I never went into town. By the time I was twenty I'd been to every big port in Europe and the States and I'd never been more than a mile from the waterfront. I never took a leave and I saved all my dough. Wasn't long before I had a handy nest egg. Then I ran across two old salts who'd been saving up for years to try and buy their own ship. They were short just the amount I had. So I put in with them. I only had a one-seventh share in the grottiest old tramp you ever saw. But I was on my way. After two years, the oldest of my partners died. He didn't have a wife or family and he left his three-seventh share to me. That made me the majority shareholder. Two years after that I bought the other bloke out and I was a shipowner. The rest's pretty much as you'd expect. I won't bore you with it now."

"You wouldn't bore me. It's very interesting."

"Think so? Claire always tells me not to bore guests with it. So whenever I can corner a guy who's on the payroll and can't wriggle out of it, I let rip. But I'll let you get to your bunk now."

"Right." Webster stood up. "By the way, you said you'd be having that tip-off letter sent on. I saw Dimitri give you a pile of mail earlier. Was the tip-off letter among it?"

"Yeah, it was."

"Then could I see it? I've had quite a bit of experience with that sort of thing. There just might be a clue in it which I could spot."

"Sure. It's upstairs. I'll show it you tomorrow."

# 6

The next morning Webster went on deck immediately after breakfast and sat down to wait for Irene. He was wondering how she would react to the prospect of his company during the morning. He hadn't spoken to her since their opening conversation, and had been hoping for a couple of days at sea in which to get on better terms with her before they put into port again. He thought that probably the best approach now would be to ignore their first meeting and if the subject came up to treat it as a joke. If she rebuffed him, however, it might be necessary for him to tag along behind her with the two musclemen; but in that case he mustn't let her catch sight of him.

At last he saw her approaching the gangplank. He went up to her and said, "I've never seen Port of Spain. May I see it with you?"

She frowned. "Sure you want to be seen in the company of such a frightful mess?"

"Certainly, if she's the daughter of the seventeenth richest man in the world. Besides, you don't look quite such a mess today."

This was true—though the improvement was not all that marked. She'd put on a yellow dress and tied her hair back with a matching ribbon. So her appearance was at least, if nothing else, a little more gay.

She shrugged. "Well, I suppose I can't stop you if you want to come."

She thawed out a little during the morning. They spent most of it on foot, wandering the streets, looking in the shops, absorbing the sights, sounds and smells. Webster caught several glimpses of the two shadowing crew members, a discreet distance away. He didn't know whether Irene saw them, but it would hardly matter if she did. Though she did not know of this specific threat, she was surely aware that as the daughter of a multimillionaire, she must always be a potential target, and that it was natural for her father to have her watched.

Once they saw Trent, who had left the yacht before them, making his way in a stately fashion along the pavement, followed by two small boys, laden with parcels. "He has to hire his native bearers wherever he goes, I suppose," Irene murmured.

They arrived back at the *Angel* at noon. Webster was very hot and tired. He went straight down to his stateroom by the aft stairway and took a shower. He hadn't realized it would be quite as hot as this, and was comforted by the thought that it would be cooler when they put to sea. Leaving his room, he ran into Quine in the passageway.

"She's arrived," Quine said.

"Karin Johnson?"

"In the flesh."

"Up to expectations?"

Quine grinned. "Not exactly. Oh, she's attractive, all right."

"But?"

"Quite different from what I expected."

"In what way?"

"You'll see, pal."

"The boy friend here too?"

"Philippe? Yes. They're all up by the pool. Go and join the gang."

Webster went up and made his way towards the swimming pool. Twenty yards short he stopped and surveyed the scene. All the other passengers, including Trent—attired in brand new clothes—and Irene, were gathered around. Webster looked closely at the two newcomers. Philippe Barrault was probably in his late twenties, broad-shouldered, with long dark hair and craggy good looks. He was dressed in rather dirty-looking shirt and jeans. Karin Johnson was a petite girl with reddish-blonde hair, a snub nose and freckles. She too was wearing jeans and a shirt, though cleaner ones than Barrault. She didn't really look like Webster's idea of a film star, but nevertheless he couldn't quite understand Quine's surprise.

Suddenly Karin glanced towards Webster and caught his eye. For a few seconds they stared at each other; then to his intense surprise she suddenly screwed up her features into a grimace and poked out her tongue. It was the first time a girl had done that to Webster for nearly forty years, and his surprise must have shown, for her face suddenly broke into an impish grin and she left the side of the pool and came across to him.

"I'm sorry," she said, "did I shock you? I was very rude. But you looked so terribly solemn and mysterious, just standing there watching, like somebody out of *The Third Man.*" She spoke English with just the barest trace of an accent.

Webster smiled. "No, you didn't shock me. I was just a bit taken aback. Sorry if I appeared to be snooping."

"You're English?"

"That's right."

"I thought you looked as though you had to be."

"Williams is my name, Alec Williams. You must be Karin Johnson."

"That's right. Hullo." She held out her hand. As he took it, she said, "Wait a minute: what do you mean—I 'must be' Karin Johnson? Don't you know for sure? Don't you recognize me?"

Webster shook his head. "I regret to say I've never seen you before."

"You haven't seen *Yesterday's Woman*?"

"No. Sorry."

For a moment he thought she was annoyed. Then her face lit up. "But that's wonderful! You're the first person I've met in months who hasn't seen it. You won't think I'm like that dreadful drag, Polly."

"Polly?"

"The character I play in the movie. Come across and meet Philippe."

In a strangely child-like gesture she took Webster's hand and led him across to the pool, where Barrault, sipping a drink, was standing listening to Roussos, who was holding forth to the rest of his guests, gesturing expansively with a cigar. Karin waited for the pause, then tapped Barrault on the arm.

"Darling, this is Alec Williams."

Barrault looked round. Webster smiled. But the smile was not returned. There was a brooding expression in Barrault's eyes, which seemed momentarily to deepen into positive anger as they alighted on Karin's hand, which was still holding Webster's. Then the impression had passed and Barrault was holding out his own hand and saying, " 'Allo."

Roussos called out, "Sit down, Alec. Have a drink. Enjoy the town?"

Webster complied and helped himself from a tray brought instantly to his side by a steward. "Yes, very much, thanks."

Muller said, "Is our party now complete, Roussos?"

"Nearly. Just one to come."

"Who's that?"

"Feller called Orchard—an Englishman. Priest, as a matter of fact."

"A priest?"

"Well, a Reverend. Don't think he hears confessions or preaches these days, so don't worry. He was a teacher of some sort at Cambridge University." He turned to Trent. "Whaddya call 'em?"

"Do you mean a don?"

"That's it. He was a theology or divinity don at Cambridge. Started off a Catholic, but then switched to the Church of England. Became a journalist and wrote a book that caused a bit of a kerfuffle in religious circles. He writes for the papers and goes on TV in Britain a lot too."

Mrs. van Duren drew her breath in sharply. "Not *Hilary* Orchard?"

"That's right. D'you know him?"

"I certainly do not. But I have heard of that book. The man's a heretic."

"Heretic?" Roussos gave a snort of laughter. "You sound like someone out of the Middle Ages."

"I'm sorry you find it a matter of amusement, George. But I assure you I would not have consented to come on this trip had I known that that man was going to be on board. It's only for Irene's sake that I don't leave now."

Roussos became serious. "Look, I'm sorry. I had no idea you'd feel that way. But you gotta be mistaken. I mean, if a guy teaches religion at Cambridge University, surely he must know what it's all about?"

"I assure you that that qualification is no guarantee of doctrinal soundness. The standards at Cambridge are deplorably lax—as bad as at some of the so-called theological seminaries back home."

Trent leaned forward. "Just what is wrong with this man's views, dear lady? I remember hearing about his book, but I can't recall just what he said in it."

"It's difficult to know where to start. He scorns the scriptural view of sin. He denies the concept of judgment and punishment. From that it follows that he cannot believe in the Atonement. I assume he does believe in God, but I cannot be very confident even of that." She got to her feet. "And now if you'll all excuse me, I am going to rest in my stateroom until lunch. I'm finding the sun a little strong."

She departed. Roussos was looking anxious. "Hey, I hope she doesn't start giving Orchard hell as soon as he gets here. She's quite likely to."

Karin laughed. "What a shock for him that would be—considering he doesn't believe in it. But perhaps she'll merely tie him to the mast and set fire to him."

Barrault was looking contemptuous. "It is unbelievable that in the nineteen eighties people can still become heated over the rights and wrongs of religious belief."

Trent said, "Happening all the time, Philippe: Palestine, Lebanon, Ireland."

Muller shook his head. "None of those are religious disputes, Lance. They're political or racial. Religion is incidental, or just a cover."

Claire said, "One of the best things about a yacht is that one can be completely cut off from all that sort of thing. If the proles start slaughtering each other where one happens to be, one simply moves serenely on and lets them get on with it."

"Perhaps one day there'll be nowhere to move on to," Irene said quietly.

"Oh, darling, don't be so dreary. There'll always be somewhere for people like us."

"I hope you're right, sugar," Roussos said.

The unexpected note of seriousness seemed to make everyone thoughtful for a few moments. But then the spell was broken as, without warning, Karin ran half-a-dozen paces and leapt into the pool. She hit the water feet first with a huge splash for such a small person, liberally showering most of the others. There was a startled silence. Then Karin surfaced and grinned up at them. "It was just so blue and cool-looking I couldn't resist it another second." She swam to the side and climbed out. She gave a wriggle and pulled her shirt away from her body. "Oo, I feel horrid now. I wish I hadn't done it."

Irene, who had received the worst of the splash, had taken a packet of tissues out of her bag, and was dabbing herself dry. "So do I, dear," she said.

"Another myth exploded," Claire remarked. "You see, it is just not true that all young actresses remove their clothes at the least excuse. Some don't, even when they might reasonably be expected to."

Barrault's face was intensely grim. He said, "Haven't you forgotten something, Karin? There are no casting directors sitting round this pool. Will you all excuse me?" And he strode off.

Webster smiled at Karin, upon whose face an expression of dismay had appeared. "You know," he said, "I was greatly tempted to do that myself. But you look so uncomfortable now that I don't think I'll bother. Thanks for trying out the experiment for me."

She attempted rather unsuccessfully to smile. "You're welcome. I—I must go and change." She turned hastily and squelched off.

There was a few seconds' further silence. Then Muller said, "When are you expecting Orchard to arrive, Roussos?"

"Any time now."

"And then we sail for Tobago?"

"That's right. I was fixing on putting into Scarborough this evening. I don't know how long we'll want to stay on the island—I got one trip ashore for us all planned, but when we've had enough we can go on to Grenada. How does that grab you all?"

"Your yacht, my dear chap," said Trent.

"Yeah, but I want everyone to do what they want."

"If you take my advice, you'll make the decisions yourself. Don't be too democratic."

Claire said dryly, "That, Lance, is rather like someone advising Jack the Ripper not to be too gentle with women."

Trent said, "All I mean, Claire, dear, is that if you try and get everybody in agreement, you'll just have arguments. Your hubby should take his guests where *he* wants to. You'll find they'll all be quite happy."

"Sounds as though you've had a bit of experience of cruising," Webster remarked.

"I wouldn't say that. But I've organized parties of people—led treks and safaries and expeditions. People need to be led. That way they stay docile."

"You make us sound like a lot of sheep."

"In my experience, people are. Nothing personal, of course."

"And what about yourself, Lance?" Muller asked him. "I've never known you particularly sheeplike."

"Depends who's doing the leading, Paul. I'll follow the right man, you know that."

Shortly afterwards the luncheon gong sounded. They all started to make their way aft. Webster went to look at his watch, and found that he didn't have it on his wrist. Then he remembered taking it off to shower. He felt undressed without it, so murmuring an excuse, left the group and made his way below. He passed Quine on his way up, went to his room, fetched his watch and was just leaving again when he heard the sound of a voice raised in anger. He stood still and listened. It was Barrault. He was in one of the opposite rooms some yards down the passageway, the door of which was open an inch or so. He was speaking—or rather shouting—in French. Normally, Webster could follow simple French, if it was spoken slowly, but Barrault was talking too rapidly and incoherently for Webster to make much sense of it. Only one thing was certain: Barrault was very, very angry. Karin's voice made occasional short interjections, but didn't get in more than two or three words at a time.

Then there came the sound of a sharp slap, followed by something half way between a cry of pain and a sob. Webster—torn between an English reluctance to get involved in private quarrels, and the habit of twenty-five years spent trying to maintain the peace—hesitated. Then he took a few steps towards the other stateroom. But as he did so, the door of it started to open wide, and he dodged back to the cover of his own doorway. Barrault came swiftly out, slammed the door after him and strode off along the passageway.

Webster wavered for a few more seconds, then walked along to the other stateroom and tapped on the door. There was no reply for a moment, then Karin called, "Who is it?"

"Alec Williams."

"What do you want?"

"Are you all right?"

"Yes, of course."

"Can I see you?"

"No, not—oh, all right. Come in."

He opened the door and went in. She was sitting at the dressing-table with her back to him. She had taken off her wet clothes and put on a blue wrap. Momentarily Webster saw her reflection in the mirror and a bright red mark on the left side of her face. She caught his eye and stood up hurriedly, moving away from the dressing-table but keeping her back to him.

"You heard, I suppose," she said. There was a slight break in her voice.
"Yes."

"Did anyone else?"

"I don't think so. They're all up top, except for the old lady, I suppose. But her room's the other end of the passage—and they all seem pretty well insulated."

"That's something to be thankful for."

"Does he often do that?"

"Do what?"

"Hit you?"

"Certainly not! Do you think I'd have stayed with him if he did?"

"Women do."

"Not this woman. No, it's the first time. And it'll be the last. I'll put up with shouting, but not anything else."

"Has there been much of that?"

"Shouting? It depends what you mean by much. You'd probably say yes."

"Well, if it happens again while you're on board the *Angel,* other people are almost bound to hear."

"I know. Perhaps I'd better leave right away."

"No, don't do—" He broke off.

She turned. The mark on her face was still visible, but less vivid. "Why not?"

For some reason, Webster felt embarrassed. "Well, I'm sure it would disappoint Roussos."

"Do you care so much for his feelings?"

"Well, it would disappoint me, too; all of us, I'm sure. You're the star of the cruise—literally."

"Thank you, but it's not true. In the first instance, Mr. Roussos didn't ask me. It was Philippe he invited. Philippe asked if he could bring me. I'm incidental, really."

"I wonder. Roussos is pretty astute. Perhaps he asked him first diplomatically, knowing Philippe would ask to bring you. I don't imagine Barrault would take kindly to coming merely as your escort."

She shrugged. "Maybe you're right. Well, if he did want me, he's probably already having second thoughts. Boy, did I goof! The atmosphere round that pool! I felt like Ida Lupino in *The Hard Way,* after she did her wild dance at the posh party."

"I think people were just surprised. You needn't worry. Claire Roussos often seems a bit caustic. And Irene is apparently determined to be a grouch. Nobody else minded. I can't think why Barrault got so upset."

"Oh, he called it exhibitionism. Perhaps it was. But really I was only trying to make people laugh. They all looked so solemn—talking about Ireland and Palestine. I thought we were here to have fun!"

"I'm sure we'll all have much more fun if you stay."

"That will depend on Philippe. I'll stay if he apologizes. Thank you, anyway—and for giving me moral support by the pool. I appreciated it."

"Would you like me to take you up to lunch? I'll wait in my room while you get ready."

"You're awfully nice, but no thank you. Frankly, I don't want Philippe to see us come in together, and know we've been talking."

"Why on earth not?"

"Well, he's terribly jealous. That was part of the trouble, actually—it wasn't only my leap into the pool. He thought from the way I took your hand that we were old friends, but that I wouldn't admit it."

"But that's absurd!"

"So I told him. But if we go into lunch together now, he'll never believe me. We must talk again later, though. I—I'm glad you're on board."

"Oh? It's kind of you to say so, but why?"

"Well, it'll be nice to have somebody to talk to when Philippe gets his moods. I don't know any of the others, and when you arrived by the pool, I was just deciding I didn't really want to. I don't think this is my scene at all."

"Do you think *I'm* your scene? I wouldn't have expected to be."

"No, you wouldn't think so normally, would you?" she said.

The Reverend Hilary Orchard arrived during the afternoon. He was in his late thirties, tall and thin with pale blue eyes and fair hair. He spoke in an exaggerated upper-class drawl, gesticulating a lot as he did so.

Orchard had, it seemed, just come from one of the new central African republics, where he had been attending a conference on "The Anti-Colonialist Church." After the cruise he was off to the United States, where he was to give a lecture tour on the subject of "The Need for a Secular Church." At the same time he would be working on his next book, which was to be on the theme of "A Non-Biblical Christianity." He imparted all this information in a matter of minutes, and had a great deal to say on all these subjects; though as Quine whispered in Webster's ear, none of it seemed to have much to do with religion.

However, the omission was perhaps fortunate, as no temptation to tackle him on any specific point of theology was put in the way of Mrs. van Duren, who, after being introduced to Orchard, contented herself with maintaining a frigid demeanour and ignoring him.

Shortly after Orchard's arrival, the *Angel* weighed anchor.

## 7

Webster leant on the rail, looking down at the sleek hull sliding cleanly through the calm and intensely blue water. They were two hours out of Port of Spain. The sun was dipping towards the horizon. There was nothing to be seen for miles in any direction but sea, nothing to be heard but the muffled hum of the efficiently silenced engines, the slap of the water, and the cries of the only three remaining seabirds which had followed the *Angel* from Trinidad.

Webster, thinking himself for the moment alone on the deck, gazed into the distance, his brain slowly ticking over. Then a low, rather guttural voice from his elbow said, "You enjoy solitude, too?"

He swung round, taken by surprise. It was Maria Muller. She said, "I'm sorry. Did I startle you?"

"Just for a moment. I thought I had the deck to myself."

"That is the best way to have it. It is very peaceful, is it not?"

"Very."

"That is a difficult thing to find these days—peace. The reason I agreed to come on this cruise was to try and find it. I wish we were not putting into port at all. I would be quite content to cruise the ocean the whole time."

"Don't you think that might become a little boring after a while?"

She shook her head. "I shall never be bored again. When one has lived a life such as I, the idea of nothingness—of doing and saying nothing, of seeing nobody—is a beautiful one."

She spoke with hardly any expression in her voice. She didn't look at him, just stared down at the water, leaning on the rail. Webster glanced sideways at the swarthy, rather flattened profile. She turned her head and looked at him from sad, inscrutable eyes. A strange woman. He'd not exchanged more than half a dozen words with her so far. Nor had she seemed to speak much to anybody else. And she claimed to desire solitude. All of which made up a consistent pattern. Yet according to Quine she had regaled him with her whole life story the first time they'd met; and now she had deliberately chosen to come and talk to Webster. He decided to test her.

He said, "Yes, I was told you'd led a very tragic life."

"Tragic? You could say so. I would not argue. But would not that word normally imply a life scarred by blows of fate? My troubles were caused by people—human beings. It is as though all my life there has been a conspiracy against me by the people of every country—Germany, England, America —even the Jews. It has been intolerable."

She stopped. Webster said hesitantly, "I can understand how you feel."

"Can you? I wonder if you can. I am a research chemist, you know. I studied at Heidelberg University before the war. Few women did science in those days. Yet my professors said I was brilliant. I graduated with highest honours. The academic and scientific world lay before me, waiting for me to conquer it. When the Nazis came to power I was pleased. They promised a renaissance of the national spirit. I thought I would be a part of that renaissance, that I could serve the Fatherland. I had almost forgotten I was a Jew. My family had never been orthodox. I myself had no religious beliefs. None of my friends were Jewish. The anti-semitic campaign did not concern me. I was a scientist. Then an uncle of mine was arrested and died mysteriously in jail. I myself was picked up by the SS and interrogated for hours before being released. It was a terrifying experience—and monstrous that *I,* Maria Epstein, should be so treated. Then I was warned by my professor that it would be impossible for me to obtain an academic post. My parents were by then dead. I resolved to stay in Germany no longer. It was clear to me that soon your country would be at war with Germany. I was determined to help her. I knew that with my ability I could be of great use to her. At last, after such hardships as you would not believe, I reached England. I arrived in London full of hope. But to my amazement I was not accepted: my services were not wanted. There were suspicions. I was actually interned. Later I was released. But I was not permitted to do important work, only routine tasks. Yet other Jewish refugees were put to work on the most vital war projects. Why not me? To this day, I do not know. After the war I went to America. I thought things would be better there—in the land of opportunity. And for a while they were. I obtained a post with a big chemical company in Chicago. I applied for American citizenship. I became interested in politics. I was happy. And then MacCarthy came onto the scene."

So far Maria Muller had not paused for a second. Her tone of voice had not varied. She had not moved or taken her eyes from Webster's face. Now with great deliberation she shifted her position, looked away, coughed, turned to face him again and resumed.

"The political group I had been associated with stood for radical policies. MacCarthy accused it of being a Communist front organization. I was brought before his committee and questioned for several days. Afterwards I was harassed and tormented for months. My employers were pressured until eventually they dismissed me. There was no chance of obtaining another position. I was at my wit's end. However, I was still a Jew. Once my

Jewishness had been the cause of my losing a homeland. I thought that now it could perhaps be the means of my finding one. I went to Israel.

"Once more, I had great optimism. But I was not well received. News of my appearance before the committee, and my dismissal, had preceeded me. I was greeted with suspicion, as a possible Communist. Nevertheless, I did my best to make a home there. But I found the militaristic, nationalistic attitude intolerable. I was not a Zionist. So after a few years the wheel came full circle. I returned to Germany. And what do I do today? I help beautify the daughters of the men who drove me out nearly forty years ago. Ironic, is it not?"

"It is indeed. You have your own company, I understand—your own factory?"

"Yes—a very small one."

"But profitable, I hope."

She shrugged. "Profitable—yes. But not rewarding. I was worthy of better things than to end my career making lipsticks and deodorants."

"Could you not branch out into medicinal products? I should think you would have a good opportunity for useful work in that field, and for some original research."

"I have considered it. I do some occasional private research. But I seem to have lost the desire. Why should I seek to benefit the human race? Since we married, my husband has tried to persuade me to start again seriously. But so far . . ." She tailed off.

"You have not been married very long, then?" Webster knew the answer to this, but he wanted to keep her talking.

"A little over three years. My first marriage. I suppose, like everybody else, you find us a surprising couple?"

"Not at all."

"No? Well, I do. Now I must go below. Excuse me."

She turned and walked away, seeming almost to glide over the surface of the deck, so smooth and silent was her movement. Webster watched her until she disappeared. As for Quine, so for him. Why this compulsion to pour out a potted life history to men who were virtual strangers? And, he wondered, only to *men?*

Perhaps it was an unworthy thought, but her troubles seemed largely of her own making. Her sufferings under the Nazis had been, compared with what many had suffered, relatively light. Moreover, she had escaped—with qualifications which ought to have given her a flying start anywhere. Yet in three other countries she had been unhappy. To Webster, such a history suggested something wrong with the individual, rather than with the countries.

. . .

The *Angel* dropped anchor at Scarborough that evening. Nobody went ashore. Dinner would be the first opportunity for all twelve passengers to be together, and plainly everyone thought it important to be present.

Webster found himself seated towards the lower end of the table, with Karin on his left and Orchard on his right. Claire was at the foot of the table, with Barrault on her right. Irene was next to him, opposite Webster.

Webster eyed Barrault with some suspicion. But the latter's bad mood seemed completely to have passed. He was evidently in high spirits, talking with animation to Irene, narrating some anecdote and succeeding in bringing a smile, even a laugh, to her face.

Webster turned to speak to Karin. "I hope—" he began.

She caught his eye, gave him a quick smile but followed this by the slightest shake of the head. Then she turned deliberately away to speak to her left-hand neighbour, Paul Muller. Webster realized that she did not want to appear too friendly to him in front of Barrault. He felt a flash of annoyance, but resigned himself to the less inviting conversation of Orchard.

"I suppose this is what the gossip writers would call a glittering occasion," he said.

"Bloody disgrace, really, of course," Orchard drawled in a loud voice. Claire turned her head and looked at him sharply.

"How do you mean?" Webster asked.

Orchard waved an arm in an expansive gesture. "All this. Luxury—leisure. A crew of twenty-five serving less than half that number of passengers. Oh, don't worry: I've said all this to our host's face. He took it in good part— even when I told him he was an anachronism."

It was at this point that Claire intervened. "If you feel like that, why are you here, Mr. Orchard?"

"I'm seeing how the other half lives, Mrs. Roussos."

"But we're all in the same half."

Orchard looked puzzled. "I'm sorry?"

"You are in the same half of society as George and I."

"Oh, come—I'm no multimillionaire."

"I didn't say you were in the same fraction of that half. But you don't strike me as being exactly among the underprivileged of this world. If you really want to see how the other half lives, you ought to be slumming it with the working classes."

"I know how the working classes live. I've studied their condition closely. And I had a great-great-grandfather who was a manual worker, so I consider myself working class."

"Really?" Claire said. "How interesting. Can we look forward to your going on strike soon?"

"You misunderstand me. Being working class is really an attitude, a state of mind—"

"Try telling that to the average road sweeper on thirty pounds a week," Claire remarked dryly.

Orchard ignored this. "It's like being a Christian."

"Oh, surely not," she protested. "Being a Christian involves certain beliefs."

"My dear Mrs. Roussos, I do not define a Christian in the old-fashioned sense as someone who blindly embraces all the dogma of the Church, but as someone whose world-view is essentially Christlike. I mean—a Jew can be a Christian, or a Hindu, or an atheist even."

"But not, apparently, a millionaire."

"I didn't say that. Your husband's world-view is no doubt admirable. I am simply blaming a capitalist system which allows one man to make so much money. That is what I meant when I said this set-up was a disgrace. There's no harm in hard-working chaps like Willerby here and me—"

"Williams," said Webster.

"Er, Williams and myself sampling this sort of life for a few weeks, but for us to have it permanently would be quite wrong."

"Not if you'd earned it."

"No one *earns* all this. Nobody in the history of mankind has ever been worth this much."

"Oh, come," Webster said. "Let's leave present company out of it, but surely in an ideal world some people would be granted this sort of reward towards the end of their life, in return for their labours?"

"I don't think so."

"What about a Livingstone or a Schweitzer? Granted they probably wouldn't have wanted it, but didn't they—"

"In the first place, I'm not a great admirer of the paternalistic, preachifying Christianity exemplified by those two gentlemen. There are people who come *closer* to earning that scale of reward than either of them did."

"Who, for heaven's sake?" Webster asked.

"Probably people whose names none of us have ever heard of. Just as an example, take an ordinary African freedom fighter, with his rifle, risking his life every day. He is doing more to advance the people's welfare than any number of missionaries."

"And you say that—morally—he deserves a yacht like this?" Claire asked.

"No, I don't; I say *nobody* does. But some come closer to it than others."

Next to Claire, Barrault had broken off a conversation with Irene and was listening with apparent rapt attention to Orchard.

Webster said, "And the terrorists with their rifles, the killers, are among the more deserving?"

"Not necessarily each and every one of them. It depends on the al's motivation, of course."

Barrault said, "But there are some gunmen who you would reward for their efforts?"

"Oh, I'm not in the business of handing out rewards, thank God."

"But you would not necessarily condemn such a man?" Barrault was insistent.

"I'm not in the condemning business, either. My duty is to ask of every action: *why?* Did the person performing it believe in his (or her) heart of hearts that it was a necessary and right action—even though he may not have been correct in that belief? That is the only criterion on which to base a modern morality."

Barrault was nodding slowly. "That is most interesting. Yes, I am sure you are right."

"Your people have a saying that sums it all up, you know: *Tout comprendre c'est tout pardonner.*" He glanced at Webster. "That is, 'to understand all is to forgive all.'"

"I know what it means," Webster said. "Actually, it's a misquotation. And I've always thought it very silly. In my view, most of your so-called freedom fighters are bloodthirsty thugs, who ought to be put away for life."

Orchard shrugged. "It seems you and I are not going to have a great deal in common."

"Oh, I don't know. Perhaps if you make an effort to understand my views you'll forgive me for them."

"My dear chap, I forgive you for them here and now. I really wouldn't expect you to have any others."

"That sounded a most stimulating conversation you and Orchard were having at the lower end of the table during the early part of dinner," Muller said, lighting Webster's cigarette with a gold lighter held in an exquisitely manicured hand.

"I wouldn't say it was particularly stimulating," Webster said. "We just disagreed and that was that. We didn't go on about it. I'm not much of a debater."

"Oh, I'm sure you underestimate yourself, Mr. Williams. But the interest for me would lie in listening to the opposing arguments of two Englishmen —what we might describe as the pragmatic and the theoretical. So often I have to listen to arguments put forward on strictly nationalistic lines—and motivated purely by national self-interest—that it would be refreshing to hear two fellow countrymen arguing on grounds of pure principle."

"You're making it sound far more significant than it really was. I'm sure the discussion at your end was just as interesting."

"Oh, no doubt, no doubt: *as* interesting, certainly. But not more so. That's the only trouble with dear Claire's functions—there's always so much good talk going on that one is bound to miss some of it. Don't you agree?"

"I wouldn't know. This is my first one."

"Well, take the present party. Have you considered how richly varied an assortment we are? Look at the number of countries that are represented. We have every age group from the early twenties to the eighties. In addition, we cover between us an extremely broad range of professions and disciplines: our host, big business; Orchard, the church; Nathan, the law and politics; my wife, science; yourself, modern technology; Philippe, sport; Miss Johnson, the performing arts; Lance, the army—and literature—er, of a sort; my humble self, diplomacy. What a range of experience we have between us! We can converse on practically any subject under the sun."

"I'm not sure you're right there."

"Oh?" Muller cocked an elegant eyebrow.

"We can between us *spout* on practically any subject. But we can't sensibly *talk* about many of those you mention because there's only one representative from each field. I mean, who among us could authoritatively discuss scientific topics with your wife, or big business with Roussos? I would say the only topics we *can* discuss are general ones—and for that we might just as well all be deep sea divers."

Muller chuckled. "You have just proved what I was maintaining about the good talk possible here. I cannot imagine why you claim not to be a good debater."

"It seems to me just common sense."

"There's little enough of that in the world, I assure you, my dear Williams. That is one of the first things one discovers in my absurd profession."

"You consider yours an absurd profession?"

"In my better moments I tell myself that it serves a useful purpose. At other times I long to be able to desist from seemingly vain attempts to penetrate wooden skulls with the light of reason and leave them all alone to go to hell in their own particular way."

"While you do the same?"

"On the contrary: while I set myself to seek a heaven on earth."

"And what would that consist of?"

"An interesting question. It was an English divine, Sidney Smith, was it not, who said of somebody that his idea of heaven was to eat *pâtés de fois gras* to the sound of trumpets? My own would be somewhat similar, I think. Drinking a Mouton Rothschild '61 while listening to Franck's Quartet and looking at a Holbein portrait perhaps? Would such a Sybaritic paradise ultimately become a hell, do you suppose? I believe it was Milton who wrote of the human mind that it can make a 'Heaven of Hell, a Hell of Heaven.' I must seek our friend Orchard's opinion on that. I think, however, that I would be prepared to take the risk of my particular heaven becoming a hell eventually if I could enjoy it for a short time first. My, my, I'm starting to sound rather like Faust, am I not? And what a poor bargain he struck! Poor fellow. I'm sure he did not deserve to end in hell. His peccadilloes were so utterly harmless."

"Who would deserve hell, in your book?"

"Oh, without doubt the bores and the philistines."

"Is that all? What about those who try to enforce their will upon their fellow men?"

"Doesn't everyone do that?"

"I don't think I do. Do you do it?"

"I have been known to try and enforce my will upon my fellow women. Oh dear, can someone of my sex use such an expression?" Muller chuckled smoothly. Before Webster could reply, Claire came up to them.

"Who's for bridge?" she asked.

Muller got to his feet. "My dear, you know I can never resist a game."

"Mr. Williams?"

"No, I'm afraid I don't play."

"Well, George will be showing a film in here for the others. Come along to the card room, Paul. I think we have just enough for two tables."

Webster went outside, glad of the opportunity to check that the guards were on duty and that unauthorized boarding of the yacht was impossible. It wasn't strictly necessary for him to do this, as Roussos obviously had it all well organized. But he felt that he had to make at least a token effort to earn his money.

Having satisfied himself, he remained outside, enjoying the coolness and silence and smoking a cigarette. Then he heard a woman's footstep. He turned, momentarily expecting Maria Muller again. But it was Karin. "Hi," she said.

"Hullo."

She came right up. "Do you have a cigarette?"

He gave her one and lit it for her. She said, "I wanted to apologize for giving you the cold shoulder at dinner. I didn't want Philippe to see us being too chummy. But he's immersed in bridge now, so I can talk to you as much as I like."

"Things are all right between you again now?"

"He apologized."

"I'm sorry to have been the cause of friction."

"Don't be silly. It wasn't your fault. Besides, as I explained, it was my plunge that really got him uptight."

"Tell me: what did he mean when he said you'd forgotten there were no casting directors around this pool?"

"Oh, it's a long story. You see, I have a reputation for being—quote—a serious actress. I made my name in Sweden in some terribly dreary imitation Ingmar Bergman things. I hated them. Of course, I never had a chance to work for Ingmar himself: that would have been different. The trouble was that I seemed to be the only person not to like them. In the States they became quite a cult. And they got me an invitation to Hollywood. Hollywood! My mecca! I was over the moon with joy. I thought at last I'd get a chance to change my image. But the first major part they offered me was Polly—which was almost a parody of my Swedish films. I nearly turned it down, but eventually my agent persuaded me to do it. Well, as you know, the beastly thing was a smash. Since then I've been offered about six parts practically indistinguishable from it. And I swear I won't do them."

"What sort of parts do you want to play?"

"Comedy! I've got the face for it—can't you see? This big mouth and up-turned nose and red hair and freckles. But what do producers want to do? Dye my hair or give me a wig, cover my freckles with make-up, build up my nose, try to make my mouth look smaller. It's crazy."

"I'm afraid I still don't see what this has got to do with jumping in the pool."

"Well, I've been doing things to try and establish myself as a funny lady—a kook."

"Oh, I see—like jumping in pools with your clothes on."

"Not actually that before. But I did try to take a chimp to lunch at the *Brown Derby*. And I threw a custard pie at Robert Redford."

"What happened?"

Karin sighed. "Nothing. The restaurant wouldn't let me in. And Bob moved at the last second, the pie hit the wall, and hardly anyone noticed. It was then I decided—or rather Philippe decided—that it was time to get right away from Hollywood for a while."

She looked so mournful that Webster laughed. "This beats everything," he said. "Here you are, a young actress with a smash hit behind you, an Oscar nomination, snowed under with offers—you ought to be walking on air."

"I know, it's awful, isn't it? Anyway, my agent has promised to fight for a comedy role for me. Trouble is, it probably won't be the right sort of comedy. I was really born forty years too late. I was cut out to play the type of part people like Claudette Colbert and Jean Arthur used to play in those gorgeous old thirties comedies. But they don't seem to make them like that any more."

"You'll have to produce your own films," Webster said. "Set up an independent company."

She gave a gasp. "What a fabulous idea! Oh, it would be super! If only I could get the financial support."

"Surely after the success of *Yesterday's Woman*—"

"Ah, yes, but that's only one film. It would be an awful risk."

Webster jerked a thumb over his shoulder towards the deck house. "There's someone in there who doesn't mind taking a few risks, from all I've heard."

Her eyes widened. "You mean Mr. Roussos?"

"Why not?"

Slowly she let the idea sink in. "Hey, I wonder if he'd play ball."

"You could ask him."

"Yes, I could, couldn't I? Of course, I'm contracted to the producers of *Yesterday's Woman* for two more films. But after that . . ." Her eyes were shining with excitement. "Alec—it's a great idea—fantastic—super. It could be the answer to everything. Thanks a million times." She gave him a sudden kiss on the cheek. Then she drew back, abruptly calmer. "Now: I must go at this very carefully. I must think how best to approach him. Trouble is, I've really hardly spoken to him yet. I must think—think." She turned away and calling over her shoulder, "See you later," ran off along the deck.

Webster grinned to himself, then went back into the main saloon. He found Roussos in solitary state, watching, and laughing immoderately at, an Abbot and Costello film. Webster sat down by him and watched it until the tape ran out. Then as Dimitri appeared, to change it, Webster leaned towards Roussos and said quietly, "I'm wondering, as this is our first night away from Port of Spain, whether you'd like me to stay up and keep an eye on things."

"No need, Alec. Everything's organized. Just relax."

The film recommenced. As it did so, Karin entered. "What are you watching?" she asked. "Oh, Abbot and Costello. Lovely. What's happened so far, Mr. Roussos?"

"I'll run the first tape over again," Roussos said.

"Oh, don't bother—"

"It's not any bother. I'd like to see it again. Dimitri!" he yelled at the top of his voice.

Webster left and made his way to the card room to watch the bridge. He found two games in progress, and it was soon obvious that they were very different types of game. One, consisting of Orchard, Irene and the Mullers, was being played in a very lackadaisical spirit. However, on the other table, where Claire and Quine were up against Barrault and Trent, the game was being taken much more seriously.

Webster settled down to watch this one, and although the finer points were largely lost on him, he was soon caught up in it. It was clear neither side wanted to lose, with Claire and Barrault being the most keen. The look that Claire once shot at her partner, Quine, when he made an error was of a shrivelling vindictiveness. As the game approached its climax, Claire grew more and more excited. She chain-smoked, her cheeks became flushed, and her eyes grew bright and hard. Barrault, on the other hand, was white-faced and grim-expressioned. Both Quine and Trent played with silent concentration.

Eventually the game ended with victory to Claire and Quine. Claire sat back, breathing hard, and smiling in triumph. Barrault got to his feet with a jerky movement. He was scowling. He said to Trent, "Settle up for me. I'll see you later." Then without another word to anybody he hurriedly left the room.

Claire was already busy making calculations. She said excitedly, "Forty dollars! I think I've won forty dollars." When settlement had been made, she started to count her money eagerly. Quine watched her and, when she finished, pushed his own winnings across the table to her.

"What's this?" she asked.

"It's yours by rights, my dear. You were brilliant in that last hand. We'd never have won if our positions had been reversed."

Her eyes gleamed. "You want me to have your winnings?"

"Sure."

"Why, thank you, Nathan. That's very generous." She gathered up the money quickly.

"Well, me for bed," Quine said. "Coming down, Lance?"

"I think so."

They said goodnight, and Trent went out. Quine had to pass close by Webster on his way to the door. He cast a surreptitious glance over his shoulder at Claire, who was stuffing money into her evening bag. He put his head close to Webster's and spoke softly. "One thing I've learnt about shindigs like this, buddy: always keep your hostess happy."

Quine left the room and Claire looked up with a smile. "I could use a drink."

She crossed the room and touched a switch on the wall. Webster thought she was ringing for a steward, but to his surprise, a section of the panelling about three feet square slid to one side, and a small drinks cabinet was revealed. Then suddenly and unexpectedly, this moved forward into the room and stopped.

Claire looked at Webster and smiled. "The wonders of modern science," she remarked. "Can I fix you a drink, Mr. Williams?"

"Not just now, thank you, Mrs. Roussos."

She poured herself a gin and tonic, saying as she did so, "You should play bridge, you know. You miss a lot."

"Oh, I don't know," Webster said, "I find just watching highly informative."

## 8

The next morning four chauffeur-driven hire cars arrived to convey the entire party, plus a steward and stewardess and all the equipment for a picnic lunch, on a tour of Tobago. Webster rode with Irene and Paul Muller. Karin, he noticed, managed to get a seat in Roussos's car, Orchard making the third.

For nearly three hours the cars bowled in stately convoy round the island, stopping at pre-determined beauty spots and points of interest for lectures by one of the drivers, who was an experienced guide. Then after ten or fifteen minutes they would start off again for the next sight. It wasn't Webster's way of seeing a new place, and he soon began to get restless. Irene, too, was plainly very bored, and after the third stop didn't bother to get out. In their car only Muller seemed to enjoy himself, staring out of the window and commenting on everything of interest that they passed.

At twelve-thirty they stopped for lunch at a pre-arranged site overlooking a beautiful bay with silver-sanded beach and surrounded by forest. Great hampers, trestle-tables, white cloths, canvas chairs and boxes of crockery and cutlery were unloaded from the car boots.

Webster was amused to note that overnight Karin seemed to have developed a high regard for Roussos's views. She constantly sought his opinion on every topic, plied him with questions about Tobago and positively hung on his replies.

After lunch most of the party lazed about in the shade of banana trees and chatted, read or dozed. It was very hot and Webster found difficulty in staying awake. However, the muscle men were not in attendance today, Roussos having decided that they'd stand out too much, and Webster remembered his responsibility to Irene.

He was never quite sure how he lost her. One moment when he looked at her she was lolling back reading a magazine about fifteen yards away; the next time he glanced in her direction, her chair was empty. He got hurriedly to his feet and looked around, wondering what Roussos would think of him. But Roussos was asleep with his mouth open, and most of the rest of the party seemed to be in various stages of somnolence. The nearest fully awake person was Maria Muller, who was sitting gazing silently and inscrutably into the distance. Trying to make his voice casual, Webster turned to her and asked, "Did you see where Irene went?"

"For a walk in the forest with Nathan Quine."

"Oh I see. Er, which way?"

Maria just pointed uninterestedly.

"Thanks." He stuck his hands in his pockets and wandered slowly off in the direction she'd indicated. He reached the edge of the forest and found a clearly defined path. He started along it, increasing his pace.

Quine. That was surprising. He wouldn't have expected Irene to choose him as a companion for a walk. Was there any significance in it? He wondered if there were any special woman in Quine's life. If not, an immensely wealthy wife would be an extremely valuable asset for any American with political ambitions. And Irene would undoubtedly one day be an immensely wealthy woman.

After about five minutes' walking Webster rounded a bend in the path and, to his relief, saw Quine and Irene fifty yards ahead. He slackened speed. He was now rather at a loss to know what to do. He didn't want to make it obvious that he was following them, but on the other hand, he mustn't let them think he was spying on them. In London there'd be no problem, but he wasn't accustomed to shadowing through West Indian forests, and although they hadn't spotted him yet, he didn't trust himself not to be seen eventually.

While trying to decide what to do, he studied them. There was no indication of affection or intimacy between them. They were walking a foot or two apart, not touching, and Quine seemed to be telling some story, gesticulating freely, while Irene just nodded occasionally.

Soon Webster's fear was justified, for suddenly and with no apparent reason Quine looked back over his shoulder and saw Webster. He said something to Irene and they both stopped and turned. His problem solved, Webster walked up to join them.

Quine said, "Dr. Livingstone, I presume."

But Irene looked decidedly annoyed. She said coldly, "Did you want something, Mr. Williams, or do you just happen to be going our way?"

"This seems to be the only path through the woods," Webster said, "but I hadn't intended to interrupt a tête-à-tête, if you hadn't waited for me."

"It's a beautifully peaceful spot," Quine said.

Webster nodded. "And cooler. I suppose it's quite safe? I'm afraid I'm woefully ignorant of the wild life in these parts."

"I don't believe there are any man-eating lions or tigers, if that's what you mean," Irene said with the slightest suggestion of a sneer in her voice.

"Or wolves?" Webster said. He regretted the words the moment they were out. They were facile and facetious; and he had no cause to be offensive to Quine, who'd only ever been pleasant to him, and who seemed to have been behaving with perfect propriety towards Irene.

To his surprise, however, Quine was clearly delighted by the implicit suggestion in the remark. "Well, of course," he said, chuckling broadly, "freedom from that particular species can never be guaranteed for a beautiful girl, wherever she goes." It occurred to Webster that he would probably like nothing better than the reputation of a wolf, without ever having had much success in that field.

Irene glanced from one to the other, with an expression of contempt. "You are both utterly absurd," she said coldly. "You know perfectly, Mr. Quine, that I am not in the least—"

"Nathan, Irene—I keep telling you."

"I prefer Mr. Quine. You know perfectly well that I am not in the least beautiful and that the only reason a man ever looks at me is because I'm George Roussos's daughter. There have been plenty of men who've done that, and I can spot them a mile off. As for you, Mr. Williams, I don't know whether you normally get your kicks by spying on people in woods and then making dirty remarks . . ."

She never finished the sentence. Her face changed and she stared over Webster's shoulder with a look of mingled amazement and fear. Webster spun round.

Standing about seven or eight feet away was a huge black man. He must have been about six feet four tall, and had the build of a heavyweight boxer. He was wearing a vividly patterned green and yellow shirt and was smiling broadly. In his hand was a revolver, which was levelled at them.

"Hi," he said.

Webster's heart gave a lurch. A wave of intense fury at his own carelessness swept over him. Stupidly, the only words he could think to say were, "What do you want?"

"Guess," said the man. "OK, fellers," he called softly, and moved two steps closer.

The next moment they were surrounded as, quite silently, three more men materialized from the shrubbery. They were all armed with heavy rough wooden clubs, which they were swinging menacingly.

Irene gave a little scream, and in a scared voice Quine said, "Listen—we don't have much cash or jewellry. And our friends are just down the path. If you harm us you'll be in deep trouble. Look—I have a watch—it's a good one—but that's about all. Now why don't you take it and go? Then we won't—"

"Man, you sure do talk a lot. And let me tell you I ain't blind. I can see your watch. When I want you to give it to me, I'll tell you—OK? Until then, just shut up—eh?"

Quine shut up.

Webster said, "What do you want?"

The man turned his head slowly to look directly at him. "Did'n you ask me that just now?"

"You didn't answer."

"Oh, I am so sorry, massah. Ain't that re-miss of me? Well, you see, sir, me an' my friends, we're just the local Baptist church on its annual outing, and we thought you might care to join us in our festivities."

The other men laughed. Irene said, "Why don't you leave us alone? He told you we don't have anything."

"Oh, now, I wouldn't say *you* don't have anything, honey-chile. You don't have much maybe, but you'd pass on a dark night."

Irene, who'd gone very pale, now flushed. "You're extremely offensive," she said loudly.

"Oh, deary me! So I'm oh-fensive, am I? Do you hear that, boys? I don't expect you'll want to be seen around wi' me no more, will you?"

The other men laughed again, and one of them said, "You're a bad boy, chief."

Irene swallowed. "Will you please let us pass?"

The big man stood aside. "You want to go that way?" He pointed along the path, farther into the forest. "But of course you can. Please go in jus' as far as you like. We'd like to have you fine people a mite further away from your friends, as a matter of fact. We'll jus' follow on behind—to, er, protect you from all them wild animals you was talking about. Then, when we know we won't be disturbed, we can all get down to business. And in particular, I can get to know you better, girl. You're growing on me, do you know that? You got a bit of fire. I reckon there's more to you than meets the eye. How about you coming away with me for a little while, eh?"

Irene was now looking decidedly frightened. She took a step closer to Webster, throwing him an appealing glance.

Webster's mind was racing. He thanked his lucky stars for the automatic stuck in his belt, hidden by the lightweight jerkin he was wearing. But given the chance, should he go for it? Irene's safety could be his only consideration, and if bullets started flying, she might be in greater danger than if he left his gun where it was. Because whatever these men were after, they were certainly not going to kill her—or at least not here and now.

At this last thought, a crazily audacious scheme flashed into Webster's head. He had no time to weigh up the pros and cons of it. He just acted.

"You're right there," he said to the big man, "she's quite a girl when you get to know her. Here, why don't you have her?" He put his arm round Irene's shoulders and pushed her gently towards the negro. A flicker of surprise showed in the man's eyes, and he took a quarter step back.

"Go on," Webster said, "don't be frightened: take her. I don't want her."

And then, with all his strength, he thrust Irene straight at the gang leader. She staggered forward, instinctively putting out her hands towards him to break her fall. The man's reaction was what Webster had prayed it would be: with his left hand he warded Irene off, pushing her to the side. And as he did so, his gun hand swung in the air.

Webster's hand flew to his belt and closed on the automatic. He brought it out, at the same time throwing himself flat onto the ground and yelling at Irene and Quine, "Run!"

He barely saw them start to sprint down the path, for as they did so, he levelled his gun at the big man and fired. The shot missed. Webster saw the negro's revolver swinging round towards him, and he rolled to his left. A bullet smacked into the ground three inches from his head. Webster aimed and fired again. The big man dropped his revolver and staggered back, a vivid crimson stain spreading over the shoulder of his shirt.

Webster had been vaguely conscious of the other men scattering as he drew his gun. Now he was aware of a blur at the corner of his vision. He rolled again, to his right and onto his back. He saw a man looming over him, club raised to strike. It swept down and took him sickeningly on the shoulder. Webster fired for the third time. His bullet caught the man in the thigh and he went down. Webster scrambled to his feet. The big man was in the act of picking up his gun. He swung the barrel round, towards Webster, who dived for the cover of a bush, firing again as he did so. The two guns barked together and both bullets missed. Webster hit the ground behind the bush. He lay panting for a few seconds then gathered himself and sprinted clear, bent low.

There was no sign of the four men.

Sending a fusillade of shots into the bushes nearest to where the big man had been standing. Webster continued to run, back down the path towards the picnic site. As he ran, he zigzagged from side to side. Every second he was waiting for further shots from the rear. But nothing happened. Then he heard voices ahead, rounded a bend, and the next moment Roussos, Trent, Barrault and two of the drivers were encircling him, pouring out questions.

Gasping for breath, Webster shook his head. "Later. Let's get away from here. Irene all right?"

Roussos nodded. "Just shaken. She had quite a fright."

"She's not the only one," said Webster.

"They were after me, weren't they?" Irene said later, back on the *Angel.*

"After you?" Webster made his face blank.

"Yes. Kidnap."

"Oh, I don't think so."

"I do. I'm a pretty obvious sort of target for that."

"Maybe. But I'd guess they were just muggers—and perhaps after you in a quite different sense."

"Well, whatever they were after, I want to thank you."

"I'd quite understand if instead you slapped my face. Some people would say I risked your life inexcusably."

"Pushing me at him like that, you mean?"

"Precisely."

"Well, I was, to say the least, a little surprised. But it was a highly original thing to do. And I can see now it was just about the smartest thing you could have done."

"Actually, it was the only thing I could think of. I just knew that whatever they did want, it wasn't your life. So you yourself were the safest weapon I could use against them. And at the same time I could give you a head start in getting away. If I'd had time to think about it, though, I very much doubt if I'd have risked it."

"Then thank heavens you didn't have time."

"I didn't hurt you?"

"Only my feelings for a moment, when you were offering me to him, like a cast-off shoe, as they say. But I guess I had that coming, the way I spoke to you just before. Sorry about that, too."

"I can see it must have looked as though I was spying on you."

"Well, after today, you're welcome to spy on me any time. By the way, I didn't have a chance to ask earlier, but why were you carrying a gun?"

"I wasn't carrying a gun."

"But we heard lots of shots as we were running away."

"The big bloke dropped his gun. I grabbed it up and took a few pot shots at them."

"But the shots came so close together! I could have sworn there were two guns."

"Just me losing my head a bit and loosing off madly without taking proper aim."

"I see. What happened to the revolver?"

"I dropped it running away. I didn't think it advisable to stop and pick it up."

"I suppose not. It might have been a good clue, though. That is, if we do tell the police about the incident. My father doesn't seem keen. I don't mind either way. What do you think?"

"Oh, let's forget about it," Webster said. "I don't like policemen."

"So," Roussos said, "you're the guy who's not a sharpshooter."

Webster shrugged. "I could hardly miss. He was as big as a house."

"I'm very grateful, Alec—more than I can say."

"You shouldn't be. I was at fault in letting Irene go off like that with only Quine for protection."

"Bull. You weren't hired as an ordinary bodyguard. I gave you the gun as an added precaution, but I told you I didn't think it would be a matter of a straightforward grab and I had a couple of guys on the payroll who could handle that. I'm mad with myself that I didn't take them along on the picnic. Only I figured the others would wonder why, and that anyway we'd all be together all day and the crooks wouldn't risk the snatch in those circumstances. Hell's bells—and I thought this gang was gonna be subtle!"

"They may still be."

"How do you mean?"

"Well, firstly, what happened today might have been nothing to do with your London friends at all. It's possible this was just an ordinary mugging attempt by the local Mr. Big and his boys. You arranged the outing and the picnic in advance with the car hire people. The whole island must have known about it."

"Yeah, advertising our movements in advance like that was a real booboo. But I arranged the outing before I had the tip-off letter. It's the only trip like that I have fixed for the whole cruise. I knew this would be our first stopover and I figured the picnic would be a good ice-breaker."

"Don't blame yourself. I could have advised you to cancel, but I didn't. I'm just saying today could have been a coincidence. Those villains could have been on their way to rob the entire party when they ran into Irene and Quine and me."

"You think it was too much of an amateur job for the London mob to have been involved?"

"No, I don't go as far as that. The London mob could have put the local boys up to it—without any real expectation that it would work."

"What for?"

"To lull us into a false sense of security They may know you've been tipped off. They might have hoped to make us think that *this* was their attempt—the one you'd been warned about—so we'd stop worrying and lower our guard."

"Hey, that's pretty smart," Roussos said admiringly.

"Irene says you don't want to inform the local police. I played along, but are you sure it's wise?"

"No, I ain't. But I'm less sure it would be wise *to* tell them. After all, you did shoot two guys, even though it was in self-defence, and there'd certainly be formalities to go through. Those thugs have already been taught a pretty sharp lesson, and I can't see it'd do much good to get 'em put away."

"Except that they're certainly known to the local force, who shouldn't have too much trouble picking them up. If they *were* put up to it, the police might be able to do a deal to find out by whom."

"I know, but then we'd have to tell the cops about the tip-off letter, and Irene and everyone else would have to know about it. You'd have to announce who you really are. Then you'd have no hope of spotting if any of the guests is involved."

"I suppose you're right. And I must admit we probably wouldn't learn about the villains behind it, anyway. It just goes against the grain for me to keep fellow police in the dark. Incidentally, talking of the tip-off letter, I still haven't seen it."

"I know. But I gotta confession to make. I've lost it."

"Lost it!"

"Well, mislaid it. It was among that pile of mail you saw Dimitri give me when we arrived. When I came to go through it all this morning, it wasn't there."

Webster whistled silently. "Could it have been stolen?"

"I suppose it could. But I didn't tell anybody else it was there. And why should anyone want to pinch it? I mean, I've had the tip-off now. Look, I'll have one more really thorough search sometime—tear the room to bits. It might have fallen down between the table and the wall or something. I'll let you know if I have any luck."

"OK." Webster stood up. "By the way, what are your plans for tomorrow?"

"We sail for Grenada first thing. I don't think we ought to hang about Tobago a minute longer than necessary now."

## 9

Unusually, Webster slept late the next morning. When he got up he was surprised to find that the *Angel* still hadn't sailed. He learned from his steward that slight engine trouble had arisen. The engineers had been working on it for about two hours, but didn't expect to complete repairs before lunch.

Hoping they didn't decide to seek the advice of Alec Williams, marine engineer, Webster breakfasted alone.

Afterwards, he was just making his way out to the deck when he heard a voice behind him say curtly, "Ah, Williams, I would like to talk to you." Webster turned round. It was Barrault and he wasn't looking very friendly.

"Oh, good morning," Webster said. "By all means. Shall we go into the saloon?"

They did so, and sat down. Barrault wasted no time.

"I was hoping to speak to you yesterday, but there was no chance. I think it was you that told Karin to ask Roussos for money to make the movies—yes?"

"I just mentioned his name as a possible—"

"You had no right. In the future, please mind your own business."

"Now hold it. She was wondering where she could get financial backing to make her own films, and so—"

"Which too was your idea, I think."

"She was complaining she wasn't being offered the right sort of parts. I suggested, not altogether seriously, that she set up her own company."

"She took it very seriously. And it is absurd! She is far too young and inexperienced to consider such a thing."

"Good heavens, surely she's old enough to decide herself. Do you run her life?"

"Yes, I do."

"How does she feel about that?"

"She has been very happy about it always. And if there is any question of her setting up her own company, I will arrange it—I, Philippe Barrault."

"Fine. Who's stopping you?"

"At the present, my own common sense stops me. But if I should decide to go ahead with it, I would not want George Roussos involved."

"Why on earth not? His money's perfectly good, isn't it? I should say you ought to thank your lucky stars if you can get him interested. With him behind you, you'd be home and dry."

"I have said I do not want Karin involved with him. Now please, stay out of the matter."

"I've never had any intention of doing anything else. It was just a casual remark on the spur of the moment, nothing more."

"Then that is all right. We will *say* nothing more. But remember, please, that Karin is impulsive, too enthusiastic, carried away easily."

"She needs you to keep her feet on the ground, is that it?"

*"Pardon?* Ah, yes. That is it."

"Bit scatter-brained, is she?"

*"Precisement.* I look after her, you know."

It was nonsense, Webster was sure. Karin had struck him as a young woman who knew exactly where she was going. But he didn't intend to start arguing the point with Barrault. He wanted to draw the man out.

"Have you been, er, looking after her long?" he asked.

"Nearly three years."

"Well before she went to Hollywood, then?"

"But yes."

Webster smiled. "Weren't you frightened you might lose her when she went there?"

"Frightened? Oh no." Barrault spoke with a quiet certainty that Webster found irritating. Karin should not be taken so much for granted.

"Not with all those handsome young actors around?" he persisted.

Barrault gave a Gallic shrug.

Webster paused, but there was no reply and he continued, "But I suppose you've been spending quite a lot of time there yourself?"

"I keep a small apartment there permanently. But I cannot spend as much time there as I would wish to."

"Your motor racing makes that impossible, of course."

"It has done. Though I will not be doing very much in the future. I intend to write on it, and on other sports. Many newspapers and magazines are interested. So I shall still be travelling a great amount."

"That should be interesting. But I'm sure the fans will miss you."

"Of course."

"The race I remember most was your Le Mans victory a few years ago. Was that your best drive, do you think?"

"It was a good one, yes, but I had to share the honour with my co-driver. I preferred races where I was the only driver."

"Won't you miss competition?"

"I do not think so. I proved years ago that I was good. After that I preferred to enter only the races that particularly interested me. Besides, the sport has become too safe—so many new precautions and regulations. And if one really tries hard to win, the other drivers, they say you endanger them. They are cowards. So one seeks new sensations."

"Like skiing—climbing?"

"Skiing was my first interest. That I grew bored with before I took up the cars. I have not skied competitively for years now. Climbing I like, but it is slow—long periods of just walking before anything happens. And again, one needs people to climb with one. And they are all so timid—so careful of their precious necks."

"So what is the next sensation to be?"

"I want to try the sky-diving. There is a sport where one is alone—dependent on nobody. Again, though people would try to spoil it. I made the enquiries about jumping with a club—just at the beginning, you understand, to learn. Do you know what I found? They insist that you wear the two parachutes. Where is the risk there? Even with only one 'chute, the odds are stacked in your favour."

"You obviously like to gamble."

"Only when the odds are so finely balanced as to make it a real gamble. To play for really high stakes, when the chances are even—that is the only thrill there is."

"I'm afraid you're not going to find this cruise very thrilling. There isn't much action on board."

"Not yet, that is true. Perhaps, though, before the end of the voyage things may become more lively."

"I hope not. I came along for relaxation."

"I thought you came as a salesman, to try to persuade Roussos to buy some bagatelle you have thought up." There was the slightest suggestion of a sneer in Barrault's voice.

"Oh no. He's decided to fit the stabilizer to some ships, on a trial basis. There are some technical details to iron out, that's all. I'm sure the details would bore you."

"I, too, am sure of that."

"You are easily bored, aren't you?"

"Fools bore me. Cautious, frightened little people bore me. Routine bores me."

"How fortunate you are not to have to pursue it."

"Yes, my talent has preserved me from that. Unfortunately it does not preserve me from the frightened people."

"Nor does it preserve them from you."

"Preserve them from me? What do you mean?" Barrault's face darkened.

"Simply that I think frightened people might be made even more frightened by contact with you."

Barrault lost his temper. He burst out in a stream of French too fast for Webster to follow. Webster smiled and held up his hand. "You misunderstand me. I was not suggesting that you're some kind of sadist. I just mean that your personality—brave, dashing, brilliant at so many activities, unconventional—must show up their own inadequacies."

Barrault immediately calmed down. He smiled. "Ah, I understand. Yes, no doubt you are right."

One thing was clear: he was a sucker for flattery. A minute or so later he and Webster parted on the best of terms.

The Reverend Hilary Orchard stretched and yawned as he reclined beside the pool. It was gleaming invitingly. But he wouldn't bathe again just yet. More pleasant to soak up the sun for a few more minutes. He reached lazily for his glass of Campari and sipped. This was the life . . .

How fantastically lucky he'd been over the past few years. Fate had certainly smiled on him. Not that he hadn't worked damned hard, of course. But however hard one worked, however gifted one was, one got nowhere in this life without sheer, blind luck. It had been luck which had led him to that Cambridge cocktail party six years ago, just when he was becoming bored with his fellowship and was looking round for a new job, and where he had met Osterlinck. That had led directly to the assistant editorship of *Religion Left*. And from that had grown everything else—especially those extraordinarily useful contacts among the left wing establishment, in the radical campaigns like the peace and race relations movements. From that base he had been able to make himself one of the most persuasive spokesmen for so many of the new pressure groups as well—abortion on demand, pot legalization, abolition of censorship, and so on—just when many of them were getting off the ground. Since then he hadn't put a foot wrong. And his first book had caused a tremendous stir. To think that a few years before, immediately after his ordination, he had been seriously considering accepting that curacy in Glasgow! He gave a shudder. All these years he might have been flicking water over bawling babies and mouthing mumbo-jumbo over death beds and open graves. And making—how much? Two thousand pounds a year? Whereas in fact it looked as though his income this year was going to top twenty thousand for the first time.

Now the big professional decision he had to make was whether his base for the next year or so should be Britain or the States. It was a tricky choice. There was the offer of the coast-to-coast TV chat-show in America. That was highly lucrative. In addition, it would make him really well known to the American masses. At present his name only meant something to a comparatively small, though influential, section of the population over there. On the other hand, would it be wise to appear in a programme sponsored by a big industrial combine—especially one which did occasionally have dealings with South Africa?

Suppose, then, that he went home again? That would be the easy option. There were certainly more varied outlets for his talents there; and if he *was* one day going to think seriously about a parliamentary seat, he ought perhaps to put down roots. But, of course, he couldn't make any firm plans in that direction until he'd decided whether or not to remain in the Labour party. It was so hidebound in so many ways. If he did resign, though, it would have to be over some really big issue, which would attract maximum publicity. The difficulty there was likely to be the lack of an issue which he could legitimately make a matter of conscience and which at the same time the proletariat would feel strongly about.

Again, which party would he switch to? The Liberals were the obvious choice. But just how radical were they going to be in the future? It would be ghastly if he tied up with them, only for them to swing to the right. It would look bad to have to change parties a second time. Nor would it be easy to find a safe Liberal seat. However, this wasn't a decision which he needed to make quickly.

What he *was* going to have to decide quickly was the question of Venetia. The six months' separation they'd agreed on would soon be up. What was their future to be? In many ways it had been a highly satisfactory relationship; but were they really compatible in the context of a meaningful, long-term commitment? If so, was that commitment going to be expressed in terms of a marriage contract? The trouble was, he'd never really formulated his views on the subject of marriage. It was ironic: he'd left the Roman church initially largely because it prohibited marriage for its priests; and now he wasn't at all sure he didn't consider marriage an outmoded institution.

Then there was Venetia's attitude to his religion. It was unfortunate that she was so militantly atheistic. To keep on at him as she did to renounce his beliefs was absurd. Besides, religion was his stock in trade. It would be extremely bad for his image to change his opinion on too many subjects.

Oh, hell! When the big political and social issues were so simple, why did little personal questions have to be so bloody complicated?

Orchard got to his feet and dived rather less gracefully than he would have wished into the pool.

The *Angel* eventually sailed for Grenada, seventy-five miles distant, just before 2 P.M., her estimated time of arrival being six-fifteen.

Webster passed the heat of the afternoon indoors, but at five-thirty he went on deck to watch the island approach. He saw Trent leaning on the rail, and joined him.

Trent took a battered old pipe from his mouth and jerked it towards the distant coastline. "Never fails to excite, does it?"

"Grenada?"

"No—no. I mean arriving somewhere—anywhere. Every time it's a new adventure."

"So you still feel that? I should have thought it would have become routine for you now, considering the amount of travelling you've done."

"Never. Hope it never does. That's when I'll know it's time to stay home and tend my roses."

"You're lucky to be able to make something you enjoy so much pay for itself."

"Yes, but it's not all luck, you know. Had to work at it."

"Oh, I'm sure you did."

"Writing's damned hard work, I can tell you. Shook me when I first tried it."

"How did you happen to start in the first place?"

"When I came out of the army I decided to blue my gratuity on seeing as many parts of the world as possible. I happened to have a couple of pretty weird experiences, and when I got home a friend suggested I write it up into a long article. I'd never written anything longer than an army report in my life. Never been much of a one for books and things at all, to tell you the truth. Always imagined authors as pale-faced, long-haired pansies. Certainly never imagined I'd be one myself. It must have been my very ignorance of the business that gave my effort some sort of freshness, because when I sent it to a literary agent, he sold it straight away and asked if I could tackle a full-length book. From then on I was in business. Though as I say, it's not all beer and skittles. Frankly, I wish I could pack in the scribbling and just go where I want not always having to be on the look out for places that'll provide good copy."

"I'm sure an awful lot of people would be disappointed if that did happen. 'The last of the mad Englishmen' has got quite a following."

"Nice of you to say so. Damnfool nickname, though. Picked up by my New York publisher from a review in some obscure rag. I'd be jolly glad to get shot of it." He lowered his voice and glanced round. "Some people have taken it seriously, you know. They think I'm *really* insane. Me! So the sooner I can lose it, the better—as well as the monocle and the OE tie. All that image is a hell of a burden."

"So I can imagine. Speaking of hell reminds me of something Muller was saying last night. He said his idea of paradise would be listening to Franck's quartet—"

"Frank who?"

"Oh, I, er, think he meant César Franck, you know."

"Who's he?"

"A composer. Classical. French."

"Ah. Sorry, go on."

"Listening to Franck's quartet and looking at a Holbein portrait while drinking a glass of Mouton Rothschild '61."

Trent chuckled. "That just sounds like old Paul."

"I was wondering what your idea would be."

"Well, he can keep his highbrow Froggy composer. I'll settle for a military band playing Souza. Scotch and soda's good enough tipple for me, thanks very much. What was the third thing?"

"A Holbein portrait."

"Oh yes. Well, I don't go much for art. To tell you the truth, I can't see a lot of point in buying paintings. I mean, photography is so good these days— it can give you a much closer representation of a thing than any painter can. I know artists waffle a lot about getting below the surface of things and all that, but I reckon it's a lot of guff. I've never been able to see it. Do you agree?"

"Some of them exaggerate, of course," Webster began cautiously.

"That's rum," said Trent.

"What is?"

Trent pointed to the coast of Grenada. "We've passed Point Salines. We should have turned starboard and stayed parallel with the coast, if we're making for St. George's. But we seem to be carrying straight out to the open sea."

It was quite true. If there'd been any doubt, the *Angel*'s long, foamy wake showed clearly that the ship was continuing dead straight in a roughly north-west direction.

There was a footstep on the deck behind them. They turned. It was Dimitri.

"Mr. Roussos's compliments, gentlemen, and he'd be obliged if all the passengers would kindly join him in the main saloon."

He passed on to speak to Orchard, who was sitting reading a few yards away.

Trent said, "Mysterious, what?"

They made their way to the saloon, where they found Roussos waiting. Within a few minutes all the passengers were present. Then Roussos stood up. "Listen, folks, sorry to call a public meeting like this. There's nothing to worry about. It's just this. You all know what happened yesterday in Tobago. We don't know exactly what those thugs were after, but let's face it, they could have been after Irene. She thinks they were, anyway. But even if they were just thieves, they obviously knew where we were gonna be at what time. Our itinerary for this cruise was planned in advance. You all knew what it was, so did the crew, and though I asked people not to shout about it, it weren't no secret. Now, what's happened once can happen again. I know that Irene's thinking that. She's a brave little girl, and she hasn't said nothing but I don't want the cruise spoilt for her through her being scared to go ashore and having to keep looking over her shoulder the whole time." He looked at his daughter and nearly every eye in the room followed his gaze. Irene slowly went red.

Roussos continued, "That goes for all the rest of us, too, to a lesser extent. So what I've decided to do is change the itinerary. As you know, we were planning to make Grenada our next port of call and from there sail north in a zigzag pattern through St. Vincent, Barbados, Martinique, St. Kitts, etc., etc., to the Virgin Isles, but now we're gonna miss all them places out. Instead we're getting right away from this part of the Caribbean. We're making straight for the Dominican Republic."

Orchard gave a whistle. "That's quite a hop."

Roussos nodded. "About six hundred and fifty miles. I just hope nobody's too disappointed at missing out the places I mentioned."

Without looking directly at anyone, Irene said quietly, "It seems this is happening on my account. I'm very sorry. I don't want to spoil anybody's vacation."

Paul Muller said, "Don't talk nonsense my dear. You aren't spoiling any vacations. We'll have a splendid cruise."

There was a murmur of acquiescence from the others, and Quine added, "I personally don't mind in the least. I guess one Caribbean island's much the same as another. But where do you intend to go after the Dominican Republic, George?"

"I figure we'll talk it over during the next day or two and follow the will of the majority. We could go on to Haiti and Jamaica or back to Puerto Rico. Then we could all sail north to the Caicos Islands and on to the Bahamas, including Nassau. There are plenty of choices. But wherever we go, nobody'll know in advance that we're coming, and none of the local punks will have a chance to plan surprises."

"When will we reach the Dominican Republic?" Orchard asked.

"Haller reckons that given continuing good conditions, the trip'll take around thirty-eight hours. It's now Thursday, which means we'll be putting in at Santo Domingo Saturday morning."

Claire said, "I hope you don't all find thirty-eight hours at sea too much of a bore."

"There'll be plenty to do," Roussos said. "There's films and cards, and tomorrow evening there's going to be a bit of a celebration. It's a red-letter day."

"George!" Claire spoke sharply.

"Sorry, honey, it's no good. You're not getting away with it." He looked round the room. "Day after tomorrow's Claire's birthday. She told me not to mention it because she didn't want anyone to feel they had to get her a present. Well, I played along. But it's too late for any of you to get anything now, so she has to put up with a bit of a shindig tomorrow night!"

"My husband, as you can see, is a great one for surprises," Claire said, and there was a cold edge to her voice. "Maybe one day someone will surprise him—with a well-aimed grenade, perhaps." She smiled very sweetly at him.

Roussos threw back his head and gave a roar of laughter. One or two of the others joined in, but a little uncertainly. When Roussos had stopped, Karin said, "I thought you said the birthday was the day *after* tomorrow— Saturday."

"Ah, there I've been clever," Roussos said. He looked at his wife. "I took the trouble to find out the exact time you were born, sugar. The great event took place in London at 3:10 A.M. British time. But London's four hours ahead of us. So the actual anniversary of your birth will be 11:10 P.M. our time tomorrow—Friday. That's why we're all going to be in here at that time to drink your health. And maybe we'll go on doing it all night, huh?" He grinned round the room.

Mrs. van Duren got stiffly to her feet. "I shall be delighted to drink Claire's health at ten minutes past eleven. But I assure you that I have no intention of staying up all night indulging in some sort of bacchanalian revel."

"That's all right, Emily. You toddle off to your bunk whenever you feel like it. When you wake up—when we all wake up—we should be safely anchored in Santo Domingo harbour."

"Poor Santo Domingo," said Mrs. van Duren.

The group started to break up. Irene hurried out alone. Webster hesitated for a moment, then followed her. She went aft as far as she could on the main deck and threw herself down on a canvas chair. Webster walked up quietly and sat down next to her. She looked at him, her face charged with emotion.

"Relieved?" he asked her.

"Relieved? Certainly not! Furious would be closer to the mark."

"Oh? Why's that?"

"Why do you think? I feel humiliated. How dare he make *me* the reason for changing everything like this? I wasn't as scared as Nathan Quine was yesterday, and I'm no more apprehensive than anyone else. *He's* decided on the change of itinerary. But it looks to everybody else like *my* fault. Brave little girl—yuch!"

"There's no question of *fault*. It won't spoil the cruise for anybody—"

"I don't care about that! I've been raised to be polite at all times, so I apologized. But I don't give a damn for their lousy vacations. They're a bunch of boot-licking, sycophantic spongers. I hate them all!" Her voice was harsh and for a moment her face looked vicious. Then she seemed to make an effort to calm down. "What I object to is being made his stooge for the dramatic announcement. I object to the pretence of consulting them all about the new itinerary—when I bet he's already decided exactly where we're going."

"At least he's shown he cares a lot about your welfare."

"That's it exactly: he's *shown* he cares a lot about my welfare. Do you know what I think? I think he's secretly pleased about yesterday. I think he sees it as a sort of status symbol. I mean, only big, important people have trouble with kidnappers, don't they? This puts him in the Lindburgh or Hearst or Getty league—or it would do if the thing actually happens."

"I think you're being unfair to him. Granted the public announcement was a bit on the dramatic side. But he did say it was for all our safety. And he seems quite genuinely to care for you. Why do you fight him all the time?"

"What business is it of yours?"

"I'm sorry, I didn't mean to pry." Webster started to stand up.

"Wait!" She put a hand on his arm, and he sank down again. "You think I'm a spoiled brat, don't you?"

"No, I don't think you're a brat. Spoiled a bit, maybe, but that's pretty well inevitable. The only daughter of a very rich man . . ."

"Ah, but you see, I wasn't always the only daughter. That's just the point. You clearly don't know about Helen."

"Your sister?"

"My *late* sister. My beautiful, chic, vivacious, witty, gay, fun-loving, altogether perfect—and very dead sister."

Webster raised his eyebrows. "But obviously not your beloved sister."

Irene flushed. "No, not beloved. But not hated. I didn't mean to sound bitchy. We didn't have a lot in common, but we got on well enough and I was very sorry when she was killed. Not only from a purely selfish motive, either—even though things were a darn sight easier for me when she was alive."

"Do you want to explain?"

"Yes, I do. I'm tired of your looking at me as though I were a cross between Typhoid Mary and Lizzie Borden. Helen was everything my father ever wanted in a daughter: a girl who'd live high, mixing with the beautiful people, jet-setting it round the world—New York, Paris, London, St. Moritz, Monte Carlo, Bermuda. He wanted to see her name in the gossip columns and her photo in the society magazines, dancing with European royalty or movie stars. Because that was the sort of life he'd always wanted himself and had never been able to have. Even when he made his pile he could never quite buy himself into the very best circles. So he wanted to live it vicariously, through Helen. And she would have done all those things, too, if it hadn't been for that car crash. It completely broke him for a while. But when he got over it a bit, he wanted *me* to take over where she had left off. *I* was to be groomed to be the high-living heiress. But you see, I'm not made like that. I'm fat. I have no dress sense—I'm not even particularly interested in clothes. I'm clumsy. I don't dance well, or ski. I'm not vivacious. I don't sparkle. And I have a homely face."

"Nonsense."

"Well, that's a matter of opinion . . ."

"What you have got is a brain."

She glanced at him acutely, as if suspicious of sarcasm; but his face was innocent of any trace of this. She said, "Well, I did have, though I'm afraid it's been rapidly becoming atrophied for the last few years. Once I wanted to go to university. I wanted it more than anything. Do you know what my ambition was?"

Webster shook his head.

"To be a teacher. Surprising, isn't it? The last thing you'd expect of the daughter of the seventeenth richest man in the world. But it was the only thing I've ever been really interested in. I'd like to start my own school—an international, completely free private school—the best in the world."

"So what was the snag?"

"My father was the snag. He wouldn't hear of it." Irene's voice became a passable imitation of Roussos's. " 'What—waste the best years of your life poring over musty old books? No way! Get out and enjoy yourself, girl. Have fun while you can. That sort of stuff is all right for a girl who's going to have to earn her own living. But not you. A degree? Who needs it?' "

"But surely, if you'd made it clear how much you wanted to go . . ."

"Oh, don't be a fool! Of course I made it clear. But there was no budging him. It wasn't the sort of life for the daughter of George Roussos. Anybody could do that sort of thing. What was the point of having millions of dollars on tap if you then go and live like any two-bit clerk? You don't know how I tried—and my grandmother tried—to talk him round."

"But could he have stopped you if you'd just gone ahead—defied him?"

"That's what I should have done. But it's not the sort of thing that's ever happened in our family. It would have meant a terrible row, and almost

certainly a complete break with him. I just couldn't face it. I guess I simply
didn't have the guts to do it. So I knuckled under. Or up to a point I did."

"You mean that even now you refuse to live the sort of life he wants?"

"Right. He could stop me going to university, but he couldn't make me
become a second Helen. So most of the time I just stagnate quietly in Boston
with my grandmother. A couple of times a year I receive a summons to join
him—on the *Angel,* or at his mansion outside Athens or at some place he's
rented in Cannes or Bermuda. I don't refuse. Like a dutiful little girl I obey
the summons. I even attend his ghastly all-night parties. And I make myself
as disagreeable as I can the whole time."

"In the hope that one day he'll relent and give his blessing to your going to
university?"

"I don't know that I even want to go now. The urge seems to have
passed."

"This war seems rather pointless, then."

"Not if I can teach him that he can't order people's lives for them. At
least, not mine. I want to do my own thing. I don't want my life ordered. I
don't even want him hiring bodyguards for me."

Webster stiffened. But he managed to keep his voice casual as he said, "Is
he planning to do that?"

"Don't pretend. *You're* one—I can tell."

Webster sighed. "How did you know?"

"You've been taking far too much interest in me—and sticking far too
close. But you're not a fortune hunter. And you're not a marine engineer
who's trying to sell him something: he wouldn't have asked you on this trip if
you were. What are you? Ex-policeman?"

"Yes. Scotland Yard. Detective Chief Superintendent."

"Hm, I'm flattered. Why did he hire you?"

"I suppose he thought I had the right qualifications."

"No, I mean why hire anyone? Did he have reason to think someone was
going to try and get me?"

"Why should you think that?"

"I don't know. But he's been different somehow this trip—just a little
*distrait;* though I doubt if anyone else has noticed it. I wondered if he'd had
a phone call making threats against me, or an anonymous letter."

"Well, I've seen nothing like that and he'd surely have shown it to me."

Irene gave an unconvinced grunt. "So you did shoot at those thugs yesterday?"

"Yes, I did. Sorry to have lied to you, but I didn't want you to know who I
really was, and you would have guessed—so I thought—if you knew I was
armed. I still don't want anybody else to know; so I'd be glad if you didn't
tell anyone—not even your grandmother."

"All right; if you promise not to tell my father that I guessed."

"May I ask why?"

"Let's just say I like to be one up on him—know things he doesn't know I know. Deal?"

"Deal," said Webster.

# 10

"Has anybody seen my heart tablets?"

The question was asked in a loud and piercing voice by Mrs. van Duren at lunch the following day. She followed it up by casting an eagle eye slowly round the table.

There was a general shaking of heads. Roussos said, "You lost 'em?"

"I would hardly be asking if anybody had seen them otherwise, would I, George?"

Irene said, "Your digoxin tablets, you mean?"

"Naturally, my dear. Those are the only ones I take for my heart, as you know quite well."

"Do you have any spare ones?"

"Yes, fortunately; but they will not last for the rest of the cruise."

Roussos asked, "When did you have 'em last?"

"I took one first thing this morning in my stateroom. I'm almost certain that I left them there. But when I returned just before lunch they weren't there."

"Almost certain?" Roussos said.

"It is possible that I slipped the bottle into my purse or pocket. But I don't think so."

"What do they look like?"

"They are very small white tablets in an ordinary pill bottle, which originally contained one hundred. I keep a close count of them and there were exactly seventy-two left."

Roussos shrugged. "Well, don't worry. They're not anything a stewardess is likely to have knocked off."

"I certainly hope not: it would probably mean she were planning to take her own life."

"Oh, poisonous, are they?"

"Highly so. I once read the report of a suicide case in which it was stated that ten are invariably a fatal dose."

"I'll see Dimitri warns the servants," Roussos said. "I bet they turn up. If not, we'll cable Boston for a new supply to be sent on. Don't worry about it."

Karin Johnson stared at Philippe Barrault disbelievingly. "You did *what* yesterday?" she demanded in French.

"Told Williams to mind his own business and not interfere in your career. He agreed to comply."

For a moment she was speechless. But only for a moment. "How dare you!" she said furiously. "Do you think you own me?" She made for the door.

"Where are you going?" he snapped.

"To apologize to him."

"Oh no you're not." He moved in front of her. "I did what was right and necessary. I will not have strange men putting crazy schemes into your head. I warned you when you first told me his suggestion that you had to forget the idea. Obviously you have not forgotten it. Very well, I'll humour you. When we get back to the States I'll go into the matter. But if I do decide the thing is feasible, the backing will not come from George Roussos."

"Listen, if Mr. Roussos and I—"

"There will be no Mr. Roussos and you. After this cruise you will never see him again."

She made a great effort to calm down, gave a gulp and said quietly: "All right: tell me why."

"If you must know, because the way you were fawning over him on Wednesday made me feel sick."

She went white with anger. "I was not fawning over him!"

"Do you deny that you—?"

"I don't deny anything. I don't have to. But just to put things straight, until yesterday I'd hardly said more than ten words at a time to him. He's your friend, not mine. I couldn't suddenly ask a virtual stranger to back me. I knew I had to get to know him first: so that I could approach him as a friend."

"Friend? Huh!"

"Just what do you mean by that?"

"It was quite clear from the way you were behaving that it wasn't merely friendship you had in mind."

"That's a swinish thing to say."

"I think you'd do anything to get backing for this damn film company."

Karin was now trembling with temper. "Philippe, I won't be spoken to like this. I'm going on deck. When you're ready to apologize, you can come and do it."

She went to step past him, but he grabbed her wrist. She tried to wrench herself free. "Let go of me!"

"I will not. Not until you promise to forget Roussos and his money and start behaving like a normal person."

"I'll promise nothing," Karin shouted. "And *you* telling anyone to behave like a normal person is really funny!"

His fingers tightened on her wrist. "What is that supposed to mean?"

"Philippe—you're hurting!"

"I said what do you mean?"

"Well, is this pathological jealousy normal?"

"You say I am not normal?"

"Yes, I do say that—all right? You're not normal. You are out of your mind. Is that clear? Mad. Insane."

Philippe's eyes narrowed into cold slits. He raised his left arm—and slapped her viciously, back-handed, across the mouth. She gave a cry of pain and shock and tried to pull away, but he kept a tight grip on her wrist with his right hand. For a moment he seemed about to hit her again, this time with the palm of his hand. Then he apparently thought better of it and released her. Karin, still tugging to get free, staggered backwards and nearly fell. She steadied herself and stood looking at him, her lips trembling, the marks of his knuckles showing red next to her mouth, like an extension of her lipstick.

"You pig," she said. "You despicable pig."

"Get out."

"Don't worry—I'm going—for good. Don't think you can say you're sorry tomorrow and everything will be back to normal. We're finished. I'll keep up appearances in front of the others for a few more days; but at the first opportunity I'm leaving. And I don't want ever to be within spitting distance of you again."

"I don't want it any other way, you tramp. And I said get out."

Karin went to the door. Her hand on the knob, she turned. "I repeat what I said: you are out of your mind, Philippe. And before very long everyone on this yacht is going to know it. You can be quite sure of that."

Webster stood by the rail, staring out over the flat, featureless blue sea under the cloudless blue sky, and yawned. He was bored. He'd spent most of the morning reading and didn't feel like doing any more. There was nobody among his fellow-passengers he wanted to talk to—except Karin, perhaps, and she was somewhere with Barrault. He couldn't talk to the crew without the risk of giving away the fact that he knew nothing about marine engineering. He wished he had something positive to do. He wasn't used to all this leisure. Or all this sun. He was beginning to find the heat rather overpowering. He thought wistfully of London at its coldest, greyest and wettest; of its villains and their victims; of long, exhausting hours among the dregs of its population; of stale cheese sandwiches and luke warm tea in plastic beakers drunk standing up; of autopsy reports, record sheets and mug shots; of drug pushers, con men, safe crackers and pimps. All that, and the constant battle of which it was a part, had been the breath of life to him. He'd been a fool to resign. This life of luxury and ease was not for him. For one thing, it left the mind too passive, too open to memories . . .

"*You knew I was a policeman when you married me.*"

"*Yes, a policeman, Alec. A uniformed bobby, who worked reasonably regular hours.*"

"*There was plenty of night and weekend work even then.*"

"*But nothing like this! And mostly we knew when it was coming.*"

"*Long hours are part of the price of success. Would you really like it if I were still a bobby on the beat? Would you be proud of me? And would you be content to live on that sort of salary?*"

"*That's not the point. Jim Lomax is the same rank as you, but Norma says he doesn't work anything like your hours. She says he told her you've got a reputation for always being on the job. It's a standing joke at the Yard. It's humiliating, Alec.*"

"*Humiliating? That I'm a hard worker?*"

"*Yes—yes—yes! Hasn't it ever occurred to you what it's like for me to be known as the wife of the man who never goes home?*"

"*Oh come on! That's ridiculous. I'm home now, aren't I?*"

"*For how long?*"

"*Would you rather I was spending my time with another woman?*"

"*At least that would be grounds for divorce.*"

"*You're not serious?*"

"*Perfectly serious.*"

"*I won't agree to it.*"

"*What on earth do you mean? You can't—*"

"*I won't agree to a formal separation, Susan. You're my wife—*"

"*Spare me the clichés.*"

"*If you want a divorce—*"

"*I don't want a divorce Alec. If I did, I'd say so.*"

"*Is there somebody else?*"

"*No.*"

"*Then why—?*"

"*I want to sort myself out. And I want to be free to come and go as I please— to be able to accept invitations without qualification, to book for a theatre knowing I'll be able to go.*"

"*Have somebody else book for you, you mean, don't you?*"

"*Probably. I'm not going into a nunnery.*"

"*You want me to give you leave to run around with other men.*"

"No. I want us to live apart—just for a while. Both be free to do what we want—within limits. You'll be free to take other women out—"

"Which you know perfectly well I won't do."

"I'll see what life's like without you. You'll see what it's like without me."

"Yes—that's it, isn't it? You want to teach me a lesson. 'I'll show him'—that's what you're saying. 'I'll teach him to stay out so much.'"

"What if I am? Is that so terrible?"

"Yes. It is terrible—when you know the work I'm doing. You don't realize what a sordid, putrid mess we've got below the surface of this city—and not always below the surface, either. Somebody's got to try to clear it up."

"Single-handed?"

"Don't be such a damned little idiot."

"Don't you give me that about 'got to.' You love it! You're only happy when you're up to your elbows in that putrid mess."

"I see. I wonder in that case why you've ever wanted me home at all."

"Right now, so do I."

"Well, you're stuck with me, I'm afraid. I'm not going to move out. I can't stop you leaving, if you're set on it, but I'm not going to say I agree to a separation, and that's that."


*Dear Alec,*

*I've done it, you see. Sorry it's got to be like this—just a disappearance while you're at work. No doubt it's a cowardly way to do it, but I couldn't face another discussion about it.*

*Believe me, I don't want this to be the end. But we can't continue in the way of the past twelve months. Our marriage had become a farce. (Funny how it seems impossible for either of us to avoid clichés in this situation.) I suggest you don't try to trace me. I don't suppose you'd have a lot of difficulty in finding me, but there's no way you could make me come back. Not yet, anyway. I will get in touch with you sooner or later. That's a promise. I realize you may not want me back then, but that's something we can discuss when the time comes.*

*Take care of yourself.*
*Susan.*


"Hullo, Alec."

"Jim! What on earth's the matter?"

"I've—Alec, I've got some news for you."

"What—What sort of news?"

"Bad news."

"Tell me. Please. Quickly."

"It's Susan."

*"Hurt?"*
*"She's dead."*

*"It was a car crash, Alec. She was with a man. He was driving. She was killed instantly. She didn't feel anything."*

*She didn't feel anything. Didn't feel anything . . .*
"I've had the most terrible row with Philippe."

"I'm sorry—what did you say? I was miles away."

"I've had the most terrible row with Philippe." Karin was pale and looked decidedly shaky. She tried a small smile. "I have to tell someone all about it. Do you mind if it's you?"

"Of course I don't mind. Please do. Look, would you like a drink?"

"Yes, I think I would. It—it was rather traumatic."

When they were settled in a corner of the otherwise deserted main saloon, Karin with a brandy, Webster with a beer, he said, "Are you sure you want to tell me? Isn't it more usual for girls to unburden themselves to other girls?"

"Can you imagine me pouring my heart out to Irene? No, you will do very well—if it won't bore you to listen."

"Don't be silly. What happened?"

She was silent. Then: "You know, I don't think I do want to go over it, after all. Not just now. I'm sorry. But he hit me again."

"Oh no! He ought to be turned off the yacht."

"Now let's not make too much of it. I'm luckier than Gloria Grahame in *The Big Heat,* after all. He didn't throw scalding coffee in my face."

"Let me speak to Roussos."

"No, please: leave things as they are. He's already accused me of trying to seduce Mr. Roussos in order to get money from him to finance my films."

"He's out of his mind!"

"I do think he's getting a bit pathological about things."

"I don't know why you've put up with it so long."

"I've been hoping he'd become more his old self again."

"He wasn't always like this then?"

"Heavens, no! I mean, he's always been what's known as a hell-raiser. He's had fights and smashed up bars and things. But that used to be more exciting than anything else—like living in a John Ford Western. And he was always terribly kind to me; I could rely on him to take my part. Once he blacked the eye of a critic who'd said something nasty about me. He was protective without being too possessive."

"When did things change?"

"I think when I had the success with *Yesterday's Woman.* Before that, you see, Philippe, was the big one—the great sportsman—and I was his companion, just a young actress. Now, well, I suppose I'm a star. I'm a bigger name than he is. When we go out, he's only like a sort of consort, and he can't take it."

"What are you going to do about it?"

"I won't be having any more to do with him after this trip."

"Do you really mean that?"

She nodded decisively. "Yes. We'll keep up appearances for a bit of the cruise. I wouldn't spoil things for the Roussoses for worlds. But then—" Karin made a chopping gesture with her hand.

"I hope you'll stick to that. He'll have plenty of time in the next few weeks to try and win you round."

"I won't be staying that long. I'm going to leave the boat as soon as I can do it unobtrusively."

"Oh, are you? I'm very sorry. Why?"

"I told Philippe I would be. It would make things very awkward for the rest of you if we were both on board."

"But why should *you* be the one to disembark? This row wasn't your fault."

"That's true," she said thoughtfully. Then she nodded. "Yes, you're quite right: why should I run away? All right—I'll stay to the bitter end. He won't like it, but he'll have to put up with it."

"Good for you. And if he gives you any more trouble, be sure and let me know."

"Yes sir." She gave him a mock salute. Her colour had returned and she was looking much happier.

"Are you going to speak to Roussos about this film company?"

"No; not yet anyway. That's the ironic part: the row was partly over that. But I'd already more or less decided to wait and see how things turn out when I get back to Hollywood. If I still can't find the scripts I want, then I might think about it again—but only if I can persuade some people who really know the business to go in with me. If that happens I'll probably mention it to Mr. Roussos, to see if he'd be interested in investing—but that's all."

"I think that's a good decision—even though it was my suggestion that sparked off all the trouble."

She gave a contented sigh. "Do you know, I feel as if a great weight's been lifted from my shoulder. It's lovely just to sit and talk to you without having to worry in case Philippe sees us and flips his lid. I only hope he's not too unpleasant to everyone else because of me."

"I should let Roussos handle things if that happens. It was he who invited

Barrault, after all, and I think he'll be quite capable of dealing with anyone who looks like spoiling the cruise."

"Yes, he'd go to great lengths to prevent that, wouldn't he? Like suddenly changing everything because of that attack—" She stopped short. "Oh, I'm so stupid! I've been longing to talk to you about that, but I didn't get a chance with Philippe watching me. And now I forget to mention it! It must have been thrilling—like something out of James Bond. I wish I'd been there."

"I don't think you'd have enjoyed it. There was no director around to call 'cut.'"

"*Touché*. But I'd loved to have seen you doing your *Fastest Gun Alive* thing. Though really it would have been more exciting if you hadn't stopped them and they'd got away with her. Then we could have all chased after them in the *Angel*. That would be a super scenario."

"You're a heartless little minx. What about poor Irene?"

"Oh, we'd have got her back unharmed in the end. That always happens in movies anyway. And it would teach her to count her blessings and not be such a grouch. What does she have to be grumpy about, I'd like to know?"

"Actually, she does have something."

"Oh what?"

"I mustn't tell you the details. But through no fault of her own, she was unable to do what she wanted to do most in life."

"That does make a difference. All right, I take back all I said. I shall be very nice to her from now on."

"Good; I think she needs a nice, bright girl-friend."

"I don't know about the *nice* part, but I suppose I'm bright enough. Or I could be the sophisticated, wisecracking friend—the Eve Arden type. What do you think?"

"Just be yourself."

"Sometimes I don't know what that is. Anyway, I can teach her how to dress better and make herself look pretty."

"Well, do it tactfully."

"Of course I'll do it tactfully! I'm a most tactful person when I wish. You know, I think I'll enjoy this. It'll be quite a change for me to have a *girl*-friend."

"Alec, I been thinking." Roussos sat down next to Webster. "What do you make of Orchard? Could he . . . ? You know."

"Well, I can't say I've taken to the chap, but I can't honestly see a clergy-man getting involved in a kidnapping caper."

"If he is a clergyman."

Webster stared. "What do you mean?"

"What I say. Do he seem like a priest to you?"

"Well, he's not like any one I've met, but that doesn't mean anything. After all, he's not an ordinary parish priest—a vicar. He's a university teacher and a writer."

"But he never talks about religion at all—it's all politics and social stuff."

"He's one of the new school, I suppose."

"OK, I'll ask another question: does he seem like an Englishman? Because he don't to me."

"I agree up to a point. His accent sounds overdone. And he uses his hands rather a lot when he talks. But look, Hilary Orchard *is* British—and a priest. So you're suggesting that this man's an imposter—right?"

"I'm wondering if he is."

"But surely you've met him before, haven't you—the real Orchard, I mean?"

"Yeah, but only once and that was several months ago. And I'd been having a bit of eye trouble round then and I wasn't seeing too good. So I didn't get too close a look at him. But this bloke strikes me as different somehow."

"I see. So, what do you want me to do—challenge him?"

"Naw—you'd have to give yourself away for that. I was figuring we might test him."

"In what way?"

"If he's a phoney, he's probably done a bit of swotting up on what Orchard thinks and believes, and how he talks; and it could be he's learnt a bit about religion and the Bible and things like that—just enough to get by. The real Orchard's radically minded, and doesn't go much for that old-fashioned religion, so people don't expect him to be always spouting texts and Bible-punching. OK?" Webster nodded. "But Orchard would have had to have learnt all that stuff once, wouldn't he? I mean he was ordained as a priest, and then he'd have had to lecture on orthodox religion at Cambridge, and mark exam papers and so on?"

"Certainly he would," Webster said.

"So though he mightn't actually believe the Bible now, he'd have to know all about it. But if this bloke's an imposter, *he won't* know all about it. He'd never be able to answer the sort of questions a real priest would."

"Are you suggesting we put him through some sort of Bible quiz?"

"No—what I mean is that if he got talking to a real Bible expert, he'd be bound to give himself away."

"Do we have a real Bible expert on board?"

"Course we do: old Emily. Listen, she spends hours reading it. She must know it backwards. And she understands all the priests' jargon too. Remember how she explained just where Orchard's book was wrong the other day?

So what I'm suggesting is that you try and get 'em together to talk about religion—and then just listen."

"Me? Wouldn't it be better if you did it?"

"Naw—that's no good. The old bag hates my guts. She wouldn't talk religion with me around—she'd think I was laughing at her up my sleeve. But you she likes. So—what do you think?"

The honest answer would have been "not much." But Roussos seemed to want it, and Webster was still harbouring guilt feelings about not earning his money; this would be *something* for him to do, at least. So he didn't intend to argue.

"How would we get them together?" he asked. "Mrs. van Duren won't willingly settle down for a theological debate with Orchard. She thinks he's a heretic and she won't have anything to do with him."

"I've thought about that. I reckon the best thing will be to take her into our confidence about what we suspect."

"And about who I really am, too?"

"Yeah. For one thing, she's taken that Tobago bother real bad. She's worried stiff about Irene, though she don't show it too much. But if she knows there's a Scotland Yard dick on board she'll be much happier—and I fancy she'll enter into the plan. We can rely on her to keep her trap shut. Suit you?"

"Sure. When do you want me to do it?"

"Might as well make it as soon as possible." Roussos looked at his watch. "After dinner, I should think. That'll give Emily a chance to prepare for a bit first—decide on the questions she's going to ask and so on. And you'll have a couple of hours to kill before the party."

"Have you thought about how to get Orchard's cooperation to this?"

"Well, not his cooperation exactly. But we can get him in a position where he'd have a job to wriggle out of it. In the library there's a book of all sorts of short pieces of stories and poems. An anthology they call it. I think Irene had it as a school prize. There are a few pieces in Latin in it. Suppose you find one of 'em, and then after dinner, ask Orchard to translate it for you? By the way, that'll be another test in itself, won't it? I'll tell Emily to give you ten minutes and then go into the library herself. Knowing her, I reckon you'll be able to leave the rest to her. All I want from you is a promise to stay with 'em right through—and watch. If he is a phoney, he's a terrific actor. He couldn't fool her if he gave wrong answers about the Bible or religion. But he might think of some way to con her—evade the questions somehow. He couldn't do that with you there."

"Oh, I'll stay with them—assuming Mrs. van Duren agrees to the scheme."

"She'll play along. I'll go and put her wise now."

And Roussos lumbered off.

Webster and Karin soon found that they needn't have worried about Barrault. That evening his behaviour was impeccable. He showed no reaction to his row with Karin, and was so cheerful and charming to everyone that at one time she whispered in Webster's ear, "This is maddening. He's behaving as though *he's* glad to be shot of *me."*

Webster was not anticipating his after-dinner task with any relish. He was well aware that the "test" could easily turn into a farce. Moreover, should Orchard—assuming he was the genuine article—see through the stratagem, he would be justified in being highly annoyed. Webster's apprehensions weren't lessened when, catching his eye half-way through the main course, Mrs. van Duren gave him a broad and very obvious wink.

By eight-twenty all the passengers had moved forward to the main saloon. Here Roussos made another of his now familiar little speeches.

"Folks, we'll be using this room for the party tonight and the servants have gotta get it ready. For one thing, we might have some dancing and the furniture must be shifted. I don't wanta keep 'em up too late, so if you don't mind we'll clear out as soon as we've drunk our coffee. You'll still have the library, the card room and our sitting-room on the upper deck to relax in. I only call it 'ours' because usually we only use it when we got the *Angel* to ourselves; it's cosier then. But feel free to use it this evening. The video's been taken up there, and I'll be showing a movie if anyone wants to watch, though I expect some of you may like to get a bit of shut-eye ready for the party. Anyway, let's all meet back in here a bit before eleven. And then we can make a real night of it, OK?"

Roussos let a minute or two pass, then approached Webster. "I've briefed Emily," he said quietly, "and for once I think I'm in her good books. Come and see me after the"—he grinned—"the Bible class breaks up and let me know how Orchard made out. I'll have something to show you too."

"Not the tip-off letter?"

"Yeah. I found it at last."

"Oh, that's fine. Where was it?"

"Between the pages of another letter. Funny, I'd've sworn I'd looked there. Suppose I musta been a bit careless. You ready for Orchard—picked out something in that book for him to translate?"

"Yes."

"OK. Best of luck."

Carefully choosing a moment when Orchard was not speaking to anybody, Webster strolled up to him, and in as casual a manner as he could
manage, said, "I wonder if I might have the benefit of your scholarship for a
few minutes?"

Orchard looked surprised, but in no way displeased. "By all means."

"Perhaps you could step along to the library with me. There's a bit of
Latin in a book there I'd like you to unravel for me if you can manage it."

"I can't imagine that'll be outside my capabilities."

They went to the library. Webster picked up the book, which he'd put
aside with a page marked, and opened it. "Here you are."

Orchard sat down and pulled the book towards him. "Now, let me see."

Ten minutes later he said, "That's all of it. Mine wasn't the most poetical
of translations, but I gave you the sense accurately enough."

"Thanks very much. Great help." Webster glanced at his watch. What
was keeping the old battle-axe? She should have been here by now. He was
just about to ask Orchard to translate another passage when the door
opened and Emily van Duren stumped in.

She stared at them with a good imitation of displeased surprise. "Oh.
You're here."

"I'm afraid so," Webster said.

"Sorry," Orchard added. "Did you want the room to yourself? I'm just
leaving."

"No, don't. As you're here you can both make yourselves useful. My eyes
aren't what they used to be. In fact, none of me is. It's a forlorn hope, I
think, but would there be a Bible concordance in here, do you suppose?
George doesn't know. I can't imagine where all these books came from. He
never reads one, I'm sure. Probably he picked them up as a job lot somewhere."

Webster and Orchard both started scanning the shelves. Mrs. van Duren
sat down and watched them. After a few minutes Orchard said, "You know,
one of the most irritating things about publishers is their failure to standard-
ize the way they print titles along the spines of books. Half of them read
from the top to the bottom and half the other way. Looking for a book on a
shelf, one spends the entire time wagging one's head from left to right like a
demented puppet."

At the end of ten minutes they announced failure.

"Oh well," Mrs. van Duren said. "Can't be helped. Suppose I'll be able to
buy one in this Dominican place. In the meantime, perhaps you can help."
She fixed Orchard with a gimlet eye.

"I?"

"Yes; you're a clergyman, aren't you?"

"Of a sort."

"Your expression, not mine."

"How can I help you?"

"Tell me where the text is found that says, 'He was numbered with the transgressors; yet he bore the sin of many.'"

Orchard smiled. "Even I know the answer to that one: it's in the book of Isaiah."

"Do you know the chapter and verse?"

"Fifty-third chapter—final verse."

"And are those words actually the last ones in the verse?"

"I think not. I believe there's one more clause; something like 'and made intercession for the transgressors.'"

"I had an idea that those first words appear in the New Testament as well, in a slightly different form."

"Yes, in one of the gospels. Jesus applies the words to himself at the Last Supper."

"Do you know which of the gospels?"

"Oh, let me think." Orchard closed his eyes for a moment. "Er, Luke, I believe."

"Tell me, Mr. Orchard, can you explain the phrase 'he bore the sins of many'? What is the original of the word rendered 'bore' or 'bare'?"

"Oh dear," Orchard frowned and for a second Webster had a stirring of excitement. But then Orchard said, "The Hebrew is, I believe, *nāsā'*, which can mean either 'bear' in the sense of simply 'carry,' or can mean 'take away.'"

"What about the Greek?"

"That I think is *anapherō.*"

"Is that the same word in the epistle to the Hebrews, in 'Christ was once offered to bear the sins of many'?"

"Yes; and in 'he himself bore our sins in his body on the tree,' in One Peter."

"So the meaning, then, is that by His sacrifice Our Lord took the penalty for our sins upon himself, and also carried them away?"

"That is certainly what the original writers believed."

"Do I gather that you don't believe it?"

"It would take me some time to explain my interpretation of the terms 'sin' and 'sacrifice.'"

"I have plenty of time, Mr. Orchard."

"But I'm sure Williams doesn't wish to hear me preach a sermon."

"On the contrary," Webster lied. "I'd be most interested."

"It won't be a sermon, either, Mr. Orchard," Mrs. van Duren said. "I couldn't interrupt or ask questions during a *sermon.*"

"Oh, it's a seminar you want, is it? Very well, if you're sure. I see it like this."

It was an hour and a half later that Orchard looked at his watch. "My word, look at the time: ten twenty-five!"

"Is it really?" Mrs. van Duren got to her feet. "Well, it's been most instructive, Mr. Orchard."

"Thank you. Actually, I'd almost forgotten how absorbing a good old Bible discussion can be. Quite takes me back to my undergraduate days. Incidentally, I must congratulate you on your Bible knowledge. Really remarkable in a lay person."

Mrs. van Duren gave her characteristic little bow of the head. "I have spent nearly—well, a considerable number of years reading it. I ought to have acquired a fair knowledge by now."

"I must admit, in view of that, to surprise at your not knowing where to find the text about being numbered with the transgressors. It's quite well known."

"At my age, Mr. Orchard, one forgets things very easily." She looked at Webster. "I'm afraid that between us we've talked poor Mr. Williams almost into a stupor."

"Not at all." Webster, too, stood up. He was feeling pretty dazed by the cut and thrust of the debate, much of which had been above him: but he shook his head as he opened the door and they all went out. "I wasn't in the least bored."

"I'm pleased to hear it. Though it might have been preferable to have had the discussion some other time. You both ought really to have slept this evening in readiness for tonight's saturnalia."

"Oh I'm used to late nights," Webster said.

"And I shan't be staying up very late, I assure you," Orchard added.

Mrs. van Duren gave him a pitying look. "Mr. Orchard, I'm afraid you are an innocent abroad. I have known George Roussos for many years, and I promise you that if you do not stay to the bitter end—probably between 4 and 5 A.M.—you will mortally offend your host, and as a result will not enjoy the rest of the cruise. I am eig—I am of advanced years, with a weak heart, so am exempt; which shows that my condition does, thankfully, have some compensations."

Orchard looked a little alarmed at her words. "Oh, I see. Thank you for the warning. Perhaps I ought to try and get at least a short nap first."

"I think that would be highly advisable."

"Then I'll see you both later." He walked away.

There was nobody in sight. Webster looked at Mrs. van Duren and smiled. "Well done. That was quite a grilling you gave him. What's the verdict? I must say he seemed pretty knowledgeable to me."

"Oh, he's genuine, of course. I knew after a couple of minutes that he was a trained theologian."

Webster stared at her. "A couple of minutes?"

"Yes—when he gave me those Hebrew and Greek words. No imposter could have done that. I mean to say, *I* didn't know them off-hand. I was able to look them up in advance."

Rather grimly, Webster said, "I think you might somehow have indicated the fact that he is OK a little earlier."

"Why?"

"I needn't have stayed."

"You said you weren't bored."

"I wasn't; but I can think of more entertaining ways to pass an evening than listening to Brother Orchard spouting."

"The evening won't have done you any harm. You heard a fair amount of nonsense from him, I agree—but you also heard some good, old-fashioned gospel from me."

Webster chuckled. "Do you think I need it?"

"Everybody needs it."

"But some more than others?"

"No; but some need to be *reminded* more than others that they need it— that young man among them. Sad case."

"How do you mean?"

"He could have made a good minister—and a powerful preacher. I think he's a genuine idealist. And I have a suspicion that deep down he still believes the gospel. But he's been so side-tracked with all this modish nonsense that he's forgotten what being a parson's all about. He's gotten into the habit of telling people what they want to hear. And people don't want to be told that they're sinners who need forgiveness."

Webster said, "Well, as you say, we both heard it from you tonight—even though that wasn't the real reason for the exercise. Anyway, I must go and report to my employer that his suspicions were unfounded."

"Could I trouble you for your arm down the stairs first? I want to rest a while before this party and I find them rather steep."

"Of course."

They made their way to the lower deck and Webster took Mrs. van Duren to the door of her room. He was about to return to the main deck, when from further along the passage there came a sudden outbreak of muffled shouting and banging.

Mrs. van Duren looked startled. "That sounds like a woman's voice."

"It is. I think somebody's got shut in."

He went along the passageway, Mrs. van Duren at his heels. The noise gradually got louder, until, with a sudden note of alarm in her voice, Mrs. van Duren said, "That's Irene."

As they went up to Irene's stateroom the noise stopped. Webster tapped on the door. "Irene? Are you all right?"

"Oh, thank heavens! At last," Irene's voice from inside came with enormous relief. "Is that Alec?"

"Yes. What's the matter? Can't you get out?"

"Of course I can't, you damned idiot. I—"

"Irene!" Mrs. van Duren spoke sharply. "I will not have swearing."

"Oh, mercy, I didn't know you were there, Grandmother."

"Obviously not."

Webster was bending down. "The door's not locked," he called.

"I know that."

"Hang on." Webster got on his knees and peered at the bottom of the door, which, like all the others to the staterooms, opened outwards. "There's something jammed here." He took hold of the small piece of wood that protruded very slightly and tried to pull it out. It was wedged firmly, but after some hard tugging he managed to get it loose. He stood up and opened the door. Irene, looking furious, said, "I suppose that was somebody's idea of a joke."

"No I don't think so." He held out the inch of wood for her to see. "It's the stump of one of those big oval carpenter's pencils. It acted as a very effective wedge, but I should imagine it was simply dropped and kicked under by somebody passing. Just an unlucky accident."

"Hm." Irene looked unconvinced.

"How long have you been here?" Mrs. van Duren asked.

"About an hour and three-quarters."

Webster raised his eyebrows. "And nobody's been along in that time?"

"Nope."

"Presumably you tried ringing for the stewardess?" Mrs. van Duren said.

Irene swallowed and seemed to find difficulty in speaking calmly. "Yes, Grandmother. Repeatedly."

"I see. Well, you're out now and no harm done, so I am going to lie down." Mrs. van Duren went away.

"Let me have a look at the bell," Webster said. He went into the stateroom and stopped short. For lying fully dressed on the bed was Karin.

"Oh, so you had company," he said.

"Company! That's a gas. She's been snoring most of the time."

At Irene's snort of derision, Karin opened her eyes. She yawned. "I'm sure I did not snore," she said. "In fact, I haven't been asleep for more than a few seconds at a stretch. You must have woken me hundreds of times with your banging and shouting."

"I'm sorry; I didn't know you'd come in for forty winks!"

"I didn't; I came in for a chat. Ten minutes later I grew terribly sleepy. Then I found I couldn't get out. I'm sorry not to have been better company. I should have done exercises to keep awake, like Margaret Lockwood in *The Lady Vanishes.*"

"Oh, that's all right. I wasn't in the mood for cosy girl-talk anyway. I just wanted to get out."

"I'm still not properly awake," Karin said. "I must go and wash my face in cold water." She left, rubbing her eyes.

Webster had been examining the bell push and the wire that led from it. He said, "Nothing apparently wrong here." He went outside, following the wire with his hand. "Ah, here we are. It's broken above the door."

"Cut?"

"It appears just to have frayed."

"Quite a coincidence, isn't it?"

"Yes." He noticed for the first time that Irene was not wearing the same dress that she'd had on at dinner. That one was lying on a chair in the stateroom, the front of the skirt badly stained. "An accident?" he asked, pointing.

"Yes, Paul Muller spilt his coffee into my lap. He was terribly embarrassed. I don't think he liked anybody knowing he could make a hurried or clumsy move."

"What time was this?"

"Just after you left with Hilary Orchard. I came straight down to change."

"I see. Well, having done my good deed for the day, I must go and have a word with your father. See you at the party."

"Thanks for letting me out."

Webster went up to the main deck, seeing nobody. He made his way along the centre passageway to Roussos's study and was about to tap on the door when it opened and Roussos emerged. "Ah, Alec," he said. "Come to report?"

"Yes."

"Fine. I just want to slip along to the saloon and make sure everything's ready for the party first. Come along."

He walked the few yards to the door of the saloon, Webster following, and went in. Dimitri and his assistants had certainly been busy. Most of the furniture had been moved to the sides, leaving a fairly large area in the centre clear. The main light bulbs had been removed and replaced by chains of coloured fairy lights, slung around the walls, giving a dimmer, but warm and cheerful, illumination. On one of the two semi-circular bar counters stood a magnum of champagne in an ice bucket, and on the other some shallow, broad-based champagne glasses. In front of the bar had been placed a large table, covered with foodstuffs—plates of dainty sandwiches, canapés, fancy pastries and a big, beautifully decorated iced cake—as well as half-a-dozen bottles of liquor and many more glasses, of different types from those on the bar.

"Very nice indeed," Webster said.

"Yeah, old Dimitri knows his stuff. Hullo, he's slipped up on the champagne glasses, though: he's only put six out." He pointed to the bar. "Careless. But I won't call him back just to get the other six now. Daresay we can find them ourselves later on. Come back to the study."

They returned. Roussos went behind the desk, opened the safe, rummaged inside for a moment and took out a large sheet of rather dirty-looking white paper. Then he sat down. Webster sat opposite him. Roussos raised his eyebrows.

"Well?"

"Orchard's genuine."

Roussos's face fell. "Is she sure?"

"She's sure. So am I. I think you would have been too, if you'd been there."

"That's that, then. Pity. Thought I was on to a good thing, too."

"You haven't been down to the accommodation deck this evening, have you?"

"No. Why?"

"I was hoping you might have seen somebody in the passage. Irene's spent most of the time since dinner shut in her stateroom." He explained what had happened.

Roussos frowned. "That's weird. You think someone deliberately jammed the door and put the bell out of action?"

"I made out to her that I thought they were just two accidents. But she realized that would be too much of a coincidence. Besides, the bit of pencil wasn't kicked under the door. It was wedged far too tightly."

"But who'd do a thing like that?"

"I don't know. But it might be possible to work out who *could* have done it. Did this incident with the coffee look like a genuine accident?"

"Yes."

"Nothing happened to startle Muller?"

"Not that I noticed."

"Irene says it happened just after Orchard and I left the saloon. That was at about eight-thirty. Did Karin go down with Irene?"

"No—followed her about a minute later."

"From what they both say, the door must have been jammed between twenty and ten to nine. Can you tell me what people were doing during those ten minutes?"

Roussos scratched his head. "Not really. We drifted off in various directions. The only one I can alibi is Muller. I was chatting to him all the time until the film started at about five to nine."

"So it could have been any of the others—or one of the crew."

"But what on earth could be the point of it?"

"I've no idea. But somebody did it."

"It must have been a hoax."

"A hoax—by Quine? Or Trent? Or Barrault? Or *Maria?* And would any of the crew risk the sack for the sake of a hoax? No, the only person I can even remotely imagine doing it for a hoax has got the best alibi of all—she was shut in the room with Irene the whole time."

"Does this mean you now think one of the passengers *is* up to something fishy?"

"I'll just say it looks rather more likely than it did a couple of hours ago. Of course, your change of route will have made a difference. There won't be a chance for any fresh plans to be made until we reach Santo Domingo, so I'd say Irene's safe enough for tonight at least."

"I reckon I'll keep the guards on duty on the deck tonight, all the same. Now: this is what you've been wanting to see." He passed the letter across the desk.

Webster studied it. It was written in a large, scrawling hand, in blue ballpoint. With some difficulty he read it through.

*Dear Mr. Roussos this is a warning. There's a mob in London what's planning to snatch your girl Irene. There already to do it somewhere in West indies when you takes your boat Angel siling there. I can prove I knows about it because her gran from Boston America Mrs. Vanduren is coming with her and there joining you in Jamika on 7 next month. They got good backing these boys and there real pros some of them bloody vicious I can tell you. Two of them's killed in the past. I think one of your boat friends helping so watch out. I knows about it because one of the mobs my fellow. I don't mean he's a killer or he planned this but he's going along with it and I'm scared he'll go down for a long stretch if there court. So I want it stopped before they does it then perhaps he'll stop going with them, there vicious. And I dont hold with kidnapping its cruel. So I thort as how if you new about the fret you can see your girls kept safe. This isn't a joke honest its dead serious. You got to believe it.*

"Well, what do you think? Roussos asked.

Webster considered. "It looks genuine enough. I'd *think* it was written by somebody British and it gives the impression, which may be faked, of being from an uneducated London girl. But that's all I can say. We can't rule out a malicious hoax. I wouldn't like to bet on it either way."

"You noted the significant bit?"

"Yes. 'I think one of your boat friends helping.' Rather ambiguous, but certainly worth noting."

"You agree I couldn't ignore it?"

"Of course you couldn't."

"What worried me specially was that though it was sent from London, and it says this is a London mob, they knew all about Irene's and Emily's plans and so on. It's pretty clear they've got contacts in the States as well."

Webster nodded thoughtfully. He ran his eyes over the letter once more, then handed it back. Roussos said, "Right, taking it seriously, then, is there any more we can do to protect Irene? If you got some advice, let's have it now, before we reach land."

"Well, I have been thinking a lot since yesterday. Now that we've openly acknowledged to Irene herself, and to everyone else, that she might be in danger, the position has changed. And there is one other step you might take."

"What's that?"

"Tell all the crew that there'll be a very large reward for anyone who proves to you that he knows of any plan to kidnap her. But you must make the reward really substantial—enough to tempt anyone to inform, however vicious these villains might be."

Roussos nodded firmly. "Yeah, good thinking. I'll put Dimitri on to spreading the word first thing in the morning."

"There's one more thing. It might go against the grain, and it's not strictly fair to the honest people, but I think it would be worth it."

"Out with it."

"Promise that if any of them's been involved in any way with a possible kidnapping, and they come to you now with the full story, they won't be prosecuted—and they'll still get the reward."

Roussos scratched his nose. "I see what you mean: it'd hurt to let any swine who's been mixed up in it get away scot free, let alone *pay* him, but anything that'll stop the attempt is worth trying."

"Of course, you must make sure your guests know about the offer too. You'll have to pass it on discreetly, as though you're simply telling them about your offer to the crew, as a matter of interest. But word it in such a way that it'll be clear the offer applies to anyone."

"OK, I'll try it."

"There's no need to mention the letter. Let them think it's just the To-bago business has got you scared."

"Anything else?"

"I don't think so. When you've done that, you'll have taken every reasonable precaution. Anything more and in my opinion you'd be over-reacting. So I'd say just carry on with the cruise, have Irene watched whenever she goes ashore, keep your sentries on patrol, let me go on monitoring the other guests—and as far as you can, try to forget about the threat. Because their chance of pulling the snatch off now is negligible."

"I'm glad I had you along, Alec. Thanks." Roussos looked at his watch. "Gone quarter to eleven. Let's move along to the saloon and get this shindig off the ground."

## 12

Webster went out of the study and waited in the passageway for a few moments while Roussos put the letter back in the safe and then joined him. They returned to the main saloon. It was empty. Roussos gave a chuckle and pointed to the bar.

"Old Dimitri doesn't slip up much." Webster looked and saw that a full dozen glasses were now standing on the counter. "He must have remembered and come back," Roussos added.

It was as he said this that there came the sudden sound of somebody moving in the small galley behind the bar. Roussos looked surprised. "Oh, he's still in there. Dimitri!" he called.

However, at that second they heard the sound of the closing of the far door out of the galley to the short passage that led to the deck. Roussos grinned. "Wants to get back to his bunk. He's conveniently deaf sometimes. Still, I did say they could all knock off early tonight."

A few minutes later Claire, Irene and Emily van Duren came in, followed by the other guests more or less in a body. Roussos got busy at the drinks table. Nathan Quine sat down at the piano and started to play softly and surprisingly well. Webster stood aside and studied the others. Irene looked cross—plainly still angry at having been shut in her room most of the evening. Barrault, on the other hand, was in high spirits, joking and laughing, and paying much attention to Claire, who, in spite of her earlier protests, now seemed far from averse at being the guest of honour. Trent was hearty, Muller charming to everybody, Orchard thoughtful, Maria away in some world of her own, and Mrs. van Duren gracious.

Karin kept yawning all the time. "I don't know what's wrong with me," she said to Webster. "My, I could have done with a nap this evening. It's all your fault I didn't get one."

"My fault?"

"Yes; I would never have been in with Irene if you hadn't said what you did about her needing a friend. I was making a start. She went to change out of that awful dress and I thought perhaps I could help her pick another one, and persuade her to do something about her hair and make-up. It wasn't a very good idea."

At about seven minutes past eleven Roussos went to the bar. "OK, folks, gather round." Everybody moved up to join him. Roussos took the magnum of champagne from the ice bucket.

Trent said, "Ah, bubbly. Good show."

Roussos wrestled with the cork, shaking the bottle in the process. The cork came out with a pop. Champagne spurted forth. There was a ragged cheer from Quine, Trent and Karin. Roussos swung the bottle round and gave Karin a spraying. She uttered an exaggerated shriek and dodged. Roussos, laughing, aimed the bottle at Quine, who pretended to hide behind Irene.

They were trying hard to make the party swing, but to Webster there seemed a forced air about the revelry. This was perhaps due to the guest of honour, who was now looking unamused at the antics and said dryly, "George, if you really want some fun, why not swap the champagne for fire extinguishers? You could soak the entire saloon then. And you probably wouldn't notice any difference in the taste."

Roussos chuckled, moved to the other counter and started pouring. He ran the bottle along the rows of glasses without stopping, spilling champagne liberally over the bar in a way that reminded Webster of an attendant pouring tea in a British Railways buffet.

"Come on, come on," Roussos boomed. "Help yourselves. Every man— and girl—for themselves here."

"I believe this is what is known as the survival of the fittest," Muller murmured in Webster's ear. They both reached for the same glass. Webster withdrew his hand.

"After you."

"Thank you." Muller gathered up two glasses and handed one to his wife, retaining the other himself. Webster picked up another glass. He looked round for Mrs. van Duren, meaning to give it to her, but he saw Trent in the act of doing so, and passed his instead to Karin. Quine, who'd been about to do the same thing, hurriedly diverted his glass to Irene. Webster noticed Orchard, holding two glasses, passing one to Trent. Webster finally took one for himself. Quine and Barrault followed suit. Two glasses remained. Roussos picked them up and handed one to Claire.

He looked at his watch. "Honey, I reckon your birthday's just about starting now. I'm not going to say which birthday it is. Not that it would matter if I did: no one would believe me. Because tonight you look about twenty-one."

Muller said, "Hear, hear," and Webster heard a barely perceptible sniff from Mrs. van Duren.

"Anyway," Roussos continued, "I wanta say how great it is for me that you're here on the *Angel* for this birthday. The old tub was lacking something until you signed up. So as they say in England, 'Here's mud in your eye.' I know all your friends wish you a very happy birthday and many happy returns of the day."

There was a murmur of agreement. Roussos raised his glass. "Claire."

A chorus of "Claire" rang out. They all drank.

Claire said, "Thank you, George. And thank you all very much. I drink to you all in turn." She raised her glass and drank from it. Then she grimaced slightly. "George where did you get this?"

"Me? I didn't get it. Why?"

"It tastes rather strange." She drank some more.

"Oh?" Roussos emptied his own glass.

Muller said, "I didn't like to mention it, but as Claire has done so . . ." He went forward and examined the bottle. Then he drank some more. "Well, if this really is a Bollinger '66, I'm Henry Kissinger."

"Yeah," Roussos said, "I reckon it is a bit queer. What do the rest of you think?"

Everybody drank judiciously. Webster said, "Champagne's a once-a-year drink for me, on average, so I'm not in a position to say." He finished off his glass. "All I can say is that it doesn't seem at all a bad drink to me."

Barrault said, "I agree. But I also agree with Claire and Paul. There is certainly something different about it."

"People have been plying me with champagne for the past few months," Karin said. "I quite like this one, but it's not the same as any other I've had." Orchard and Quine both nodded their agreement.

Roussos was looking a little embarrassed. He poured some more into his glass and sipped at it. Then he said, "Seems OK, now. Try some more, Paul."

"Must I?"

"Just a bit. Come on." He refilled Muller's glass.

Muller drank. Then he nodded. "That *is* a Bollinger '66. How odd."

Roussos went round filling up all the others' glasses. Everyone, even Webster and the others—Mrs. van Duren, Irene, Trent and Maria Muller—who hadn't expressed an opinion before, had to agree that it did now taste somewhat different.

"Ah well," Roussos said. "Let's not worry. Perhaps the glasses weren't washed all that clean."

"What a charming thought," Mrs. van Duren said. She laid her glass down hurriedly, as though she had suddenly discovered it was encrusted with filth.

Roussos reached into his pocket and brought out a small packet. He handed it to Claire. "I won't wish you health to wear them out, honey. That would be a bit optimistic even for a twenty-one-year-old."

"That sounds very exciting," Claire said. While everyone watched, she tore off the paper and opened the square, hinged box that was revealed. Then she gave a gasp. "Oh, George! They're magnificent!"

She drew from the box a dazzling necklace of large, perfectly matched diamonds. Webster was no authority on jewels, but he, as well as everybody else in the room, knew that he was looking at something special. There was an outbreak of exclamations and whistles. Claire's eyes were shining almost as brightly as the diamonds. She ran them through her fingers and stroked them, whispering to herself as she did so. Then she looked at Roussos with the first sign of affection Webster had yet seen from her. "Thank you, George, they're absolutely gorgeous." She gave him a kiss, handed him the necklace and turned her back to him. "Put it on me, please."

Roussos encircled her neck with the brilliantly sparkling cord and fastened it at the back. Claire hurried from him across the saloon, to the mirror. She stood quite still, staring at herself for about a quarter of a minute. Then, obviously suddenly becoming aware that every eye in the room was still on her, she turned with an embarrassed smile.

"Rather nice, aren't they?" she said.

Irene went across to her. "Grandmother and I have a small present for you, but it would be rather an anti-climax to give it to you now."

"That's all right, dear. Give it to me tomorrow, if you prefer." Claire spoke almost absently.

"Sugar, come and cut your cake," Roussos called.

Claire made her way to the table. Karin said, "Oh, good, I'm longing to try it. It looks delicious."

"You'll have to watch your figure, my dear," Mrs. van Duren told her.

"Don't you bother, beautiful," Quine said. "Let me watch it for you, instead."

Claire cut the cake. Slices were handed out. Then Orchard went across to her, holding out a white envelope. "Have you seen this, Mrs. Roussos? Looks like a birthday card. It was on that small table."

She put down her knife and took the envelope from him. "Probably from the servants," she remarked, tearing the envelope open. She drew out a white card, glancing casually at it. Suddenly her face changed. "What on earth—?" Everybody looked at her.

"What's the matter, honey?" Roussos asked sharply.

Claire had gone quite pale. "It's horrible," she said.

Roussos snatched the card from her. "Let me see that." He looked at it and his expression turned to one of intense rage.

"What is it?" Irene asked.

"Yes, come along, George—give." This from Nathan Quine.

Claire said, "Might as well show them."

Roussos silently handed the card to Quine, who read out loud, "Many happy returns of the day? Perhaps. If you are one of the lucky six in this room. If not, by tomorrow morning you will be dead. So will five others. Good luck."

There was a chorus of exclamations. Roussos said, "Now there's no cause for alarm. I'm pretty sure I know who did this. It's one of the servants. He's got a chip on his shoulder, according to Dimitri. He talks a lot—but he's quite harmless. I'll see him in the morning. Try to forget about it now, OK?"

Webster went across to Quine and took the card. The writing had been done with a fibre-tipped pen in large black capitals. He picked up the envelope from where Claire had let it fall. It was simply addressed MRS. ROUSSOS with the same pen. Thoughtfully Webster put card and envelope in his pocket. The party continued. Liquor flowed in quantity. Gradually the nasty taste left by the card faded, and perhaps as the very result of the card, the atmosphere grew warmer—warmer, in fact, than it had been at any time since the cruise started. Quine returned to the piano and started to play bouncy, cheerful tunes. Roussos danced with Claire, then with Maria; Barrault with Irene; Webster, clumsily, to general amusement, with Karin; Muller with each of the women in turn. Mrs. van Duren forgot to go to bed and watched benevolently.

Suddenly Roussos shouted, "Now I'll show you all how we dance in Greece." He hurried to the record player, selected a disc and put it on. Claire, standing near Webster, closed her eyes. "Oh dear. He's reached his Zorba the Greek stage."

The strains of a Grecian folk song at nearly full volume blasted the saloon. Roussos danced—energetically, heavily and badly for several minutes. Then he roared, "Come on—everybody join in."

There was no denying him in this mood. Within a minute everyone else in the saloon, except Mrs. van Duren, was attempting with various degrees of unwillingness to follow his steps. Karin alone succeeded in making the dance look good and seemed to be enjoying herself. Gradually, the others dropped out, leaving only the two of them on the floor. Eventually, even Karin collapsed laughingly into a chair.

Roussos, though, still had apparently boundless energy. He gave a few more triumphant hops before running across the room and turning off the record player. Then he went to the buffet and cut himself a huge slice of cake. He grinned round the room. "OK—what we do now?" Webster noticed that his accent was becoming decidedly thicker and he was sounding more and more like a Greek.

Claire said, "How about something nice and quiet like a game of Rugby football?"

Roussos gave a guffaw. "How about a singsong?"

Hilary Orchard murmured, "I don't believe it."

"I gave you fair warning," Mrs. van Duren whispered.

"I know!" Roussos snapped his fingers excitedly. "We all sing a song in turn. One from our own country, eh? Nathan an American one, Paul a Swiss, Karin a Swedish, Philippe a French, Maria a German, and so on. You can choose a Greek or American one, honey," he said to Irene. "And Claire and Lance and Hilary and Alec can form a quartet and give us something British, eh?"

Claire said, "George, we can't possibly—"

"Sure you can. You ought to have a go, too, Emily. Didn't your folks come from Holland way back? Give us a rendition of something Dutch. Whew, I'm hot." He dropped into a chair. "What I want now is an iced beer." He looked at Irene. "Honey, there should be some cans in the fridge in the small galley. Do you want to fetch a few in here?"

"Oh, all right." With bad grace, Irene got to her feet, slouched across the room and disappeared through the door behind the bar.

Roussos clapped his hands. "OK—who starts? Nathan—how about it?"

Quine gave a shrug. "It's your funeral, George." He went back to the piano, sat down and started on a tolerable rendering of "Yankee Doodle."

When he was on the second verse, Irene came back, carrying a tray with half-a-dozen cans of beer. She gave one to her father, then looked enquiringly round as if to see if anybody else wanted beer. There were no takers, but to Webster's surprise, Irene seemed to gain the impression that he wanted one. She came across to him and, before he could say anything, bent down and whispered in his ear, "Come and look at something, will you?" Webster noticed that she'd gone slightly pale.

She straightened up and returned to the galley. Webster let half a minute pass then, as the applause for Quine broke out, went as unobtrusively as possible after her.

Irene was waiting for him. "Close the door," she said. "Now come over here."

She was standing by the small sink. He joined her. She just pointed.

Next to the sink was a red formica-topped table, with a number of objects on it. There was a half-empty bottle of vodka, a glass jug, a large spoon, and, surprisingly, a wooden rolling-pin. There were also slight but noticeable traces of a fine white powder on the surface of the table. But it was none of these things that caused Webster's heart to beat a little faster, but a pill bottle, the stopper off, with a few tiny white tablets in it. He bent to look at it more closely.

In a curiously unemotional voice, Irene said, "My grandmother's digoxin tablets."

"Sure?"

"Of course. I've seen her take them hundreds of times."

"How many did she say were left in that bottle?"

"Seventy-two."

Webster picked up the bottle, tipped out the remaining tablets onto his hand and counted them. "Just twelve here now."

He put one of the tablets on the table, took a second spoon from a drawer and crushed the tablet. The resulting powder matched identically the odd traces previously present. He stared down at the table, then looked at the window just above it. This was open a few inches and a gentle breeze was blowing in. He got down on one knee and peered at the table surface from level with it. As well as the more noticeable traces of powder, a thin film of it covered the entire table-top. Or almost the entire top. For in the film could be clearly seen the sharp outlines of six rings, about three inches in diameter, where the surface was dust-free.

Webster straightened, fighting down a sudden rising tide of panic. Holding it carefully by the rim, he picked up the glass jug. Where it had been standing, a larger but otherwise identical ring was left on the surface of the table. He replaced the jug. Incredible and horrifying thoughts were forcing their way into his mind and sending small ripples of fear up his backbone.

*"Ten are invariably a fatal dose."*

*"He's slipped up on the champagne glasses, though. He's only put six out."*

A footstep in the galley, a closing door, an unanswered call . . . Not Dimitri, after all.

Champagne that had tasted odd. And now six rings in the dust. Sixty crushed tablets. *"Ten are invariably a fatal dose . . ."*

Keeping his voice quiet and steady, he said, "How many champagne glasses do they have here?"

"I don't know. All the glassware is kept in that closet."

He opened the cupboard she indicated and took out a champagne glass matching the ones in use in the saloon. He placed it with great precision over one of the six rings in the powder. It fitted exactly.

"We've been poisoned, haven't we?" There was a slight catch in Irene's voice. "Or some of us have."

Trying hard to fight off the clutch of cold dread that was creeping over him, Webster played for time. "I don't know. Not necessarily."

Before she could reply, the door to the saloon burst open and Roussos charged in. "What the hell are you two up to in here? Trying to get out of doing your numbers? No way! Come on."

Then he seemed to notice their expressions. "What's up?"

"George"—and for the first time Webster used the name unselfconsciously—"will you please go and ask Maria Muller to come in here?"

Roussos gave him a surprised look but, obviously sensing Webster's urgency, didn't argue or ask questions. "Sure," he said, and went out.

Webster and Irene stood in silence until a rather bewildered-looking Maria entered. Webster wasted no time on explanations. "Frau Muller—what do you know about digoxin tablets?"

"The old lady's heart tablets, you mean?"

"Yes."

"What do you want to know? Digoxin is obtained from digitalis."

"It's poisonous?"

"In a large enough dose, certainly."

Webster looked at Irene. "What strength are your grandmother's tablets?"

"A quarter milligram, I believe."

"She said ten of them would be fatal," Webster said. "That's two and a half milligrams." He turned back to Maria Muller. "Would you agree with that?"

"That two and a half milligrams of digoxin would be a fatal dose? Certainly. But why do you ask all this? Has she taken an overdose?"

Webster ignored the question. "Any antidote?" he asked.

"Remember, I am no physician—no toxicologist. I think if you acted quickly, one of the usual emetics—"

He looked at his watch. It was twelve-ten. "How quickly? An hour?"

"No, no—it would then be too late to do anything. The poison would have been absorbed into the system."

Webster nodded. He'd had some experience of poisoning cases in his career, and had expected this answer.

"These tablets would dissolve in vodka?"

"Vodka? Yes, I'm sure they would."

"Leaving no taste?"

"I don't think there would be any taste. But what has happened? You must tell me."

Webster hesitated, throwing a glance at Irene, who said: "He won't say it. But I will. Yes: six of us have taken a big overdose of digoxin. It's the only explanation."

For a moment Maria Muller did not react at all. Then without any warning, she turned on her heel and hurried back into the saloon. The next second they heard her voice raised: "Poison. Half of us have been poisoned. Digoxin tablets. A fatal dose. There is nothing we can do."

Webster gave an exclamation. "Damn! The fool!" He hurried after Maria, Irene at his heels.

The scene that met his eyes in the saloon was like a tableau: people were frozen in mid-movement, some with glasses half-raised. Some of the faces were frightened, but most were just blank. Maria's own usually impassive face was flushed and animated as she faced them.

Webster said loudly, "Please—we don't know that. It may be a mistake—or a hoax."

Orchard was the first to find his voice. "But—but what's happened? I don't understand."

At this it was as if a spell was broken. Nearly everyone in the room surged forward, exclaiming, throwing questions at Webster and Maria. For thirty seconds there was pandemonium. Unavailingly Webster tried to calm them. Then from the back, one voice rose above the babble. "Quiet!"

It was Roussos. Webster looked up. The others swung round. Roussos said, "Alec—tell us everything you know."

Webster took a deep breath. "It looks as though earlier this evening somebody crushed up sixty digoxin tablets in the small galley and then dissolved them in vodka. In addition, he—she—had six of our champagne glasses out there. I should explain that before the party George and I saw that there were only six glasses on the bar. Later when we came back there were twelve. We thought Dimitri had come back, and we heard somebody moving out there. But when George called out, there was no answer and we heard somebody go out by the back door into the short passage."

In a horrified whisper Muller said, "The champagne. I knew there was something wrong with it."

Quine said hoarsely. "The card. The birthday card. It said six of us would be dead by tomorrow morning."

From Claire there came a harsh scream. Her hands clutched at her face, which was deathly white and gaunt as a skull. She started to babble hysterically, "I've been poisoned. I must do something. A doctor. Antidote. Anything. We must stop it working. George . . ."

Roussos crossed to her side. "It's all right, honey, we'll do all we can."

He tried to put his arm round her, but she thrust him away.

Maria Muller said, "There is no antidote. A doctor could do nothing now. There isn't anything we can do but wait."

Incredulously, Orchard said, "You're saying we—six of us—are doomed, *dying?*"

"Yes."

"But—an emetic . . . ?"

"Too late. The poison has been absorbed into our systems. If you wish to occupy your time in futile action, you can drink warm salty water. But it will be quite pointless."

Claire said, "Yes. Salt water. Yes, that's it. I must. There's got to be a chance." Staggering a little, as though she were drunk, she half ran from the saloon.

Quine said desperately, "We must try. We must." He hurried after Claire. Without a word Orchard followed him.

There was a kind of numbed silence. It was broken by Trent, who turned almost fiercely on Webster. "Look, are you saying the poison was already in the glasses when the champagne was poured?"

"I believe so, yes."

"But we'd have seen it."

"I thought that at first, but the lights aren't very bright in here tonight and vodka is quite colourless. To the best of my knowledge nobody looked at the glasses closely before George poured the champagne. Did anyone?"

He looked round. There was no answer. "I thought not. So I doubt very much if any of us would have noticed if there'd been a few drops of vodka in the glasses already. They're flat and broad-based and the glass thickens towards the stem. I think the vodka would look like slightly thicker glass."

Muller said, "But *all* the champagne tasted wrong."

"I know. I would guess there was plain vodka in the other glasses. The poisoner wanted to make quite certain we wouldn't know which of us had taken it."

Trent said, "How do you know only six glasses were poisoned?"

"Ten tablets are a fatal dose—everybody heard Mrs. van Duren say so. The poisoner deliberately used only sixty of them. And if you go behind you'll see the rings where six glasses stood."

Again nobody answered. Maria Muller moved slowly to an upright chair which was standing against the wall, and sat down. Her husband said, "Look, we don't *know* any of this is right, do we? We haven't got proof we've been poisoned."

"Not scientific proof," Webster said, "but I can't think of any other explanation. Believe me, I'll be overjoyed if you can."

"A hoax? You said yourself . . ."

"I know I did. It's possible—"

"It's not," Irene said harshly. "Why on earth would anyone plan a hoax so utterly vicious as this?"

"Well, why on earth would anyone want to *poison* six of us?" Muller ran a hand through his hair.

Irene said, "Yes, and *any* six of us. It just didn't matter to him who took it. Nobody could possibly have known who was going to drink out of which glass. Remember how we gathered round: we were helping ourselves, passing glasses to each other."

Webster nodded. "Poisoning those glasses meant killing six people utterly at random."

Trent brought his fist down hard on the back of a couch he was standing by. "But who?" he shouted, "by all that's holy, *who?* He swung round on Roussos. "This servant—do you still say he's harmless?"

Roussos seemed to be in a semi-trance. Then he gave himself a shake, like a dog waking up. "I—I don't know. I thought he was. Perhaps I was wrong."

"Well, let's go and find out." Trent started towards the door.

Webster caught his arm. "Hang on. We've got no proof it's him. Let's think before we start throwing accusations."

"Maybe we haven't got time to waste thinking," Trent said.

Webster turned to Maria Muller again. "Can you say how long before we become ill?"

She looked at him without great interest. "I should think about four hours from the time of ingestion."

"Till about ten past three, then."

"Naturally I cannot be so precise as that. It might be a little longer or shorter."

In a very low voice, Irene asked, "What—what will the symptoms be?"

"Nausea, I should think. Stomach pains. Vomiting."

"And how long will we have then—I mean, before . . . ?" Irene tailed off.

"Before we die? Perhaps another four hours. But I repeat, I am not a physician."

Again there was complete silence. It was as though the emotions of everyone had been flattened, deadened, by the appalling, and so far not fully assimilated, knowledge. Then Irene suddenly swung round on her father. "Well? Aren't you going to do something? You're the seventeenth richest man in the world, aren't you? Let's see you buy your way out of this."

Roussos seemed about to make an angry retort. Then he appeared to take a grip on himself. He nodded. "Yes, I must do something. Can't just wait here. I'll go and see Haller. Get a message sent out for assistance or something. Change course for the nearest port. Something." He made his way slowly and uncertainly from the room.

Webster looked round at each of the others: at Trent, screwing his left fist into the palm of his right hand and taking little indecisive steps back and forth; at Paul Muller, sinking slowly down into a deep chair, taking out a packet of cigarettes and lighting one; at Irene walking across to him, and asking for one, waiting as he lit it for her, inhaling deeply, straightening and walking slowly away across the room; at Maria Muller, still sitting in the upright chair, her body as motionless, her face as impassive as a wax dummy.

Three people had not said a word since Webster's explanation. Emily van Duren was sitting as still and quiet as Maria; yet hers seemed the stillness not of passivity but of alertness; it was as if she were tensed, straining every one of her senses to take in everything that was happening. Philippe Barrault had at some point moved unnoticed to the bar and seated himself on a high stool; he had a pack of cards and was apparently calmly playing patience; however, a closer look showed Webster beads of sweat on his forehead.

Webster continued to scan the room and then suddenly realized that one person was missing. Karin had left.

He found her on deck, leaning on the rail looking out over the dark water. She didn't turn her head as he approached, but she plainly knew it was him, for she said, "I couldn't bear it in there another second."

"I know how you were feeling."

"I suppose for once everybody really does know exactly how everybody else is feeling."

"I wish there was something I could say to make things better."

"I wish there was too. Never mind, I suppose if I should come through this, it'll be a very valuable experience for me as a dramatic actress. It's a pity there isn't a writer or director among us, someone who could really make use of the experience."

"Is there anything I can do—anything I can get you?"

"Just a large slice of luck. And if you had one of those, you'd need it yourself."

"You'd be most welcome to it."

She paused, then said quietly, "Thank you."

"Look, there's something I want to do, but if you'd like me to stay with you, it'll keep."

"No; go and do it. I'd like to be alone for a little while."

"Very well. I'll see you shortly." Webster walked away.

It was a little more than twelve minutes later that he came back along the deck. He felt a stab of alarm when he saw that she was no longer by the rail, and he hurried into the saloon. But then he saw her curled up, her shoes off and her legs under her, in the corner of one of the big couches. She looked hopelessly small and vulnerable.

Claire, Quine and Orchard, all pale and ill-looking, were present again. The others were still as when he'd left. Roussos also was back. He looked more his usual decisive self, though his expression was grim. He glanced round as Webster entered.

"Oh, Alec," he said, "good. That means we're all here. I just got back. I gotta few things to say."

"So have I, after you." He sat down.

Roussos looked round the room. "The news isn't good, I'm afraid. First of all, we can rule out the possibility of immediate help—and the idea that this business is a hoax. The radio's been put out of action."

There was no chorus of exclamations at his words. It was as if all shock had been expended by now. Webster just asked quietly, "How?"

"Somebody's forced the lock of the radio room and been to work with pliers and a chisel. Thousands of dollars' worth of damage. I can't see anyone doing that just to back up a practical joke, can you? Anyway, there's no way we can get a mayday call out now."

Nobody spoke until Irene licked her lips and asked, "Then—what is the plan?"

"Haller's trying to raise help. He's going to keep sending up distress flares and if another ship comes close enough he'll signal asking for a doctor, if she's got one; or if not, ask for her to send out a radio call on our behalf. We're still roughly a hundred and sixty miles from Santo Domingo, but only about a hundred and twenty-five from Puerto Rico. So he's already changed course. Our top speed is fifteen knots, so we should make it around 8 A.M."

"By which time it will be too late for anybody to be helped," Muller said.

Roussos turned on him with something very close to a snarl. "So what? It's too late now, isn't it—according to your wife. I can't do any more."

Muller looked shaken. "All right, all right," he muttered.

Roussos mopped his brow and sat down heavily. "What do you want to say, Alec?"

"I've been to see Dimitri. I didn't tell him exactly what's happened—there didn't seem much point—just that some of the passengers have apparently been poisoned. Incidentally, he wanted to rouse all his staff to come and help, but I told him there was nothing they could do just now and that we'd send for them when there was. I hope that was right."

Roussos gave a nod and Irene said, "Quite right. I'd hate to have a lot of stewards and stewardesses fussing round now."

There was a murmur of agreement. Webster went on, "That's by the way. I asked him about the preparations for the party. He says that he and the other stewards left here at about nine-thirty—when there were definitely twelve glasses laid out on the bar next to the champagne, and everything was tidy in the small galley. I then asked him if he knew of any of the kitchen or cabin staff who had a grudge against the passengers. Right away he mentioned Constantine."

"Who's that?" Orchard asked.

"The youngest steward—slim, long dark hair." He looked at Roussos. "Was he the one you meant?"

Roussos nodded silently.

Irene said, "I thought he was a bit weird; he's polite enough, but he looks at you in a queer way."

"Dimitri had decided to get rid of him at the end of this cruise," Webster said. "Apparently he's got hold of a lot of half-baked Marxist ideas, and he's been sounding off about capitalist dogs, and so on. It seems the other stewards think he's a bit unbalanced. Well, Dimitri took me along to his cabin. We found him unconscious. It looks as if he's taken an overdose of something. No way of telling how much, or if he'll recover. There are some cards there like the one that warning message was written on, and a black, fibretip pen that could have been used to write it. He's only got a few books, mostly popular left-wing revolutionary stuff. But there's one novel there— Agatha Christie's *Ten Little Indians*. As you may know, that's a story about somebody who gets the idea of meting out justice to a lot of wealthy or powerful people, and kills them—mostly by poison, if I remember rightly— at a house party on an island which is cut off from the mainland. The similarity to our situation is quite marked."

Roussos said, "And then he found the tablets somewhere and that put the idea into his head."

"Would he have known about the tablets being poisonous?" Karin asked. "Was he in the dining saloon when we were talking about them?"

"One of them was," Irene said. "I don't know if it was him. But it's just the sort of thing they'd talk about. Can't you hear them? 'Old lady's in a fluster. Lost her pills. Says they're poison. Ten would kill you for sure.'"

"He took quite a chance," Webster said. "He might easily have been seen. If any of us had happened to come in here or the galley during the half hour prior to the party, we'd have probably spotted him and become suspicious. But, of course, nobody came near here, did they—or even into the short passage?" He looked round the room. There was a general shaking of heads.

"I hope they hang him." The words, low and venomous, came from Claire. "I'd like to do it myself."

"They won't," Trent said bitterly. "If he comes to, they'll probably just put him on probation for a couple of years."

"It—what he did—it was a sort of cry for help, I'm sure," Orchard said thickly. "It's society that's to blame."

"Oh, what's it matter who's to blame, or what they do to him?" Irene shouted. "None of that's going to help us, is it? Six of us in this room are as good as dead—*dead*. Can't you realize that?"

"I realize it very well," Orchard snapped. "But if I don't occupy my mind in some way, I might go off my head. Can't *you* realize that?"

Roussos said, "What's being done about Constantine right now, Alec?"

"Dimitri and some of the others are trying to bring him round, and someone is going to stay in his cabin for the rest of the night. There's not much else that can be done, is there?"

Roussos shook his head. "No, there's nothing much else anybody can do about anything."

"You are both wrong." It was Philippe Barrault speaking from the bar. "I for one can finish my game of solitaire—by putting a black ace on a red deuce. Can anybody guess which ace it is?" He held up the ace of spades. "Funny, eh?" He put it down in its place, then swept the cards together, gathered them up and threw them onto the floor behind the bar. "I wonder if that will be the last game of solitaire I shall ever play," he said.

He walked across the room and went out by the aft door.

## 13

Barrault's exit seemed to act as a sort of trigger, for no sooner had he left than Trent made his way rapidly to the forward door, saying as he did so, "Can't stay in here any longer. Must get some air."

Webster, too, made a great effort and forced himself to his feet. "There are one or two jobs I've got to do," he said. "I'll be back shortly." He left by the same door as Barrault.

Eventually he made his way to the main galley, aft of the dining saloon. Here, after a minute or two's searching he found a supply of plastic bags. He selected a quantity of different sizes, including one large bin-liner. Then he returned to the main saloon. To his surprise he found that the only person still present was Karin. She was sitting alone and forlorn among the debris of what had been the party. She looked up as he entered. "I'm terribly frightened," she said.

"I know. I'm sure we all are. Though that doesn't make things any better, does it?"

"The terrible thing is that you keep hoping it's someone else, not you, who's been poisoned. That's awful, isn't it?"

"No, I don't think it is. It's part of one's natural survival instinct."

She dredged a smile from somewhere. "I know one good thing," she said. "If they ever re-make *I Want to Live,* and I'm still around, they'll have to give me the Susan Hayward part. I'll be the only actress in the world who could do it justice. I know what it's actually like waiting to find out if you've been sentenced to death."

"I'll come to the premiere." He glanced round the room. "Where's everybody got to?"

"I don't know. They just went out in ones and twos. I think everyone got sick of everyone else and wanted to be alone."

"But you stayed."

"Well, when they'd all gone I was alone too. Besides, you said you were coming back and you had jobs to do. I thought I might be able to help. Can I?"

"Of course."

"Are those bags to do with the jobs?"

"Yes. You see, somebody ought to take charge of the evidence and put it away safely, so that the police can examine it."

"What can I do?" She stood up.

"Well, first I want all the used champagne glasses. Pick them up by putting your fingers inside and pushing outwards."

When all the champagne glasses were in bags, Webster and Karin went to the small galley and put the jug, the vodka bottle and the other utensils into bags too. Finally, Webster placed all the bags in the large bin-liner, the neck of which he tied up.

"What will you do with that now?" she asked.

"Give it to Haller to take charge of."

He carried the bag up to the wheelhouse and asked the captain to hand it to the police when the yacht reached port. Karin followed him like a shadow the whole way and waited outside the wheelhouse for him to emerge afterwards. They went down to the main deck.

"Why should you bother yourself with this?" she asked.

He stopped and looked round. There was nobody in sight, apart from one of the sentries, still on duty with his rifle twenty-five yards away and apparently oblivious to the events that had been taking place inside. "You might as well know," Webster said. "I'm not a marine engineer. I'm a detective, ex–Scotland Yard. George hired me as a sort of bodyguard for Irene. My real name is Alec Webster."

"Oh." She gazed at him, round-eyed. "Any normal time I'd have been terribly thrilled at meeting a real live Scotland Yard detective."

"Don't mention it to the others, will you? I'll probably have questions to ask them. They might not want to answer if they know what I really am."

"What sort of questions?"

He looked at her appraisingly before replying. "I want to try and find out who the poisoner is."

"But—but you know who it is: Constantine."

"No. I let him think that was what I believed, because if I'd said what I really think and told all I know, I'd probably get everybody hurling accusations at each other. And I'd rather the innocent ones believe that the poisoner has been found."

She gave a gasp. "You mean it's one of *us*—one of the passengers—not one of the crew?"

"That's right."

"But why? And why not Constantine?"

"There's no real evidence against him at all. He's a bit mixed up, and he's a Marxist. He's read an Agatha Christie novel, and has a fibre-tipped pen and some white cards in his cabin. That's all. He's never uttered threats. There are no witnesses to his having done anything. Above all, he left no suicide note: which I'm sure, if he were guilty, he'd have been psychologically compelled to do. Again, that birthday card was written by someone with a fairly good knowledge of English—which Constantine certainly hasn't got. Finally, why should he poison only six of us? Why leave twelve tablets in the bottle, when he could have used them to poison another glass? No; Constantine has been skilfully framed."

"You said you know something nobody else knows."

"There's nothing secret about it. It's this. Roussos and I heard the killer moving in the small galley at just after ten forty-five. He must actually have started his preparations well before that, and he was in there when we looked into the saloon earlier—at about ten thirty-five: he'd already taken the six glasses from the bar. Then he crushed up the tablets, mixed them in the vodka, put the poison in the glasses, took them back to the bar and returned to the galley, probably meaning to clear up. But before he could do that, Roussos and I arrived in the saloon and heard him. So he left quickly through the back door of the galley."

"But why do you say it has to have been one of the passengers? If it wasn't Constantine, why couldn't it have been another member of the crew?"

"If it had been one of the crew, the obvious thing to do after leaving the galley would have been to turn right along that short passage and go out through the door at the end onto the port side of the deck. He'd have been only a few feet from the stairs leading down to the crew's quarters, and with just a little luck he could have got back to his cabin without being seen. But our man didn't do that."

"How do you know?"

"The door to the deck is bolted—on the inside. Dimitri bolts all the unnecessary doors at night—I suppose in case of storm. I checked it just now before I fetched the bags from the galley. The bolt slides quietly and easily. So, if it was a member of the crew we heard, why didn't he go out that way?"

"Perhaps he did, and then somebody came along after and bolted the door again quite innocently?"

"Who? The staff were all off duty. I asked just now if any of the passengers had been in that passage this evening, and no one would admit it. No; the man Roussos and I heard must have turned left in the short passage and entered the main passageway outside the aft door to the saloon. For a crew member, that would have been absolutely crazy."

"But aren't we dealing with a maniac?"

"Yes—but a clever maniac, not a stupid one—not so utterly stupid as deliberately to choose to go all along the passageway, past the dayrooms— the card room, Roussos's study, the library—the stairs up and down—before he could get out on deck. He might have to run into one of the passengers at any moment. Even if he made it outside unseen, he'd have then had to go right back along the deck—and almost certainly be seen by one of the guards. Besides, I've spoken to the guards: they didn't see anybody. No, it only makes sense if it was one of the passengers we heard and he hid in the library, say, or went down to his stateroom and then joined us all for the party a few minutes later."

"You can't be absolutely sure he was the murderer, though, can you?"

Webster shrugged. "He took the six glasses into the galley, replaced them later and went out of the back door to avoid Roussos and me. Then, later, he was present when I asked if anyone had been near the saloon, galley or short passage before the party—and he said nothing. All that leaves not an atom of doubt in my mind as to his guilt. He intended Constantine to carry the can, but he slipped up—especially on that fact of the bolted door."

"You've worked it all out, haven't you?"

"Far from all of it. All I know is that there's a killer on board this vessel—a killer who has in effect already murdered half our number. There's a fifty-fifty chance that I'm one of the victims myself. And I'm not going to sit back and wait for the poison to start working. I've been a detective for over twenty years and I've no intention of dying not knowing who murdered me. So in whatever time I've got left I'm going to get the swine."

She was silent for a few seconds before asking, "When we drank the toast, do you think the poisoner could have known which were the dangerous glasses?"

"He'd have had to watch very carefully. Even then, I don't think he could be absolutely sure of getting a safe one."

"So he might have only pretended to drink?"

"Perhaps. Though there is an alternative."

"You mean he could have chosen this way to commit suicide?"

"Yes."

"So he may never be brought to trial."

"I know. All the same, I've got to find out who he is—for sure."

"You keep saying 'he.' Is that just shorthand, or do you really think it's a man?"

"I think it's a man."

"Do you have a principal suspect?"

There was a perceptible pause before he nodded slowly.

"Is it Philippe?"

"Yes. I'm sorry."

"Why him?"

"As you said, the poisoner has to be insane. And Philippe does seem to me definitely psychotic. Then, there's this obsession he has with danger—with risking his life. He told me there was no thrill to touch it—but that the odds had to be very finely balanced. Well . . ." Webster shrugged.

"But if he *knew* which were the poisoned glasses, there wouldn't have been any finely balanced chance."

"Ah, but he didn't *have* to know that. He could have deliberately kept the knowledge from himself—jumbled the glasses after putting the poison in, or purposely kept his head turned away while they were being picked up and passed round. The only thing I'm doubtful about is whether Philippe *really* wanted to risk his life in that way—or whether it was just talk."

"It wasn't just talk: I've seen him play Russian roulette."

"Have you indeed? Now that is interesting. Still, even Russian roulette wouldn't be such a risk as drinking that champagne: it is, at the very worst, five to one against the gun going off."

"No, he played with two bullets in the gun. I was nearly frantic, but I couldn't stop him. He even wanted to try it with three. I threw a convincing fit of hysterics to stop that, and made him promise never to try it. But I don't know if he kept his word."

"How did he load the revolver when he played with two bullets?"

"What do you mean?"

"Well, the theory is that the weight of the bullet will always take the loaded chamber to the bottom, so the hammer falls on an empty chamber. If Philippe put two bullets in opposite each other, their weight would cancel each other out, so he'd increase the chance of the gun going off to only two to one against. With *three* cartridges in alternate chambers, it really would be an even chance. But with two *consecutive* chambers loaded, the extra weight would be still more likely to take them to the bottom. So, in fact, you'd be safer with two than with one."

"You mean he would know that—and was just showing off."

"Could be."

"I don't think he'd do that. I think he really wanted to make the chances as near to evens as possible."

"Well, you know him better than I do. But it points even more to him being the poisoner. Tell me, do you think he'd worry about killing five or six other people in the course of the experiment?"

"I don't think he'd care two hoots."

"Even if you were among them?"

"I think he'd hope I was. He hates me now."

"Then why not just kill you outright?"

"There'd be no sport in that—no kick. I bet now he's absolutely revelling in not knowing who is going to die."

"It's pretty horrible."

"I know. And I don't see how you're going to get evidence against him. I'm sure he won't have left fingerprints on those things."

"You won't mind if I do nail him?"

"Mind? Are you joking?"

"I was thinking—old times perhaps."

"Auld acquaintance? Auld lang syne? When he's put me through this? I may be a romantic, but I'm not that much of a one."

"Right. Now: if Barrault himself does turn out to be one of the lucky ones, he presumably won't *want* to be found out, will he—or he'd never have framed Constantine?"

"Oh no—that would spoil everything for him. If you gamble and the gamble comes off, you have to win completely. It wouldn't be a victory to be charged with murder, and then perhaps be locked up for life."

"Suppose, then, on the other hand that he *has* taken the poison: will he *then* want to die with nobody knowing he was responsible?"

Karin frowned. "I see what you mean: you think he might want to have some posthumous fame?"

"Yes."

"Yes, I think he would like people to know of his courage and the great gamble which he took."

"So, it's on the cards that he will have left some record, some letter or statement or tape revealing the truth—meaning to destroy it if he does come through after all?"

"I see now what you mean. I would say it's very likely."

"Then the first thing for me to do is see if I can find it."

Then they both looked up sharply, as, before Karin could reply, there came the sound of loud voices from above their heads. A woman was screaming and shouting hysterically, and a man apparently trying to calm her. It took only a few seconds for them to recognize the voices of George and Claire. Then there was the sound of footsteps rapidly descending the stairs from the upper deck, and Claire's voice, the words now clear. "I can't stand it," she was screeching. "I can't put up with not knowing any longer. I'm going to end it, I tell you."

She suddenly appeared, half-falling down the stairs, dishevelled, her eyes wild.

Roussos's voice called desperately, "No—Claire—honey—stop!"

But it was no use. Claire reached the deck and made a frantic dash for the side. Webster sprinted to try and cut her off. She reached the rail, clambered awkwardly up onto it and prepared to jump. In the nick of time Webster's outstretched arm caught her round the waist and jerked her back. They both fell sprawling onto the deck. Webster sat up shakily but Claire lay still. Then Karin came running up and knelt down by them. Roussos arrived at the bottom of the stairs and lumbered panting across. "Is—is she all right?"

Karin had one hand on Claire's pulse, the other on her forehead. "Yes, I think she's just stunned."

Together Roussos and Webster carried Claire inside and laid her down on a big settee. By then she was showing signs of coming round. Roussos knelt down by her, holding her hand.

"Get some brandy or whisky, will you, love?" he said to Karin. "An unopened bottle. And a clean glass from the galley."

"Sure."

A few seconds later Claire opened her eyes. She stared up, looking puzzled and bewildered. "What . . . ?"

"It's all right, honey. Just relax. You knocked yourself out, that's all."

She said, "I fell backwards—somebody pulled me." Then full recollection returned. Horror came into her eyes. Her whole expression changed to one of abject fear. She gave a sob. "Oh no—no. Please God no."

At that moment Karin arrived with a bottle of brandy and four glasses. While Roussos comforted Claire, Webster opened the bottle and poured out a stiff tot, which he handed to Roussos. Roussos held it to Claire's lips. Webster charged two of the other glasses for Karin and himself, put the bottle and an empty glass down beside Roussos and drew Karin to the other side of the saloon.

She looked enquiringly at him. "What do you want?"

"Drink some of that first." She took a sip. He said, "I want to search Philippe's stateroom. But I don't want to go there if he's in it. He'd be most suspicious if I were to call on him."

"*And* if I were."

"Less so."

"All right. I'll try and find out." She took another drink of brandy, put the glass down and hurried out. To his surprise she was back in less than a minute. "Luck. He's playing cards with Quine and Muller in the cardroom. I heard voices and just peeped in."

"Well done." Webster emptied his glass and put it down. "I'll go and do it now."

"Can I come?"

He hesitated.

"Please."

"All right. You can stand guard in the passageway—in case he comes back."

They went downstairs to the accommodation deck. Barrault's stateroom was at the extreme end of the passageway, next to Webster's own. Outside Webster whispered, "Better make sure he didn't leave the game while you were talking to me." He tapped loudly three or four times on the door. There was no reply. He opened the door and switched on the light. The room was empty. He turned to Karin. "Wait here. If he should come along, speak to him loudly. And then can you ask him into your room, to give me a chance to get out?"

"All right. I'll make him think I want to apologize."

Webster went right into the room and closed the door behind him. He looked round. There was no written document or tape visible anywhere. The room was laid out on exactly the same lines as his own, and there weren't a lot of places to hide things. He went first to the clothes cupboard, opened it and started to go through the contents. This turned out to be a maddeningly lengthy job. Barrault had brought a lot of clothes, and Webster couldn't afford to miss a single pocket in either coats or trousers. But in none of them did he find anything remotely incriminating. Next he turned his attention to the dressing-table, rummaging hastily through the drawers. Again, however, the contents were quite innocuous. He went to the bed. He put his hand under the mattress and slid it along. Almost immediately he felt something smooth and flat. He drew it out. It was a loose-leaf notebook in black leather. A picture of a racing car was embossed in gold on the cover.

Webster straightened up and opened it. As he did so, Karin's voice, unnaturally loud and harsh, reached him through the closed door. "Philippe! I was just looking for you."

Webster froze. There was silence for a few seconds, then Barrault's voice reached him. "I cannot understand why you should look here—when not fifteen minutes ago you saw me playing cards upstairs."

"But you are here, aren't you, so I was right."

"What do you want?"

"To talk."

"I have no wish to talk to you, Karin. Please leave me alone."

"But we may not have very long left. And we meant a lot to each other once. I would like us to end up friends."

"That is impossible."

"But I know there are things I must apologize for."

"I also know that."

"Then come into my stateroom for a few minutes. Let us make up."

"No, I wish to be alone—in my own room."

"But Philippe, please—just for five minutes—"

"Let go of my arm."

"Philippe—"

The next instant the door opened and Barrault stood in the doorway. Webster looked up at him from the chair in which he was sitting. "Ah, Barrault, I wanted to see you. Hope you don't mind my waiting."

Barrault stared at him without speaking. Then he turned slowly round to Karin again. "I should have guessed. Friends! You help him to spy on me. You bitch."

"Now hang on." Webster got hurriedly to his feet. But before he could take a step, Barrault had spun back to face into the room. He made a sudden cat-like movement and his right hand disappeared inside his jacket. It came out gripping a long, narrow-bladed dagger.

Karin gave a gasp of horror, stepped forward and grabbed his arm. "Phillipe, don't be a fool!"

He pulled his arm away and turned on her. He gave a snarl. "Shut up!" Then he flung a punch at her head.

Karin had no time to dodge, and the blow caught her square on the jaw. She went flying back and fell down as though shot. She lay motionless. Webster hurled himself across the room towards Barrault. But as he approached, Barrault thrust the blade of the knife forward, straight towards his stomach. Webster stopped dead. Barrault smiled, reached behind him, pulled the door to and locked it. He took out the key and dropped it in his pocket, all without shifting his eyes from Webster's face.

Webster tensed himself and raised himself onto the balls of his feet. He cursed himself for leaving the gun in his stateroom. "Isn't this rather stupid?" He said quietly.

"I do not think so. And I keep things like this until I know what you are doing here, and why she tried to stop me coming in."

Barrault's gaze flashed round the room—and alighted on the bed. About halfway down, the sheet was caught up at the side where Webster had groped for the notebook. Webster stood quite still, waiting for Barrault to break forth in an outburst of fury and a demand for the return of the notebook. But instead the cold eyes merely narrowed.

"What have you been doing to my bed?"

Webster said nothing. He waited, expecting Barrault to investigate and discover that the notebook was missing. But the Frenchman just nodded slowly. "Ah, I begin to see, I think. You search my room—eh? You think I am to blame for this poisoning. Well, you are out of luck. You will find nothing here."

The cool certainty of his manner intensely irritated Webster, whose nerves were already getting close to the snapping point. He knew Barrault was bluffing, relying on Webster's not having had time to locate the notebook, but nevertheless he felt a sudden strong urge to break down the other's veneer of calm, superior confidence. Hardly pausing to think of the consequences of his act, he slipped his hand into his pocket and brought out the notebook. "Oh, I don't know," he said, "what about this for starters?"

Barrault's expression changed instantly to one of intense surprise. He stepped forward and made a grab for the book. Webster skipped back and dropped it into his pocket.

"Give that to me!" Barrault demanded angrily. "Where did you get it?"

"Where do you think I got it, you fool? Stop play-acting."

"Oh, very well—if that is how you want things, I will stop anything so gentle as play-acting." He raised the dagger threateningly. "I don't know what the game is you are up to with my notebook. But I want it back. Now."

Webster licked his lips and flashed his eyes back and forth, taking in the furniture and obstructions in his immediate surroundings. Then he looked Barrault straight in the eyes. "Come and get it," he said.

He just had time to think that there were worse ways to go when the other man was on him.

# 14

Barrault brought the knife round in a flashing uppercut towards the pit of Webster's stomach. Webster side-stepped to his left and made a grab for Barrault's wrist with his right hand. His fingers missed getting a grip by an eighth of an inch, and then Barrault was behind him. They both spun round and Barrault lunged a second time. Again, on tiptoe now, Webster stepped aside and this time did manage to grasp the flailing wrist. Using Barrault's momentum, he forced the knife hand up and above his head, at the same time trying to hook his foot behind Barrault's leg and topple him backwards. But Barrault was ready for this and jerked his foot away. With his left hand he clawed painfully at Webster's face, his index finger gouging at the eye.

Webster shook his head madly and with his left punched with all his strength at the region of Barrault's kidneys. He had the satisfaction of hearing his adversary grunt with pain, and he punched again, still jerking his head violently from side to side and trying to force Barrault's hand away from his face with his upper right arm, which was still raised high, grasping Barrault's wrist. He hooked a third time with his left fist. As he did so, Barrault suddenly stepped backwards, forcing Webster's hand down and making him topple forwards. Barrault was still desperately trying to get his knife hand free and at the same time he attempted to turn to his right and crook his left arm around Webster's neck. But Webster was ready for this and, still bent over, he hurled himself to his right, his shoulder catching Barrault full in the midriff. They both fell, Barrault's back coming up against the wall, and the force of the impact wrenching his wrist free from Webster's fingers. But he kept a grip on the knife, and sprawling back stabbed again at Webster with it, this time aiming at the face. Webster raised his left arm in defence and managed to deflect the blow. But he felt the razor-sharp blade cutting through the sleeve of his tuxedo and drawing blood from his forearm.

With his right Webster aimed a punch at Barrault's face. His knuckles caught the other's chin a glancing blow, but he couldn't follow it up because Barrault's knife hand was coming in again, to his left. He pulled himself backwards and the blade flashed past an inch in front of his forehead. Webster fell back onto the floor in a sitting position and kicked upwards at the knife, falling onto his back as he did so. His hard toecap made sharp contact with Barrault's fingers, gripping the dagger, and it went flying from the hand, to land behind Webster's head.

The next moment Barrault was on his feet again. He stepped towards Webster, raised his foot and stamped down at Webster's face. The heel of his shoe smashed agonizingly against Webster's mouth. Webster grabbed the foot and, exerting every scrap of strength he still possessed, heaved it up and away from him. Barrault fell onto his knees and scrambled forward yet again, straining to reach the dagger. Webster grabbed him by the collar and with his other hand smashed a punch into his face. Barrault shook his head and once more threw himself at Webster, both hands outstretched for Webster's throat. In the nick of time Webster got his own arms up and caught hold of Barrault's hands. He started to force the fingers back. Barrault resisted and for seconds they both remained motionless, hands straining against hands. Then Webster felt his strength beginning to go and the next moment Barrault was free. He scrambled forward, over Webster's body, and his clutching fingers managed at last to reach the handle of the dagger. Clasping him round the thighs, Webster drew on unknown reserves of strength and swung him over, rolling on to his side as he did so. Before the movement was complete, he realized he'd made a terrible mistake. His back was exposed, and Barrault had the knife.

Webster could do nothing to prevent the stab coming. He had one second in which to act. He released his grip round Barrault's legs, at the same time hurling himself clear of the other man. He saw the knife glint in the air again, flashing through the space his body had been occupying an instant before. Then there came a grunt of pain. Barrault, unable to check the blow, had stabbed himself in the thigh.

Webster forced himself to his knees, staggered to his feet and nearly fell. Then Barrault, on the floor, was lunging at him once more, thrusting upwards with the knife, as though it were a sword. Webster stepped back. Again Barrault came forward, on his knees, jabbing with the dagger. Webster moved to his rear again—and found his shoulders pressed into the corner of the room. This is the end, he told himself; his strength would not hold out for more than a few seconds longer, and he knew Barrault had no intention of letting him out alive. The same thought must have come to Barrault, for he gave a gasp of triumph as he realized Webster was trapped. Remorselessly he came forward again. Webster raised his foot and kicked out despairingly. His foot caught Barrault square on the point of the jaw. Barrault, half dazed, fell sideways and rolled onto his back.

Webster just let himself fall forward. He landed right on Barrault, the upper half of his body pinning down Barrault's head and left arm. He caught hold of Barrault's outstretched right hand, which was still gripping the knife, and pressed down on it hard. Barrault tried to rise, but his strength, too, was clearly almost exhausted and Webster's weight was too much for him. He gave a muffled gurgle and threshed wildly. But Webster didn't move. He *couldn't* move. He was incapable of fighting any more, and if he allowed the other man to get free now, he knew it would be all over for him. So he just lay, concentrating his final resources on holding down Barrault's straining right hand.

Gradually Barrault's struggles grew weaker; the muffled sounds lessened. The movements in the hand became spasmodic. Eventually the fingers loosened and the knife rested free on the palm. Without easing his downward pressure on the hand, Webster managed to flick the knife away across the floor with the back of his finger. Still he wasn't prepared to risk shifting his position, although now Barrault had become perfectly still and quiet. Several minutes passed. Then Webster suddenly became aware that somebody was hammering on the door and calling his name over and over again. Karin. He gave a croak-like shout: "All right. Wait." The banging stopped.

Very cautiously he moved the position of his hands, feeling for the pulse in Barrault's wrist. It took him another sixty seconds to be quite sure there wasn't one. Then, slowly and shakily he unpeeled himself and heaved himself to his feet. He gazed with a curious lack of emotion at Barrault's white, dead face. With a great effort, he bent down, groped in Barrault's pocket and extracted the door key. He straightened again, limped heavily across the room and opened the door.

Karin, looking none the worse for the punch on the jaw, gave a gasp in which relief and shock were equally mingled. "Oh, Alec. Thank God."

She threw herself against him, almost knocking him backwards, so weak did he feel. She was sobbing. "I thought he'd killed you."

He put his arm round her shoulders. "I—I'm afraid I've killed him."

She cast a brief glance at Barrault's body, then turned her head away.

"He tried to murder me," Webster said. "With a knife. I had no choice."

She took his hand. "Come to my room."

He let her lead him out to the passageway and along to her stateroom. Here she helped him off with his blood-stained jacket and made him lie down on the bed. Then she hurried out. Webster lay with his eyes closed. His heart was still pounding. His left arm was bleeding. Blood was trickling down his face from a gash where Barrault had clawed him. He could hardly see out of one eye, which was smarting and watering as a result of Barrault's gouging; and his mouth was ramping from the effects of Barrault's shoe. He was aching in every muscle.

Karin came back after two or three minutes. She was carrying one of the first-aid kits, which were placed in prominent positions throughout the yacht. She also had a bowl, a bottle of whisky and a clean shirt, which she put on the bed, saying, "I got this from your room." She handed him the whisky bottle before disappearing into the bathroom. He extracted the cork with his teeth and took a swig.

She returned with the bowl full of water and a clean towel. She put them down, sat on the bed and took hold of his shirt sleeve. "I've always wanted to do this," she said, and tore it open to the shoulder.

"I could have taken it off," Webster said.

She washed and dressed his wound and made a cold pad out of lint for him to hold to his eye. When she'd finished she said, "There."

"Thank you very much."

"How do you feel now?"

"Better. But still terrible. I'm not used to this sort of thing. And I'm much too old for it."

"I thought detectives had fights like that all the time."

"You've been seeing too many movies. The last time I was involved in a real scrap was trying to evict some drunks from a pub when I was on the beat. And I've never killed anybody in my life before."

"Don't think about that. Did you find anything?"

"Look in the pocket of my jacket."

She did so and brought out the notebook. She stared at it. "Where did you find this?"

"Under the mattress."

"But he lost it days ago."

"Lost it?"

"Yes, almost as soon as we arrived. He was quite upset. He'd been using it for years—always putting in fresh paper when it's full."

"He must have found it again—probably after you had the row; you haven't been speaking to him, so you wouldn't know."

"I suppose that must be it."

"Have a look inside—see if there's anything interesting."

"All right." She opened the notebook and started to flick through the pages. "Doesn't seem to be anything. This is all motor racing stuff—his times at different tracks, car performances. Then addresses—phone numbers. Then a lot of figures—to do with gambling, I think, roulette or something. Wait a minute—" She stopped abruptly, her eyes darting down the page.

"What is it?"

"I—I think this is something."

"Don't keep me in suspense."

"All right. Do you want it in English?"

"Can you manage a translation?"

"I think so. I trained as an interpreter once—Swedish, English, French— before I went on the stage." She paused. "It's—er: *Twelve passengers on board. Twelve meals—or drinks—served. Six of them poisoned. Not known which six. Passengers select plates (cups? glasses?) by chance—* no, better *at random. The perfect gamble. Even chances. Six people will die. Who will they be? Will I be among them?"*

Webster closed his eyes. "So I was right. It was him. Is that all?"

She turned over the pages. "No there's quite a lot more. Shall I go on?"

"Yes please."

"Um—*the idea grows on me. I cannot stop thinking about it. The poison must not be too quick—there must be uncertainty. Is there anything suitable on board? My sleeping tablets, perhaps, but I may not have enough. The others must know some of them have been poisoned. I must be able to watch their reactions —and my own."*

Karin turned the page again. *"If I do not die, I must find a,* er, *bouc—goat? —oh, scapegoat, as I must not be suspected of murder.* That's all on that page. There are three more. *Luck. The old woman takes digoxin tablets. Have read of them—highly poisonous. Maybe a chance very soon—a party for Claire's birthday. Must find scapegoat."* She turned over once more. *"Have taken old woman's tablets. And have found scapegoat—one of the stewards. Will plant things in his cabin. Will poison him, too—make it seem like suicide. He drinks orange juice at night. I will—*er, let me see, oh—*lace it. Will use my own sleeping tablets for him, as he must just go quickly to sleep and not wake.* Last page. *Everything planned for tonight. If I find I have lost the gamble, will end it before symptoms become too bad—but not before I know who else is dying. It had to come to this. My destiny."*

Karin closed the book and looked at Webster. "That's all."

Webster took a deep breath and let it out slowly. "What can you say? Mad, of course. You can't hate him."

Karin was silent. She was looking away, twisting the book in her fingers. Then she turned her gaze directly on Webster again. "Philippe didn't write this."

Webster jerked his head up. *"What?"*

"I'm sure Philippe didn't write any of that I just read."

"But—but it's his handwriting, isn't it?"

"It looks like it—exactly."

"Well, then—"

"But it's not his style. I've had dozens of letters from him and he just doesn't write like that. The—the vocabulary's wrong. Besides, he wasn't the type to make notes, except for purely factual things, like at the beginning of the book—records, figures."

Webster stared at her helplessly. "Are you quite certain?"

"Yes, I am. Those pages are out of character."

He closed his eyes and tried desperately to concentrate. "In his room, just now: he saw the bed had been disarranged, where I'd fumbled under the mattress for the notebook. Yet it didn't seem to occur to him that I'd taken it. He was really staggered when he saw it in my hand."

"There you are: that supports what I say. I told you he lost the book—he didn't know it was under the mattress. Besides, why should he leave it there in the first place if there was all this incriminating stuff in it? Why not carry it with him?"

Webster nodded resignedly. "You're quite right, of course." He tried to straighten his tangled thoughts. "This means that somebody has framed him —as well as framing Constantine. It doesn't make sense."

"It must make sense. Because it's happened."

"It also means I've just killed an innocent man."

She shook his shoulder. "Stop it. You didn't kill him because you thought he was a poisoner—but because he came at you with a knife. Remember?"

"Yes—but he knew he was innocent. He didn't know I'm a detective. He found me in his room with a stolen notebook of his. For all he knew, I was the poisoner—and trying to frame him. Perhaps he had a right to attack me."

"With a dagger—without giving you a chance to explain, or explaining himself? If the positions had been reversed, would you have done what he did?"

"No, but I'm not mentally unstable. Philippe was—and he couldn't be blamed for that."

"He wanted to die, Alec. He's been living incredibly dangerously for years. It was bound to come to him sooner or later. That last sentence in the notebook was the only true part."

He gave her hand a squeeze. "You're a very comforting person. Thank you."

"What's the next move?"

"I don't know," Webster said wearily. "I suppose I ought to start looking for the person who framed Philippe."

"You don't sound very eager."

"Frankly, I'm very, very tired and at the moment all I want to do is lie here, drink Scotch and smoke." He looked at his watch. "I've wasted twenty-five precious minutes on a wild-goose chase. I may have less than two hours before the symptoms hit me. If I'm to do anything, it should be preparing myself for death. And there are letters I ought to write."

"I seem to remember something about 'I've got no intention of dying not knowing who killed me.' You do have that intention now, do you?"

Webster looked at her steadily, then heaved himself up and swung his feet onto the floor. "You're a slave driver. But you're quite right. OK—what do we have? It has to be between eight people."

"Only eight?"

"Yes; what I said earlier about the way a crew member would have left, and that bolted door, still applies."

"But who among the passengers are you omitting?"

"Apart from myself, Roussos—I was with him all the time—and you."

"Why me?"

"Because if you'd framed Philippe, you'd hardly then have done all you could to convince me that the entries in the notebook were faked."

"Oh, I see." For a moment she looked a little disappointed, as though she'd been hoping for a different reply. So he added:

"Even without that, though, I could never believe someone who looked and talked like you was a murderess."

"I shouldn't go by that. Did you never see Jean Simmons in *Angel Face*?"

"No; but I have known a few real-life murderesses. And you're not one."

"Thank you. You obviously still don't think that it has to have been a man, though?"

"Far from it. It was only my preconceived idea of Philippe's guilt that made me keep saying 'he.' There was nothing involved in the crime that a woman couldn't have done."

"And you still think we're dealing with a maniac?"

"We have to be. Think: there were sixty tablets used and twelve left in the bottle. That means the poisoner intended to kill exactly six people. Why—if he or she's not mad? I agree it is possible that one of those eight people wanted to kill one specific person, worked all this out as a blind, then mentally marked the position of the poison glasses, and when the champagne was poured, leapt in and quickly passed one of them to the victim."

Webster stood up and tucked in his shirt. "But it would have been a ridiculously uncertain way to kill someone—and would show a callousness about the rest of us that to my mind would amount to madness anyway."

"Of those eight, who seems the sort of person who could murder six people?"

"Any one of them could."

She looked startled. "Do you think so?"

"I do. And I don't think there's anybody who hasn't said something which in the light of what's happened since doesn't sound suspicious to me now; though no doubt I'm reading in meanings that weren't there."

"So what are you going to do now?"

"I honestly don't know. Just play it by ear."

"Well, whatever it is, can I tag along?"

"Sure you want to?"

"Yes; I'll go crazy if I don't keep active. At the moment, I can't think of any better way of trying to help you—if you think I can be of any use."

"I'm sure you can. OK, let's go. Of course, it's crazy to try and crack a case from scratch in less than two hours. But if that's all we've got, let's not waste another second of it."

Lancelot Trent rummaged in the bottom of his duffel bag. His fingers found what they were groping for and drew it out. It was an old Webley service revolver. He'd been carrying it for years. Funny, in all the dangers he'd faced during his travels he'd never once had to fire it in anger—drawn it and waved it about a few times, but that was all. But now at last the time might have come. He looked at his watch. A few hours yet before he knew. All the same, better be ready.

Slowly and carefully, he cleaned and oiled the gun. When he'd finished he extracted a box of cartridges from the duffel bag and methodically loaded all six chambers. Then he sat down at the desk. He took the draft of *South American Way* and some blank paper from a drawer. He inserted a sheet of paper in the typewriter. As he stared at the white page, collecting his thoughts, there was a tingling of excitement within him. The words that were shortly going to fill that page could be the most important he had ever written.

He raised his hands, flexed his fingers and started to type.

"I only pray that I'm one of the people to die," Mrs. van Duren said vehemently.

"Don't say that!" Irene's voice was unnaturally high-pitched.

"Why not? I'm nearly dead anyway. And I'm prepared for it. It would— oh, it would be all *wrong* if I were spared and you or any of those other people were killed."

"I thought you were always prepared to accept God's will."

"I try to be. But what—"

"It might be God's will that you're spared."

"No—no." Mrs. van Duren shook her head vigorously. "It can't be. I must be one of those to die. Apart from everything else, the whole thing is my fault."

"How on earth do you work that out?"

"They were my tablets. If I hadn't been so criminally careless with them, and then gone on chattering about how dangerous they were, none of this would have happened."

"Oh, that's nonsense. If someone sets their mind on doing a thing like this, they'll find a way to do it."

"But I made it so much easier for him. Not only am I to blame for six deaths, I'm also responsible for making that poor boy a murderer."

"Poor boy? Constantine? *Poor?*"

Before Irene could say any more there was a knock on the door. Mrs. van Duren, in whose stateroom they were sitting, called: "Come in."

It was Roussos. He said, "Sorry to interrupt, but I want Orchard, urgent. He's not in his room and I was wondering if you'd seen him."

"No, not since we were all in the saloon," Irene said.

Mrs. van Duren said, "George—does this mean somebody's already—already been taken ill?"

"No—no, nothing like that yet. It's Claire. She's getting kind've edgy. She wants help. He's not the guy I'd go to myself, but . . ." He shrugged. "Don't worry, I'll get the stewards up and have them look for him."

"I thought we agreed we didn't want them around," Irene said.

"I know, but I want to get back to Claire. She shouldn't be left."

Irene said, "Have you tried the main deck—aft? He sits there quite a lot, looking out over the stern."

"Oh thanks."

"Irene, why don't you go and look for him?" Mrs. van Duren said. "Then your father can go straight back to Claire."

"I don't want to leave you."

"I don't mind being alone for a short while—in fact, I would welcome it."

"Very well, if you're sure. I won't be long." She went out to the passageway, closing the door behind her.

"Bring him to the saloon, will you?" Roussos said.

"Right." Irene started to turn away. But then her father caught her arm. "What's the matter?" she asked. He didn't reply, just stared into her face, more deeply than she ever remembered him doing before. A little alarmed, she said, "You all right?"

"Yeah. I just wanted to—to say sorry."

"What for?"

"This. All this. And—well, everything, I guess."

Irene swallowed. "That's all right. I guess I have things to apologize for too."

"No nothing. Nothing." He released her. "I must get back to Claire."

They walked off in different directions.

Hilary Orchard stood hunched over the stern rail of the main deck and tried to thrust away from him the reality of recent events. It couldn't, it just couldn't have happened. Before, everything had been so good, the path ahead so clear and sunny. And then the nightmare. Why, why, why had he ever come on this ghastly boat? Since the moment he'd stepped aboard, everything had happened with such remorseless inevitability. There had just been no way to avoid this hideous situation. Had there?

At that moment he heard footsteps on the deck behind him. He turned with relief to see Irene approaching.

"How are you?" she said, and the hackneyed phrase bore a significance it had never had before.

"All right, I think—so far. What about you?"

"All right. I'm sorry to disturb you."

"It doesn't matter."

"Do you think you could come and speak to Claire?"

"Speak to her?"

"Yes. It seems she's very upset—needs some spiritual comfort."

"Oh, but look, I don't really think I'm the right one to—"

"You're a parson."

"Technically, yes, but I've never served in a parish. I've never dealt with the sick or dying. I'm an academic."

"Listen, you may be the wrong sort of parson, but you're the only one we have. Surely you can mumble a few platitudes, at least, to help a scared woman."

"I'm scared myself. I need someone to help me."

"So do we all. But Claire needs it more than most."

"I daresay, but—"

"Do I have to go back and tell them you won't come?"

Orchard got to his feet. "No, I'll come. But don't expect me to be a lot of use."

"Just do what you can, that's all."


"This isn't having any effect on you at all, is it?" Paul Muller shouted. "You just don't care that you might be dead in a few hours!"

"That is true of every single person in the world."

"Oh, don't be clever—you know what I mean. You may in effect have already been murdered. But you're just not worried about it."

"Do you want me to be worried?"

"I just want you to show some emotion."

"But I do not feel any emotion."

"You're unnatural."

She gave a shrug. "What would be natural? To scream and shout and rave? To roll on the floor, beat my breast, tear my hair, babble and screech? Would such behaviour on my part make your happiness complete?"

*"Happiness?"*

"Yes; are you not already partly happy that so many bores and philistines are going to die tonight?"

"But I may be among the victims, you fool!"

"I wonder."

"What do you mean?"

"You're a survivor, Paul. People like you always come through crises. You're the organizers, the manipulators, the smooth men. The day after the Bomb falls you'll be sitting unscarred on the edge of a crater, sipping a glass of Madeira, stroking the hair of the last stenographer left alive and dictating a memo for another man exactly the same as yourself on the opposite edge."

"How long did it take you to compose that exquisitely phrased piece of venom?"

"Not long. I've studied you doing that sort of thing for some time now."

Paul looked at her with hatred in his eyes. "I hope to heaven you're among the ones who buy it."

"So do I, Paul. At least we agree on something. And by the way, I find I am experiencing some emotion now. I am obtaining mild pleasure at seeing your sang-froid shattered for once."

Paul got to his feet with a jerky movement and strode to the door. "I came down here with you because I thought in this situation we ought to make at least some effort to be kind to each other. But there's no point in continuing. I am now going to do my best to drink myself unconscious. If I'm lucky, I shall wake up and find the whole affair over. If not, I'll know nothing about it. It's unlikely that we shall both come through this, so I'll say goodbye. I'm sorry I can't say it's been nice knowing you, because frankly it's been hell."

He went out, slamming the door. Maria sat quite still and expressionless for several minutes. Then a slight change came over her face. There was nobody present to see them, but tears appeared in her eyes.

"Oh, thank God!" Claire Roussos struggled to a sitting position on the settee as Orchard and Irene entered the saloon. "You must help me."

Orchard moved reluctantly to her side. "How can I help you?"

"I'm dying. I know I'm dying. I must confess. Can you hear my confession?"

"I'm not a Roman Catholic priest, Mrs. Roussos. I started to train for it, but—"

"I'm not a Catholic."

"What is your religion?"

"I was christened—and married the first time—in the Church of England. Can you hear my confession?"

"Well, yes, I can do that. Shall we go somewhere more private?"

Roussos, who was standing near, a glass almost full of brandy in his hand, said hastily, "Irene and me'll clear out."

"No," Claire said, "we'll go." She scrambled to her feet and started for the door. Suddenly she stopped and turned almost fiercely on Orchard. "Will I have to confess everything?"

"You haven't got to confess anything if you don't want to."

"But you can't give me absolution for sins I don't confess, can you?"

"No priest could give a blanket absolution for sins he knew nothing about."

"But suppose I tell you about—about things and then I don't die at all?"

"Oh, I assure you, anything you said would be in the strictest confidence—"

"Yes, but you'd *know*, wouldn't you? And this isn't a church, there's no confessional. Suppose you decided this wasn't a proper confession? You might feel you had to tell somebody."

Orchard was looking annoyed. "I didn't want to come in here, and I'm not trying to persuade you to say anything."

Claire gave a wail of anguish. "Oh, I don't know what to do." She clutched eagerly at Orchard's sleeve. "Can you just pray for me?"

"Pray?"

"Yes—here—now."

"You mean out loud—extempore?"

"Yes—yes."

"Oh no, I don't think I could do that. Look, there are some excellent prayers in the Anglican prayer book. There must be one on board. Why don't you read some of those? I'm sure you'd find it a comfort."

"Oh, that's no good at all!" Claire flung herself back down on the settee. "Why couldn't we have had a real priest on board?"

Orchard stood gazing down at her helplessly. He looked at Roussos and Irene and made a despairing gesture with his hands.

"You don't need a priest."

The voice came from the aft doorway. Orchard, Roussos and Irene turned towards it and Claire looked up. It was Emily van Duren. She walked slowly across the room and sat down by Claire.

"Look at me," she said. Claire did so. "Listen. You have spoken to a priest, who hasn't been able to help you. So I'll tell you what to do. Confess your sins to God. Truly repent of them. And put your trust in Christ alone to save you."

Wide-eyed, Claire said, "Is that all?"

"Yes. But you must admit your guilt and that you can do nothing to absolve yourself. You must put your whole faith in Christ. He died for your sins. You must believe that. You must commit yourself to Him. Do you understand?"

"I'm—I'm not sure. Tell me again, will you?"

"Would either of you mind if I listened?" The voice, almost a whisper, was Nathan Quine's. He'd come silently into the saloon while Mrs. van Duren was speaking. He slipped into a chair near the settee.

Emily van Duren said, "I'll be very pleased if you do."

As she started to talk again, she had an audience of five.

## 15

Webster and Karin left her room together. She was carrying the notebook. They made for the stairs leading to the main deck, but when they were passing Trent's room, the faint sound of a typewriter reached them. Webster stopped. He said quietly, "I'm going to be very unpopular, but I've got to ignore people's feelings and ask some questions. Might as well start with Trent. To save time, while I'm with him, will you check if any of the others are in their rooms?"

"OK." She turned away.

Webster tapped on the door. The typing stopped and Trent's voice called, "Come." Webster opened the door and entered.

Trent, at the desk, turned round. There was a strange, half-wild, half-excited expression on his face; he looked only partially present. He said, "Ah, Williams."

Webster said, "Heard your machine. Thought I'd see how you were feeling."

"What? Oh, not bad, not bad. Good of you. Might not have enough time, though."

"Trying to get something finished?"

"The greatest thing I've ever done."

"Really? What's that?"

"An account of all this. The whole thing. It'll be unique. The diary of a murder victim. What it's like waiting as the hours tick by for the first signs to hit you. It was the very climax I needed for the book—for my whole career. Think of it! It'll be a sensation. Lancelot Trent's last and greatest adventure. Bound to put me back in the best seller lists."

"But you may not be one of the victims."

For a moment Trent seemed taken aback. Then he shook his head. "I can't believe that. Got a feeling. I'm for the chop this time."

"You seem remarkably calm about it."

"No point kicking up a fuss. If your time's come, that's that. Can't do anything about it. If I can just get this chapter finished, I'll be content. Had a good life. So, sorry and all that, but I must—"

"Would you mind answering a couple of questions first?"

"What sort of questions? Why?"

"I'm writing out an account of the whole evening, too—for the police. We want the case against Constantine to be absolutely watertight. We must prove no one else had a chance to do it. So I've got to put down as far as possible just what everybody was doing throughout the evening, and with whom. How did you spend the time between dinner and the party?"

"Watched the flick upstairs."

"What time did that start?"

"About ten to nine, I suppose."

"Who else watched it?"

"Roussos. Claire. Paul and Maria. Philippe. Nathan."

"And everyone watched it from beginning to end?"

"Yes."

"And it finished when?"

"Twenty—twenty-five past ten. But, listen, I—"

"What did you do then?"

"Went out onto the upper sun deck and had a smoke and a think about my book for half-an-hour. But now I really must—"

"One more question only: did you see anybody else during that time?"

"No. Not until the party—except those sentry chappies wandering about below now and then. Is that everything?"

"Yes. Sorry to have disturbed you. Best of luck."

"What? Oh, thanks. You too." Trent swung back round to his desk. Before Webster had closed the door, he'd started typing again.

Karin was waiting outside. "Find out what you wanted?" she asked.

"Yes; he could have done it. He's got no alibi for that vital period immediately prior to the party. What about the other rooms?"

"Only Maria Muller's down here. She's just sitting in her room alone. It's awful. I tried to talk to her, but it wasn't any use. She obviously didn't want me, so I didn't stay. She thinks Paul's upstairs somewhere. Are you going to question her?"

"I don't think there's much point. Let's go up."

They went to the main deck and entered the saloon. Six people were already there and none of them did more than momentarily turn a head when Webster and Karin came in. The centre of attention seemed to be Emily van Duren. She was seated on the big settee, while gathered around her were Roussos and Claire, Irene and Nathan Quine, all apparently listening to her intently. Such was the atmosphere that automatically Webster and Karin stopped and started to listen too.

Five minutes later Webster gave himself a mental shake and with an effort forced himself to withdraw quietly into the passageway. Here he hesitated. Then he walked along to the cardroom, opened the door and looked inside. Paul Muller was slumped in a chair at one of the tables, his hand resting on the table-top loosely encircling an empty tumbler, his eyes fixed glassily on a bottle with two or three inches of brandy in the bottom, which was standing beside it. Next to the brandy was an unopened bottle of whisky. He glanced sideways just for a moment as Webster entered, then let his eyes return to the bottle. Before Webster could speak, he said huskily, "Anyone dead yet?"

About to say yes, Webster changed his mind. There was no point in trying to explain about Barrault. So he just said, "No poisoning symptoms so far."

Muller gave a grunt. "Wondering if I'll have to open the Scotch. Not much brandy left and still conscious. Annoying."

"But fortunate for me. Because I want to ask you some questions."

Muller emptied the brandy bottle into the tumbler with an unsteady hand, picked up the glass and swallowed noisily. Then he said, "Questions?"

"Yes. You watched the film upstairs after dinner, I think."

"Film?" He frowned. "Seem to remember something about it."

"What did you do after?"

"After? Came down to party. Someone poisoned us—remember?"

"There was about half-an-hour after the film before the party started. What did you do during that time?"

"Do? Nothing."

"Where were you?"

"Don't know. About."

"Was your wife with you?"

"Wife? Dear Maria? Unlikely. We see as little of each other as we can, you know. Very little."

"Did you see anybody else?"

"Who?"

"Anyone—between ten-thirty and the party?"

Muller blinked. "Maybe. Why—why you . . ."

His voice tailed off. Almost mechanically he somehow managed to raise the glass to his lips. He poured a drop or two down his throat, but a lot more down his shirt front. Then his hand fell, the tumbler dropped to the floor, his eyes closed and his head lolled forward.

Webster bent down, picked up the glass and replaced it on the table. He took a long look at Muller, shrugged and went out.

In the passageway he met Irene, who was coming from the direction of the saloon. "She has them in the palm of her hand in there," she said abruptly.

"Your grandmother?"

"Yes. It's rather terrific, really."

"I know. I'd like to have stayed and listened myself."

"I can't stay in there any longer. It's all too painful and tense. I'm going outside to get some air."

"May I ask you a question first?"

"I guess so."

"After I unjammed your door earlier, did you stay in your room until the party?"

"Yes."

"Did you see anybody else during that time?"

"Not until I collected my grandmother at about five to eleven."

"And she'd been in *her* room—alone—ever since she'd left us?"

"Yes, I'm sure she had."

"I see. Thanks."

"I suppose you have a good reason for asking all this."

"I'm not at all sure that I have," Webster said.


It was fifteen minutes later that Karin found Webster in the writing-room. He was sitting at a table, a pen in his hand, with several sheets of paper, some covered with writing, in front of him. He looked up as she entered.

She said, "I've been looking for you. I didn't notice you leave the saloon. What are you doing?"

"What I should have done a long time ago: trying to use my brains."

"What do you mean?"

"Well, all this checking on movements and alibis is getting me nowhere. Besides, it isn't really right to grill people at a time like this. I haven't even got the authority to do so. Nor have I got the facilities for physical investigation: I can't test for fingerprints, or send objects for scientific examination. I'm on my own. So I've decided the best thing I can do is try and dig the answer out of here." He pointed to his head.

She frowned. "I don't quite understand."

"Among all the things I've seen and heard since I came on board the *Angel* there must be clues to the truth. What I've got to do is recall them—and interpret them properly."

"Are you getting anywhere?"

"I don't know. I think I may be. I've evolved a crazy sort of theory. It answers a great many questions. But there are facts which just don't fit in. If only I had more time."

"Is there anything I can do?"

"I don't think so. It's just a question of thinking, and no one can help me do that."

"Do you mind if I hang around? I won't disturb you."

"Of course I don't mind."

She sat down and Webster bent again over his papers.

Unobtrusively she watched him as he sat there, sometimes writing, sometimes just staring in front of him. At last, however, he straightened the papers, put them in his pocket and stood up. She looked at him expectantly. He gave her a tired smile.

"Well?" she asked.

"Time for action. I've got to go and ask some more questions."

"But you said—"

"I know what I said. But I have to ask just three questions of three different people—Roussos, Mrs. van Duren and Irene. Were Roussos and the old lady still in the saloon when you left?"

"No; Mr. and Mrs. Roussos went up to their suite and I think Mrs. van Duren returned to her room."

"Right, I think I'll take her first. Still want to help?"

She nodded.

"Then I'd like you to find Irene—she's probably out on the deck—and ask her these questions."

Ten minutes later Webster and Karin met on the main deck. "Did you find her?" he asked.

"Yes. I put your questions. I don't know what answers you wanted, but they are: 'Yes—twice. And the second time she knew all about it.' "

"Thank you. Now let's go and have a word with Roussos."

On the way up he said, "I'll have to tell him about Philippe's death and about Constantine being framed. But at this stage I'm not going to tell him what we discovered about Philippe being framed as well. For the time being I want to let him think I believe Philippe was the poisoner."

"Why?"

"I don't want to give him grounds to go rampaging all over the ship hurling questions at everybody—which is probably what he would do if I informed him the killer was still at large."

They reached the door of Roussos's suite and Webster tapped on it. Roussos opened it himself and looked a little surprised to see them. "Oh, hullo. Come in."

He stood aside and they went through into the sitting-room. Nobody else was there.

"How's Claire?" Webster asked.

"Calmer. She's resting now. How are things below?"

"Quiet. Muller's drunk himself into a coma. Trent's working like mad. And Barrault's dead."

Roussos drew his breath in sharply. "So soon!" He looked at his watch. "It's only eight minutes past two."

"He didn't die of poisoning. I killed him."

"*What?*"

"I had no choice. It was self-defence. He came at me with a knife."

Roussos sat down slowly. "You'd better tell me about it."

"OK. Firstly, though, Constantine is not the poisoner."

Roussos looked up sharply. "He's not?"

"No; he was framed. As soon as I realized that, I suspected Barrault. I decided to search his room."

He told the story concisely, Roussos listening in silence.

"After Karin had patched me up," Webster concluded, "she had a look through the notebook. We found something extremely interesting." He turned to Karin. "Read it again, will you?"

She opened the notebook and read the passage aloud. Roussos listened as though stunned until she'd finished. Then he gave a sigh. "It's better he's dead. Don't blame yourself, Alec. You did the only thing you could."

"Thanks. I haven't told anybody else yet, but I thought you ought to know. Now, will you tell me one thing: was it Barrault whom you suspected of being involved in the kidnap plan?"

Roussos didn't answer. He got to his feet, walked across to a cocktail cabinet and poured himself a whisky. "Either of you want anything?"

They both declined. Roussos came back to his chair and sat down again before saying, "I had no reason to suspect him particularly."

"Did you have a reason to suspect somebody else?"

"No."

"Sure? It's important I know the truth now. This isn't the time to worry about prejudicing me against anyone. If you have any grounds—however flimsy—for thinking a specific person is involved, you must tell me."

"I haven't, Alec, I promise."

"So Barrault could have been the one?"

"Well, yeah, I guess so. But look, now the guy's dead, I don't wanta—"

Karin interrupted. "There's something I have to say."

She blurted out the words and they both shot her surprised looks. She glanced from one to the other, then, stammering slightly said, "He was. Philippe, I mean. He was involved in some sort of plot to kidnap Irene."

Roussos gave a gasp. Webster said sharply, "You've known about this all along?"

"No! I swear it. I knew nothing about it until I saw it in here." She held up the notebook. "I didn't read everything out. I was scared. I thought you'd think I was mixed up in it, too. But I can see it'll have to come out eventually." She held the notebook towards Roussos. "Do you want to read it? It's in French, of course."

Roussos shook his head. He seemed dazed. He muttered, "Can't understand the language."

Rather grimly Webster said, "I think you'd better read it to us."

"All right." She opened the notebook again and flicked through the pages. "It's nearer the front than the other bit—among a lot of motor-racing stuff. Here we are. It's quite short."

Webster moved behind her and looked at the page over her shoulder as she read aloud.

*"I am making friends with Irene as planned. She, of course, is flattered, but rather nervous of me at present. I must break down her reserve quickly and gain her trust or the plan won't work. Roussos also must trust me, as no suspicion must fall on me after she is taken. I only hope the London boys don't mess things up."*

"What's that?" Roussos's eyes were fixed on Karin in an expression of utter disbelief. *"London boys?"*

"That's right."

"But—but it's incredible!"

"We knew it was a London mob who were behind it," Webster said.

"What? Oh, yeah. But—for him to write it down like that . . ."

"I know. It was extremely rash. He was insanely over-confident."

Roussos just shook his head. He looked bewildered—disorientated. Then suddenly a thought seemed to strike him and he heaved himself to his feet. "But this means Irene's in danger. Someone ought to be with her. Alec—"

Webster raised his hand in a calming gesture. "Take it easy. Obviously the plan depended on Barrault. He had to do something—take Irene some-where—before they snatched her. He won't be doing that now."

"Oh. I suppose you're right." Roussos relaxed a little. "But listen, when we get to port, you'll stay with her all the time, won't you? I mean, when the crooks learn Barrault's dead, they might just go ahead anyway, without him."

"Of course I'll stay with her," Webster said, "if it's possible. Let's face it: neither she nor I may reach port alive."

Roussos flopped back down into his chair and closed his eyes. "The poison . . . Would you believe I actually forgot about it there for a moment?"

There was silence. Karin looked at Webster uncertainly. He said, "We'd better get back downstairs."

Roussos opened his eyes. "No—stay a bit. Talk. I can't go down because of Claire and I want company. Sit down."

They did so. There was silence. Karin said, "What do you want to talk about?"

"Anything. Anything except this business."

"Oh." She looked helplessly round the room. Her eyes alighted on the video. She made a great effort. "What—what was the film?"

"Eh?"

"The movie you showed earlier: what was it?"

"Oh, I can't remember the name. Old Hollywood musical—thirties stuff. Lots of girls forming patterns."

"Sounds like Busby Berkeley."

"Who?"

"The man who created all those effects: teams of girls made to look like flowers opening, great set pieces on revolving turntable stages with different lots of girls each side, waltzing pianos, huge winding staircases up to the clouds, and so on."

But having asked for talk Roussos now seemed uninterested. He just gave a grunt. Rather desperately Karin turned to Webster. "Do you like those old musicals, Alec?"

He didn't answer her. He stood up. "Sorry," he said. "I've got to go downstairs. I've just had an idea." He looked at Karin. "You'd better stay here for the time being. I shan't be long."

He hurried from the room.

Webster looked round at the five puzzled and apprehensive faces. His mouth felt dry and there was a tight band round his heart. Suppose he were wrong? It was an unbearable thought. But he was committed now. He spoke with difficulty.

"Thank you for coming. I asked you to my room because I want to be sure of privacy. I won't keep you in suspense. At present I can't prove what I'm about to say, but I'm pretty certain it's right. As we thought, six people on this yacht have been poisoned. But not us. We're the other six, and we're going to be all right."

At first, for all the effect they had, Webster's words might have been addressed to wax effigies. Then Karin sat down suddenly on the bed, next to Irene, who just gulped. Hilary Orchard closed his eyes. Emily van Duren in the armchair said, "Thank God." And George Roussos swayed slightly and put a hand against the wall to steady himself.

It was Irene who found her voice first: "The—the others?"

"I'm afraid they are dying."

In a hoarse whisper, Roussos said, "You mean—including Claire?"

"Including Claire. Also the Mullers, Trent and Quine. The only exception is Barrault, who as two of you know, is already dead. I killed him in self-defence. He attacked me with a knife after I found his notebook—which contains the outline of a scheme for the random poisoning of six people."

Orchard said, *"Barrault?* You mean Barrault was the poisoner? What about Constantine?"

"Constantine had nothing to do with it."

Roussos said: "Alec told me a little while ago that Barrault framed Constantine."

"No, I didn't say that. I did say Constantine had been framed, but I didn't say by whom. Barrault was certainly insane. But in fact he and Constantine were both framed by a third person."

Roussos's eyes bulged. He gasped, "But that's impossible."

Orchard said, "Are you saying we've had two insane people on board?"

"No—just one: Barrault. You see, I was wrong. The poisoning wasn't the work of a maniac. It was the carefully planned murder of six deliberately chosen victims. I know by whom it was done, how it was done, and I think why it was done."

Emily van Duren said, "You say you have no proof of this?"

"Not yet. And at this time there's only one way to get it."

Irene licked her lips. "Which way is that?"

"To ask the murderer."

He turned and looked at Roussos. "What about it—George? I'm right, aren't I?"

Roussos stared blankly at him. "What you asking me for? You ain't suggesting I poisoned them?"

"I'm suggesting exactly that."

"You're out of your mind! I was with you the whole time—while the champagne glasses were being tampered with and—"

"The poison wasn't in the champagne glasses. That was all camouflage. You poisoned your victims upstairs earlier, having got the five of us safely out of the way. Later you set me up to give you a perfect alibi."

"Aw, Alec, come on—"

Webster lost his temper. He took one step towards Roussos, grabbed him by the collar and hurled him back against the wall with a thud that shook the room. "Stop play-acting," he shouted. "You've put us through two hours of anguish. Look at us. An old lady with a weak heart. Two young girls—one your own daughter. Not to mention Orchard and me. Now tell the truth or so help me I'll beat you to a pulp."

He released Roussos and stepped back. "And just in case you still doubt that I know the truth, I've found the switch inside the safe."

At these words Roussos's resistance crumpled. For a moment he seemed about to sag. Then he squared his shoulders, put his coat straight and looked Webster directly in the eye. "You're a clever devil, Alec. If only I'd had the sense to choose a *dumb* cop."

Irene was gazing at her father, her face a mask of disbelieving horror. In a hoarse voice she said: "You purposely poisoned six people—murdered them?"

"That's right."

"Including Claire—your own wife?"

"Including Claire—that's the reason I made her my wife. I only married her to kill her—and all her stinking cronies."

She raised a hand to her forehead. "But—but *why?* You must have had a reason."

"Yeah, I had a reason. A good one." Roussos let his gaze swing round the room. "For nearly seven years, those six honourable and upright citizens have been running one of the slickest narcotics rackets in the world."

There was a hush. It was broken by Emily van Duren. "I think I understand," she said quietly.

Irene seemed to be having difficulty in speaking. She stammered as she said, "But w-what's that to you? Why should *you* want to kill them because of that?"

"I'll tell you, honey. We always kept this from you, and Emily won't like me talking about it now. But the fact is your sister was a hopeless addict. When she had that crash she was stoned out of her mind."

Irene froze. It was left to her grandmother to say, "And Claire and her friends supplied the drugs that killed her?"

"Yes—almost certainly."

*"Almost?* Does that mean you aren't sure?"

"I know they supplied dope to Helen's pusher. Maybe other people did, too. I got no absolute proof that the actual stuff Helen was on when she was killed came from this lot—though I'd say it was ten to one that it did. But what of it? Somebody sold the junk that killed her. And this lot supplied junk that killed somebody's kid somewhere. What difference does it make?"

"You may find it makes a great deal of difference."

They all swung in the direction of the voice. The door was open and standing with her hand on the knob was Maria Muller.

For a moment after Maria Muller's intervention no one moved. Then Webster stepped forward. "Frau Muller, you weren't—"

She waved him down and continued as if he hadn't spoken. "From the start I suspected your motive in having us all aboard together, Roussos. I sensed danger. But because the prospect of death was not abhorrent to me I came along. Well, I was right about you. And you have won. You have liquidated us. You've closed down our operation. You have avenged your daughter. But don't imagine that is the end of the matter."

Roussos said hoarsely, "Whaddya mean?"

"You don't really think that we were a completely independent organization, do you? Oh, we were quite self-contained: there were just the six of us in the team. But we did have friends—backers, if you like. They didn't have any part in organizing our operation, or in the day-to-day running of it. But they did finance us at the start. They have always taken a substantial cut of our profits. So you could say that ultimately we were responsible to them."

"I don't believe you!" Roussos snarled. "You're making it up."

She gave a barely perceptible shrug. "I don't expect you to believe me—yet. You've never set eyes on these men—never even heard of them. They are hundreds of kilometres away at this moment. But they have been keeping events on board monitored, and before very long they will learn what has happened. They won't be pleased."

Roussos had been looking shaken, but now he rallied a little. "If what you say is true, why did you want *my* backing, too?"

"I didn't. Neither did Philippe. But Claire talked the others into it. She had ideas of breaking free from our backers eventually, once we had your money behind us. A crazy scheme, of course—they are not men who ever let go. But now you have smashed our operation. And that will cost them a lot of money. It will hurt them. They are not used to being hurt. They are men of considerable power. I wouldn't want to be in your shoes, Roussos, I really wouldn't."

Roussos gave a sneer. "I've never heard such a load of crud."

"You will soon find out if that is what it is. One thing I slightly regret is that I will not be here to see you make the discovery. You did your best to cause me a lingering and painful death, Roussos."

"You deserve it."

"Deserve it or not, that isn't the death I intend to die. For years I have carried with me a cyanide capsule. It is a hackneyed but most effective tool for ending one's life. I have often thought of using it, but have always lacked the courage. But I am now beginning to feel the effects of the digoxin. It will therefore require greater courage to remain alive than to end things quickly. So I am now going to my room to put the capsule to the use for which it was made." She backed out of the room and closed the door.

A dazed silence followed her exit. Then Orchard made as if to go after her. Webster put a hand on his arm. "Let her do it. It's the best way. And she won't want anyone with her."

Mrs. van Duren's head was bowed and her eyes closed. She opened them, looked up and got stiffly to her feet. She stared at Roussos. "At what time was the poison actually administered?"

"About ten twenty-five."

"And what time is it now?"

Webster looked at his watch. "Nearly two thirty-five."

"Hm—four hours. It seems Frau Muller's forecast was accurate. That means the other victims will fall ill very shortly—if they haven't already done so. They must not be left alone. They will need help." She started for the door.

Orchard took a step towards her. In a strangely diffident voice he said, "Do you think I could be of any use?"

"Surely you are the best judge of that."

"I was pretty hopeless earlier on. But since then I've listened to you, and I've learned a bit. If you think I can help, I'll be quite willing to follow your lead."

Mrs. van Duren looked him up and down. "Let's go and do what we can, Mr. Orchard."

## 16

Karin's red-gold curls were spread in rumpled profusion on the pillow. She looked absurdly young. Webster stood watching her for a few seconds, smiling. Then he bent down and gently shook her shoulder. Without opening her eyes she snuggled deeper into the bed.

"Hey," he said quietly, "time to wake up."

She murmured something incomprehensible and turned onto her face.

Webster changed his tactics. Loudly he said, "They're waiting for you on the set, Miss Johnson. Early call today. You've overslept."

Then he stepped back hurriedly as Karin's head shot upwards and she gave a panic-stricken squeak. She blinked round, bewildered for a second or two, before her eyes alighted on Webster and she got her bearings. She slumped back and yawned hugely. "Beast!" she said.

"Sorry. Emergency measures seemed necessary. I've brought you some coffee."

"You have? In that case, all is forgiven." She sat up and took the cup from him. She sipped from it. "Oo, that's good. Thank you. But where's my stewardess?"

"I volunteered for the duty. I wanted to speak to you and see how you were."

"How I was? Why—" She stopped short and went suddenly pale. She closed her eyes and whispered: "I'd forgotten. Did it really happen? Or was it a nightmare?"

"It happened. But it's over now."

She opened her eyes again. "Thank God. Oh, what a night!"

"One I certainly wouldn't want to repeat."

"I feel as though I've been given the chance to live again after having had it taken away from me. I know just how Jimmy Stewart felt at the end of It's a Wonderful Life." She frowned suddenly. "But what happened to me? I don't remember going to bed."

"You suddenly went out like a light. I carried you in here and Irene got you to bed."

"How humiliating. Why did I have to be the only one to pass out?"

"Because you were the only one to be given a sedative earlier in the evening."

"I was? When?"

"In something you ate or drank at dinner or immediately after. It was Roussos's method of keeping you out of the way. But he didn't know that when it took effect you'd be shut in with Irene and so kept awake. So through all the trauma you were fighting a drug. Then when you discovered you hadn't been poisoned, your mind automatically relaxed and your body gave in. At least, that's my strictly non-medical explanation."

"How do you know about the sedative?"

"Roussos told me. I've been having a long talk with him while you've been asleep. He's explained a lot of things."

"What happened exactly—towards the end? It's all muddled in my mind."

"How much do you remember?"

She screwed her eyes up. "You made him confess to being the poisoner. You were great—just like Bogie. Then Maria Muller came in and talked a lot about—about having friends. I couldn't understand it properly—I was really muzzy by then. The old lady said something about going to help the others. That's about all. Were they really poisoned?"

Webster nodded.

"What happened to them? Are—are they dead?"

"Yes. We found Trent at his desk. He'd shot himself. Maria swallowed that cyanide capsule, as she'd said she would. Paul Muller never regained consciousness after passing out in the cardroom. Nathan Quine and Claire have both died within the last few hours."

She shook her head slowly. "It's terrible. Unbelievable. And Mr. Roussos really did it all?"

"Yes."

"He's mad, of course."

"I don't think so. I get the impression that he's completely sane."

"That makes it worse. What have you done with him?"

"I haven't done anything with him. He's agreed to stay up in his rooms."

"Isn't he locked in?"

"No."

"But he might come down and kill us all! Think what we know about him!"

"There's no danger of that. He swears he never had the slightest intention of killing anybody but those six. I believe him."

"Well, I'll take your word for it. Where are the—the bodies?"

"In the other staterooms. Orchard and I brought Muller and Claire down, so they would all be in one section of the yacht. Irene's put this passageway out of bounds to the servants. It seemed best—and it gave me a good excuse to bring you your coffee."

"What have they been told?"

"Just the bare facts—who is dead. Irene got all the crew together and explained that there'd been a terrible accident. No doubt there are wild rumours flying about, but as they can hardly be wilder than the truth, we might as well let them carry on flying for the time being."

"What about Constantine?"

"He's OK."

"Oh, good. What time is it?"

"Half-past eleven."

"Heavens! Shouldn't we have arrived in Puerto Rico by now?"

"Several hours ago, but we aren't going there now."

"Why not?"

"Irene's more or less in charge of the *Angel* now, so we're going to St. Croix, the nearest of the Virgin Islands, which is very small, but which is an American possession."

"I thought Puerto Rico was too."

"Not apparently in such a full sense. Puerto Rico's autonomous. But in St. Croix the U.S. Department of the Interior has full jurisdiction. Perhaps it won't really make a lot of difference, but Irene wants to be on the safe side."

"How long will it take to get there?"

"We should arrive between three and three-thirty."

"Where are all the others now?"

"Mostly in bed I think."

"Have you had any sleep?"

"About an hour."

"You must be exhausted."

"No, I'm used to working all night and most of the next day. I've had a shower and I feel wide awake and extremely hungry. So I'm wondering if you'd care to join me for what used to be called brunch. We must give the kitchen staff something to do."

"I'll be with you in ten minutes," she said.

Karin was as good as her word, turning up in the dining-room looking incredibly fresh and bright in vivid yellow trousers and a blue shirt. Before she and Webster had finished their meal, Orchard, Irene and Mrs. van Duren had joined them. Afterwards they all made their way to the saloon and sat down. Irene looked at Webster. "Right," she said, "we all know now who you are and what you've been doing on board. Now we want explanations."

"Well." Webster collected his thoughts. "The whole object of this cruise was what your father calls the 'execution' of those six people. But he couldn't afford to have the police probing his or their backgrounds, looking for a motive, so he decided to make the killings look like the random work of a maniac. He knew about Barrault's obsession with risking his life on even chances, and he set out to create the impression that Barrault had gone right round the bend and had tried a mad gamble—that between ten-thirty and ten forty-five last night, he'd taken six champagne glasses to the small galley, added poison and replaced them."

"And it was George who took my tablets?" Mrs. van Duren asked.

"Yes; though he had some of his own as well."

Karin was looking perplexed. "You said Mr. Roussos was in the clear—that you were with him when the champagne glasses were being tampered with."

"I know; I was wrong. Nobody went near the glasses at that time. I was conned. There's an intercom in the study which communicates with every other room on the ship—including the small galley. Roussos also has a tape recorder on his desk. He pre-recorded the sound effects—footsteps and galley door closing—two minutes from the start of an otherwise blank tape. Before he left the study he switched both machines on. When he and I got to the saloon, the sounds came through loud and clear from the galley."

"Then who moved the glasses?" Karin demanded. "There were only six when you looked in at half-past ten, but twelve when you came back later."

Webster got to his feet. "Come over here."

The others looked surprised, but followed him across the room to the bar. He pointed to the semi-circular counter on which the champagne glasses had stood. "Watch that," he said. Then he went out by the aft door.

They waited, puzzled, for a minute. Then suddenly there came the sound of a low but noticeable electrical humming. The next moment, one of the wall tiles to which the bar counter was apparently attached slid silently upwards. The dark square hollow in the wall thus exposed revealed that the bar counter was in fact fully circular, but with half of it normally hidden behind the tile. On that half, they could now see, stood six champagne glasses. For three seconds nothing happened. Then the bar counter started to revolve. The six glasses emerged into the light, and having completed a one hundred and eighty degree turn, the counter stopped revolving. The tile in the wall came down and the humming ceased. Their exclamations had not died down when Webster rejoined them. "So easy when you know, isn't it?" he said.

Irene said, "Surely my father didn't have that installed especially?"

"No; he tells me the *Angel* was originally designed for a millionaire who was a fanatic for electronic gadgets—magic-eye doors, voice-activated lights and so on. But he died before the yacht was completed. Your father took it over. He cancelled all the devices except those which were already in operation: several things in the main galley and the sliding drinks cabinet in the cardroom. This thing had been installed but not wired up. When your father decided to make use of it, he did the job himself—last time the *Angel* was laid up and the crew ashore."

Karin said, "But what was it originally for? Did Mr. Roussos tell you? It seems pointless."

"He thinks the first idea was not to have a bar as such in here, but to keep the drink in the small galley, have a corresponding hatch the other side and use the turntable as a gimmicky sort of drinks dispenser. But the original owner was a bit of a practical joker apparently and perhaps he was going to use it to play tricks on his guests—make their drinks change or disappear when they weren't looking."

"And I bet the switch that operates it is in the study safe," Karin said. "That would explain what you said last night."

"Right. Luckily I'd made a mental note of the combination when he opened it in my presence earlier."

Orchard said, "So he used it last night just to give himself an alibi?"

"Yes: to convince me that somebody—whom I was supposed later to believe was Barrault—had been in here, playing about with the glasses, at a time when Roussos himself was in his study with me."

"Could you explain very simply just how it all worked?" Orchard asked.

"The servants laid out twelve glasses. Later Roussos went to his study safe and pressed the switch that spins the turntable, so that those twelve glasses disappeared. Then he came in here, laid out an additional six glasses on this other half of the turntable." Webster picked one of them up. "At ten thirty-five he brought me in here and carefully drew my attention to the fact that, surprisingly, only six glasses were on the bar. He and I then went to his study and he immediately opened the safe and spun the turntable again, making the original twelve glasses reappear. So that when we returned here ten minutes later, there were twelve glasses on the bar—which was apparent proof that while we were in the study, somebody had been meddling with them. In addition, I actually (so I thought) heard the person moving. As a result, for a long time I was absolutely convinced Roussos was in the clear."

They returned to their chairs. Karin said, "How did you get onto that gadget?"

"Through a remark of yours."

"Really?" She looked excited. "What was that?"

"We were upstairs with Roussos. You were making conversation, talking about films. I was hardly listening—just thinking about the problem of who'd moved the glasses. I was picturing the bar with them on it. At that moment I heard you say something like: 'set pieces on revolving turntable stages, different girls each side.' I thought of the unusual design of that bar. I remembered the moving drinks cabinet in the cardroom—and something clicked. I rushed down, and after about five minutes found the switch in the safe."

Irene said, "You must have suspected my father before that, though."

"Oh yes; when I settled down to think last night, I set myself the job of trying to remember anything that had struck me as in any way odd since I'd first come aboard."

"I should think the oddest things were the passengers—all of us," Irene said.

"Precisely. Not so much individually, but as a group. There was such a diversity. There seemed to be no common denominator. It wasn't simply that your father liked to invite any celebrities, as you suggested—most of us weren't celebrities. Nor had he deliberately invited a mixture of celebrities and old friends; because one of the odd things was the fact that about half the guests were obviously well known to each other, were on first name terms, while the rest of us were strangers to them and largely to each other. It was as if there were six insiders on board and six outsiders. Odder still, the host himself seemed to be one of the outsiders. He knew the insiders, but he wasn't one *of* them. Claire, on the other hand, *was*.

"Taken as a group, the insiders seemed to have even less in common than the rest of us: different interests, jobs, nationalities. For example, no two men could be more different than Muller and Trent. Yet they talked to, and of, each other as if they were old cronies. It was the same when Maria arrived: Claire greeted her like a long-lost sister—though she never normally gushed. Yet it seemed inconceivable that those two women could ever be close friends. I could give more examples. In fact, the only thing the six seemed to have in common was a sort of callousness—an indifference to right and wrong, and to the welfare of others. And that is a thing I've noticed in hardened villains. I asked myself if these people could actually be criminals—crime is a thing which links the unlikeliest people together—and if so, what racket they might all be in: an explorer of remote parts of the world; the owner of a laboratory; a UN official, who spent most of his time jetting round the world on a diplomatic passport; and two people who obviously had opportunities for making underworld contacts—a New York criminal lawyer, and the widow of a London club owner. It spelt one thing: drugs. I wasn't able to work out Barrault's precise role, but he seemed the type to fit in, too.

"All that was suggestive, but didn't give me the name of the killer—and remember, at this stage I still believed Roussos was in the clear. All I was sure of was that the murderer had gone to a lot of trouble to frame Barrault —while making it seem that Barrault had framed Constantine. I realized that what he must have been doing was providing an interim suspect, so that Barrault wouldn't be suspected too soon. But until when? Presumably until it was too late for Barrault to clear himself—which could only be when he was dead. Someone, then, had *known* Barrault was going to die. They couldn't have known *I* was going to kill him. So they must have known he was going to die from another cause—in other words, they knew that he was going to be poisoned. Yet thinking back, I was certain nobody could have known Barrault was going to get a particular glass when we drank that toast. Which indicated that he hadn't been poisoned *then* at all, but at some other time."

Irene said, "And if Barrault, why not the others?"

"Exactly. And if so, when? Not too much earlier, or the stuff would have already by then taken effect. It would have had to be shortly before the party. Well, *I'd* taken nothing between dinner and the party. Neither, I was pretty sure, had Orchard, nor Mrs. van Duren. And you two girls had been shut in Irene's cabin most of the time. If I was right, it looked as though we five might be in the clear. Then it occurred to me that the same five of us were the ones I'd previously marked off as the outsiders. Could we have been deliberately got out of the way? That would explain the jamming of Irene's door. But it was Roussos who'd arranged the quizzing of Orchard by Mrs. van Duren—and insisted I be present the whole time. It was he who had invited all these diverse people onto *his* yacht, and changed course unexpectedly, with the result that we were a long way from medical help when the poisoning was discovered. On the other hand, Claire was apparently among the victims, and it's unusual for a man to get tired of his wife after only a year of marriage. Then I remembered how he'd used a rather odd form of words when toasting her—neither giving her his love, nor wishing her many happy returns. By now I was growing highly suspicious of him. Yet there was still the matter of those glasses being moved."

Karin said, "But by then you'd decided the poison wasn't given in those."

"Nevertheless, it appeared that somebody—not a servant—had tampered with them at a time when Roussos was with me. That had to be significant. However, I put the problem aside for the moment, and thought instead about motive. Assuming that the six *were* drug traffickers, the only motive that made sense was revenge. I knew Irene's sister had been killed tragically some years ago. Could she have been on drugs? I went and asked Mrs. van Duren straight out. And—very reluctantly—she told me yes."

Karin said, "When you were speaking to her you asked me to find out from Irene whether there'd ever been any specific threats to kidnap her, and if so whether she'd known about it at the time. Why did you want to know that?"

"Because another big problem was this: if her father was the killer, why had he brought *me* along as her bodyguard? Surely no one in his right mind who was planning a multiple murder would arrange for an experienced detective to be present at the time. It would have been infinitely better to leave Irene at home. So—could he have had a special reason for wanting me on board? In fact, as he's confirmed to me this morning, he had two."

Orchard said, "First, I suppose, he wanted someone to give him an alibi—a trustworthy outsider, whose word would be accepted anywhere."

"That's right; though you would have done for that. I think the other reason was the primary one: he had to have somebody present who would think to do what I did: gather all the glasses together and put them aside for print-dusting and scientific analysis later on. He thought the only type of person who'd be sure to think of that was a policeman.

"Once I'd come to the conclusion that he'd had a secret reason for inviting me, it followed that the ostensible reason was a blind. Now: he'd been very insistent that I told nobody else about the kidnap threat—and especially you, Irene; he said he didn't want you upset. But it occurred to me that there might well have been such threats against you before. So I asked Karin to find out."

"And I told her there had been—twice," Irene said, "when I was ten, and again when I was fourteen. And I'd known about the second one from the start."

"So why weren't you to be told about this one? It suggested strongly that the kidnap threat *was* untrue—but, of course, it didn't prove it. So I decided to stage a test. According to the supposed tip-off, it was a London gang who were planning the snatch, and your father had suggested to me that one of the passengers might be involved. So Karin and I went up to see him, and I asked if the passenger he had suspected was Barrault. He couldn't say 'yes,' because he would then have had to give his grounds. On the other hand, the only logical reason he could have given for saying 'no' was that he suspected someone else—and he knew I'd immediately ask who. So he hedged. As a result I was able to make him admit that Barrault *could* have been the one. Then—well, Karin can tell you what I asked her to do."

Karin said, "I had to pretend I'd found a passage in Philippe's notebook which was an admission that he was collaborating with a London gang in a plan to kidnap Irene."

"Roussos was absolutely staggered," Webster said, "and couldn't avoid showing it. He'd made up a story—and now he'd discovered it was true! But, of course, if his story to me had been genuine, there wouldn't be any reason for surprise. Therefore, I knew he'd invented it. Next, he started talking as though he'd just learnt for the first time that Irene was in danger—and secondly as though there was no doubt she and I were both going to be alive when the *Angel* reached port."

Irene said, "Which meant he knew we hadn't been poisoned."

"Which meant he *believed* we hadn't been poisoned. But—was he right in that belief? For I hadn't forgotten those champagne glasses: somebody had moved them. Was it possible that another person had discovered Roussos's plan, stepped in and somehow twisted it to his or her own advantage? Until I had the answer to that I couldn't accuse Roussos, or tell the rest of you that you were safe. And then, as I explained, Karin gave me the answer. After I found the switch in the safe, I got you all to my room, together with Roussos, and told you the truth. If I'd been in any doubt about his guilt, his failure to rush to Claire the second I told him she was dying would have been enough to dispel it." Webster paused. "That's it. All the rest you know."

"Well, not quite all."

They looked up. It was Roussos.

## 17

Roussos was standing in the doorway. His face was unshaven, white and haggard. He was still wearing his evening shirt and trousers, and clearly hadn't undressed or been to bed.

There was a tense and embarrassed silence. "I couldn't take it up there on my own any longer," Roussos said. His manner was cautious, even diffident. "I been listening to Alec. It's all true enough, but it leaves a few loose ends. I figured you might like to hear my side of it."

He glanced from one to the other, looking finally at Karin, seeming to put on her, presumably as the only woman guest not in some way related to him, the onus of saying if he could remain.

She grasped this, looked for a second at Emily van Duren before pointing to a chair and saying, "You'd better sit down."

Roussos looked relieved, came forward and took the seat. He said, "Thanks. I appreciate it. I know I owe you all an apology for last night. You probably think I'm either some kind of monster, or a nut. Perhaps you'll think different when you've heard me out."

He cleared his throat nervously, then said, "Up to the time Helen died I'd lived a pretty useless sort of life. All I'd done was make money and spend it. But then she was murdered—murdered by drug traffickers as much as if they'd put a gun to her head. There and then I swore I was gonna use some of my money to fight the stinking trade. That's what I've been doing for more than six years now. I've spent over five million bucks on it. I learnt everything I could about the racket. I worked undercover through agents who didn't know my real identity—or each other. Through them I bought information. I hired private detectives all over the world. I bribed cops for photostats of secret records. I bribed lawyers and government officials and customs men and small time crooks. I've organized burglaries. I've used blackmail. I've planted bugs. And when it was necessary I've had people beaten up. Thanks to it all, I've gathered together more facts about the narcotics business than most police forces have got."

He was rapidly gaining confidence. He tapped his pockets, then said, "Got a fag, Alec?"

Webster threw his cigarettes across. Roussos took one and lit it. "Narcotics is a part of organized crime generally, of course. Mostly it's run by big syndicates, who are into all the other rackets as well—gambling, girls, protection and so on. But after a while I started to hear whispers of this outfit that was different—in that the organizers were *only* in drugs—and weren't professional crooks, but what you'd call respectable citizens. That seemed to me real wicked. I mean, to be raised knowing no other life but crime, to make it to the top as some sort of racketeer, and then to branch out into narcotics is bad enough. But to be straight most of your life, to be well off and educated and highly placed socially, and then deliberately become a drugs dealer—that was ten times worse. What's more—and Alec knows this —villains like that are the toughest sort to nail. They're literally above suspicion. The usual police informers just don't know about them. Eye-witnesses can't pick 'em out of mug books—their photos aren't in them. Their prints aren't on file. And so on.

"Well, I concentrated my whole operation on getting this particular group. I won't go into all the details of how I gradually uncovered them. But eventually I had a pretty good picture of their set-up. Like to know how it worked?"

"Yes I would," Webster said.

"Right. It was Trent's job to find sources of raw materials and arrange for transportation. He was perfect for that: he could go anywhere, see anyone, without raising the least suspicion. He'd been hob-nobbing with bandits and brigands quite innocently for years and if the cops had questioned him he'd only have had to say he was writing a book on the international drug scene. His stuff eventually found its way to Maria's lab, where it was processed and refined. It left in neat little packets in the bottom of Paul Muller's diplomatic case—chiefly for New York and London. Incidentally, that's why Paul and Maria got married: he had to keep visiting her place all the time, which would have looked kind've odd—unless they were having an affair. But nobody would have believed that a guy with his reputation had fallen for a dame like Maria Epstein. The only way to convince people he'd done just that was by marrying her. But that's by the way.

"In the States, distribution was Quine's baby. He'd got all the right connections—mostly with people he had too much dirt on for them to be a threat to him. In England the original distributor was Pete Ferris, Claire's first husband. His clubs gave him two outlets: young, wealthy swingers, and the criminal world. Claire knew the business as well as he did, and after he died and she sold the clubs, she still carried on with the drugs distribution."

Karin said, "Philippe—was he a distributor, too—in France?"

"That's right. But he had another job as well. He was the hit man."

Karin's eyes widened in horror and her hand went to her mouth. "You mean . . . ?"

"Yeah—the killer. You see, they had to deal with lots of small-time crooks and pushers, and them punks sometimes gave trouble. It was Barrault's job to deal with them—in his own way, without involving the others. He did at least five killings for them over the years."

Karin turned her head away. Quietly, Irene asked, "Why did they do it?"

"Barrault for kicks—and because he was unbalanced. Maria out of hatred —for the whole world. The others for money: Trent and Quine because they needed it—Trent's books weren't selling, and Quine had to finance a political campaign; Paul Muller and Claire from sheer greed.

"Well, I had all this data. Trouble was, the way it had been obtained meant that hardly any of it would ever be admissible as evidence in court. In addition, if I did give it to the cops, I might lay myself open to criminal charges. So I knew I had to take the law into my own hands—or these six were never gonna get what was coming to them."

"George." Emily van Duren broke her long silence and fixed him with a piercing gaze. "Was that the only reason you decided to take the law into your own hands. Didn't you *want* to take revenge yourself—for Helen?"

"Yes, I did. But I wouldn't have done it if I'd thought the law could give 'em their deserts. And I mean deserts. They were cold-blooded killers, and I wanted them to die. *Their* victims had died slowly, their minds and bodies poisoned by drugs. I made up my mind this lot had to die the same way— slowly. They had to know they were dying. And they had to be cut off from any chance of medical help.

"I thought for a long time about the best way to execute them. I could have hired a pro to do it, but I'd never ask anyone to kill for me. I had to do it myself. But I'm no martyr. I wasn't going to sacrifice my own life, or end up in prison. So I had to act real careful. I had personal dossiers on all of them, and I studied them for hours. At last I decided my best opening was with Claire. The main thing about her was that she loved money. I got the impression she'd do anything for it. She also liked men; but she wasn't a chicken no more, her looks were starting to go and she had a bitchy tongue. So she wasn't much liked, and there wasn't a special man in her life. I told myself that if I couldn't get her to marry me within a year, I ought to give up the whole campaign. Well, in short, I could—and she did.

"She didn't like me, of course—she thought I was dead common. But she couldn't resist my money. She hated herself for that—and she grew to hate me for having the money which she couldn't resist. That was the reason for all those digs at me—she had to get back at me for the fact that I'd been able to buy her. I used to enjoy overplaying the loud-mouthed slob, just to needle her. Because I tell you, she was just about the nastiest person I've ever met."

Roussos stubbed out his cigarette. "After we got spliced, I had to convince her I was a crook. The charades I went through! Eventually she must have thought she'd married Al Capone. Sometimes I'd get onto the subject of drugs and say if people got hooked it was their own stupid fault and good luck to anyone who took the dopes' money off 'em. For months she didn't rise to it. Then at last she came out with it—proud, you know, that she was as smart as me: she was one of the leading lights in a dope ring. I pretended to be real impressed, and then told her I'd like a piece of the action. I pointed out that if I could inject some capital into the operation, we could put it into the really big time. She was all for that. You'd think as my wife she'd have had all the money she wanted. But no. She'd had to give up her distribution duties temporarily when she married me—the others were sharing the work—and apparently there'd been talk of them dropping her from the team permanent. But now she saw a chance of getting right back in again. So she started trying to talk the others into taking me on as a sort of sleeping partner. They weren't any too keen at first, but in the end she persuaded them to meet me. I saw them individually over a period, but I made sure nothing was ever decided firmly. Eventually I told Claire the only way we were going to settle anything was if we all got together for some really long talks. They were reluctant because they'd made it a rule never to all meet together unless it was really vital. But at last they agreed. I suggested the *Angel* as the venue . . .

"I think it was the name of this yacht and the old legend of the angel of death that gave me the idea how to do it," Roussos continued. "I liked to think of myself as the angel, bringing the death. Then, at sea was the best place for being out of reach of doctors. Also, there was that turntable bar nobody knew about; I was sure I could utilize it some way, if I was going to give the poison in booze, which seemed best.

"Trouble was if half of my cruise guests died of poisoning, I'd be number one suspect—no cop would buy that being an accident. What's more, if those six found out that all of them had been poisoned, and nobody else, they'd realize that that couldn't be chance—and they'd finger me. Then I had the idea of framing one of the six and making it look like he or she had turned on the others. But there was going to be that time-lag between the poisoning and the deaths—which would give the fall-guy a chance to convince the others he wasn't guilty. And I'd be straight back in the hot seat. Then I got the idea of a stop-gap fall-guy—one just to fool the victims themselves—but who wouldn't be suspected by the cops once my phoney evidence against the real fall-guy came to light.

"The obvious choice for the real fall-guy was Barrault. I knew from my investigators all about his obsession with risking his life. If I could make it look like he'd been playing some maniac's game and that the identity of the victims was pure chance—that I myself, and my own daughter, could just as easily have been among them—then I'd be in the clear. The first time I met him he happened to write an address down for me on a page he tore from his notebook, and that gave me the idea. I had a sample of the paper and his writing. I got one of my agents to pay a forger to write out that poisoning scheme in French on a similar piece of paper.

"Planning everything took months. The only real stroke of luck I had was over the digoxin tablets, Emily. I'd figured on having to do a lot of research into poisons, but I remembered you talking about your pills years ago, and when I looked them up they turned out to be perfect for me. And I thought using them would make it look still more like it was all planned after the cruise started. I made sure you had spares before I pinched yours, of course."

"Most considerate of you," Mrs. van Duren said drily.

"You played into my hands, you know—coming out later in front of everybody about them being so poisonous. But don't blame yourself: if you hadn't mentioned it, I'd have worked the conversation round to how dangerous they were myself. Anyway, that's jumping ahead. I picked on Constantine as the stop-gap fall-guy because I knew he was a bit weird. I found out he always had a glass of orange juice last thing, and my dossiers told me Barrault sometimes took sleeping pills; I got hold of some of the same.

"I knew I had to make up the number of passengers to twelve, so it'd look feasible that Barrault should have had the idea of the fifty-fifty poisoning gamble. Also, I needed some reliable independent witnesses to everything that went on, to give me an alibi, and so on. And Alec's told you why I wanted a cop, and so made up all that malarky about a kidnap threat. I wrote the tip-off letter myself. I was pretty proud of being able to fool you with that, Alec. But as I told you, one of the ways I learnt English was by listening to girls in dockside pubs."

"I did say I wouldn't want to bet on it being genuine."

"Yeah. Anyway, I wanted you to keep quiet about the threat. I couldn't have Claire and the others thinking I knew about a possible kidnapping and hadn't told them. They'd be pretty mad—and suspicious—if it looked like I'd got 'em all together, knowing there could be an incident which might involve calling in the cops."

Irene said, "The attack in the forest must have been just an ordinary mugging, a coincidence."

"No," Roussos said. "I arranged that."

She stared. "What?"

"I had to back up the kidnap threat, and have an excuse to change course for the Dominican Republic. I wanted to make sure we were at least eight hours from port when the poisoning took place—I was determined there was gonna be no chance of medical help before they were dead—and no one would normally *plan* to start a cruise by sailing over seven hundred miles non-stop across the Caribbean."

"But I don't understand," Irene persisted. "You mean those thugs weren't crooks?"

"Oh, they were crooks all right. But they were put up to the job. They were told to put the frighteners on, but not harm any of you."

"And I shot two of the poor devils," Webster said grimly.

"I know. I don't figure they bargained for that. I'm gonna see they get compensation."

"I might have killed them."

"Don't think so. You'd never shoot to kill, Alec—even though you might think you were doing so."

"How did you know I'd be going for a walk?" Irene asked.

"I got Quine to invite you—told him you were depressed and I thought perhaps he could pull you out of it."

"That should have made me suspicious," Webster said. "Your letting her go for a walk with only Quine for protection, and not even alerting me."

"You had no cause to think I was up to anything at that time. Anyway, after that nobody thought it was queer when I changed the itinerary. So then everything was set. D'you wanta hear about just what I did?"

He looked round. Irene said, "You might as well finish the story now."

"OK. On Friday afternoon I crushed up sixty of Emily's tablets, dissolved them in vodka and put equal quantities of the poison in six glasses on the cocktail cabinet in my private sitting room upstairs. Then I told Claire and the others we had to get down to serious discussion about my joining their outfit, as I had some important propositions to put to them. I suggested we spend the evening upstairs, and say afterwards we'd been watching a movie. I said we had to see that you five were kept out of the way. They all agreed, and later they co-operated: Claire slipped the sedative in Karin's dinner wine, Muller spilt his coffee on Irene's dress, and Barrault followed her down and jammed the door. Course, we didn't know you two kids were gonna be together or we'd never have bothered lacing the wine. Afterwards, the others all went upstairs. I said I'd join them in a few minutes, when I'd had a word with the stewards who'd be getting the saloon ready for the party. I did that, then went to Constantine's cabin and drugged his orange juice with the tablets I'd got like Barrault took. I meant it to be thought later that Barrault had tried to kill him, but hadn't given a big enough dose."

Irene asked, "What about the book and cards and marker Alec found there?"

"I planted them before the cruise, so that if Constantine found them he'd think they'd been left by the previous occupant—this was the first trip he'd had that particular cabin. From there I went to Barrault's stateroom. I'd lifted the notebook several days ago and inserted the bogus pages. I put it under his mattress. Then I joined the others upstairs. We talked until about nine-forty, when I left them to discuss some matter in my absence. I came down to the small galley and made up more of the digoxin poison by crushing up some of the additional tablets I'd got hold of before the cruise."

Irene said, "Why did you want more of it?"

"I'm coming to that. I had six champagne glasses on the table while I was doing it and I purposely spread the powder round as much as I could."

Orchard said: "That was simply so that there would be six ring marks left in the powder?"

"That's right. I wanted Alec to work it out exactly as he did. I put the new poison in a small medicine bottle. Then I went to my study safe and fetched a bottle of vodka I'd put there some days ago after seeing Barrault handle it. I came back and poured a little plain vodka into each of the twelve champagne glasses Dimitri had laid out on the bar."

"Why?" Karin and Irene asked this together.

"So that when we came to drink the toast the champagne would taste strange to all of you. It was essential to my plan that everybody knew six of us had been poisoned, but not which six. Anyway, I left the vodka bottle in the small galley, together with the other things—and Emily's pill bottle, still containing her remaining twelve tablets. Then I spun the turntable—you can do it manually from underneath the bar if you know how—and set out the extra six glasses—empty—on the other side. When I'd done that I went to the radio room and put the transmitter out of action. I rejoined the others at about five past ten."

Orchard said, "Suppose we'd come out of the writing-room and seen you?"

"It wouldn't have mattered terribly. It's unlikely that after what I'd said earlier any of you would have come in here, let alone go to the small galley. If by some chance you did see me—well, nobody'd been poisoned at that stage and at worst I could have abandoned everything. The cruise had a long time to run, and I had several other plans up my sleeve if last night's fell through. But no one did see me."

"It could have come out later that you'd left the others for nearly half-an-hour," Orchard persisted.

"No reason why it should. If my plan worked, nobody would have ever thought that that period—nine-forty to ten-five—had any connection with the poisoning. Anyway, we carried on the discussion until about ten-twenty. Then I gave way on several points, so we came to agreement quickly. They were all bucked, and I said we'd better seal the compact with a drink. I went to the cocktail cabinet and got those six glasses. No one was standing near me or even watching me especially closely and they never saw there was already something in the glasses. I topped them up with ordinary liquor and passed them round. A minute later they were all as good as dead."

Everyone was silent. Roussos went on hurriedly. "We split up then. But remember I was fixing things so it would look like Barrault came straight down and poisoned the champagne glasses in the galley. I had to make sure nobody would later be able to alibi him. So I asked him to do me a favour—give an expert opinion on the blueprint and description of some new type of car engine I'd been asked to invest in. I told him that I'd only just remembered I'd promised to cable a reply first thing next morning. He was flattered. I got the papers from my study and suggested he read them in the cardroom, which was quiet and empty. I knew it couldn't take him much less than thirty minutes. He'd just gone in there when Alec arrived. I then made sure I was with Alec every second until the party started—in order to have a good excuse to talk to him I'd deliberately kept back a letter he'd been asking to see.

"Just after ten forty-five Alec and I came in here and then the rest of you arrived. Apart from placing the envelope containing the warning message on the table there were only two more things I had to do. After the toast, I made a mental note of where the six had put down their glasses. I had that little extra bottle of poison in my pocket; and during the confusion following Maria's outburst, when everyone was crowding round her and Alec, I slipped a couple of drops into each of those six glasses. Get the point?"

Orchard said, "It ensured that when the dregs were analysed, poison would indeed be found in the champagne glasses carrying the fingerprints of the six victims."

"Yeah. I was pretty sure a detective like Alec would see to it they were stashed away without being handled too much or washed."

"How long did adding the poison take you?" Webster asked.

"Not much more than half a minute."

"It must have been the riskiest part of the whole operation."

"Maybe. But I got away with it. The only other thing I had to do was go back upstairs later on in the night and wash those other six glasses—the ones the poison had really been given in." He paused. "And now I guess you do know everything."

Again nobody spoke. It was difficult to think of any suitable comment. At last Orchard asked, "Why did you invite me on this cruise—I mean me specifically?"

"I figured there ought to be a priest on board, in case any of them wanted one when they were dying. Condemned prisoners always have that right."

"You just invited me in a professional capacity?"

"More or less. I read you'd started off as a Catholic and then switched to being a Protestant, so I figured you'd know how to deal with both kinds. I gotta kind've reputation for hunting celebrities, so I didn't figure anyone'd think it odd my inviting you. It worked out very well."

"Don't you mean it would have done—if I'd had the faintest idea of how to deal with the situation? In fact, I was no help to anybody."

"That suited me fine. I didn't want them really helped. I just meant you to go through the motions. I never figured on Emily stepping in like she did and preaching to them. I didn't want them comforted. I intended them to suffer."

"And it didn't matter to you," Webster said, "that we five were going to suffer too."

"It did matter to me. But it was only gonna be for a couple've hours. Then, as I figured it, they'd develop poisoning symptoms—they'd know they *were* dying, and you'd all know you *weren't*. That was when the real punishment was gonna start."

"But think what you put us through before that," Orchard said.

"I did think—in advance—about you all. And I figured you were a priest and shouldn't be scared of dying, and Emily's been rabbiting on for years about soon going to be with the Lord, so it oughtn't to be too much of a shock to think she was going straight away. Alec was as well fitted to handle the situation as anyone I'd ever met. Karin wasn't supposed to be involved—it was only after I'd made all the arrangements that Barrault asked if he could bring her. I couldn't say no, and it was too late to cancel everything. I'm real sorry, love," he added, addressing her.

"I'll forgive you. But you haven't mentioned Irene."

"Irene was necessary. Nobody was going to suspect me of risking the life of my own daughter. So having her on board would be something else to help keep me in the clear. Besides, she always comes on these cruises, and I had to keep things looking natural." He looked at her. "I worried over it a lot, honey, before making up my mind. Then I thought: so what? It won't do her any harm, and it might even do her a bit of good—teach her to count her blessings in the future. If I didn't think you had the backbone to come through it none the worse, I'd never have done it."

"I suppose I should be flattered," she said.

"Look," Roussos said, glancing round the circle, "I know I treated you all badly, and on certain conditions I'm willing to try and make it up to you."

There were some puzzled looks at this and Webster asked, "What do you mean? What conditions?"

"I mean I wanta know what's gonna happen to me. I'm in your hands—the five of you. If you spill the beans, I'm in trouble. But have you got to? I had Barrault all set up to carry the can. He could still do that—the crew don't know what's happened, so I can square them. Remember, I can prove to you he's a multi-murderer, so you won't be doing his memory an injustice. It'll be worth a million bucks apiece to you—in cash, in any currency you like, deposited in any bank in any country in the world." He looked at Irene. "And for you, my blessing for a college education. So—how about it? Alec?"

"Nothing doing. I killed Barrault. I know too much about police methods and forensic science to imagine that fact can't be proved. I'm not unduly worried, because Karin can testify that he came at me with a knife—and because of what'll be known of my past character, and his. But my only chance is to tell the absolute truth. If I were to lie in any particular and be found out, I'd ruin my chances."

Emily van Duren said, "And I should have hoped, George, that you knew me well enough to realize that I would never—"

"OK, OK." Roussos cut her short. "You'd all have to agree for the thing to work, so that's that. Well, it was worth trying."

He suddenly sounded subdued again—and a bit frightened. "Looks like I'm just gonna have to fight it through the courts, don't it?"

Karin said, "You'll have lots of people on your side, I'm sure of that."

He looked a little more cheerful. "Yeah, I will, won't I? Say, it could be quite a fight. And, after all, I did do what I set out to do—I'll have that satisfaction."

"And just how satisfying has it been so far?" Emily van Duren asked him. "Eh?"

"You set out to avenge Helen's death. You wanted to see these people suffer and die. I'm asking if you enjoyed the experience?"

Roussos took out a handkerchief and blew his nose. "Well, it didn't work out as I meant it to—"

"It did in the case of Claire and Mr. Quine. Did you enjoy seeing them die?"

"Well, let me say—" He caught Emily van Duren's eye and stopped short. His own eyes dropped. Then: "No, I guess not," he said quietly.

"You felt sorry for them?"

"OK—I felt sorry for them. So what? You can feel sorry for a pig, can't you, when you see it being slaughtered? That don't stop you eating pork. And remember this: I've closed the operation down—saved perhaps hundreds of lives—that's the important thing. I reckon people'll call me a benefactor."

"Not all people," Webster said.

"Well, no, of course, there'll be sticklers for the law—"

"No I'm thinking of those men Maria Muller mentioned last night—those backers."

"Aw, they don't exist. She made the whole thing up."

"With what object?"

"Spite. So that I shouldn't think I'd beaten them completely. And to keep me on edge. Listen—I've been studying this outfit for nearly four years. There were no backers."

Webster shrugged. "You should know."

"I do. The only people I gotta worry about now are the judge and jury I'm gonna have to face."

"Well, you haven't *got* to face them," Webster said.

"Eh?"

"There is a possible way out for you."

"What's that?"

"I don't see why I should point it out. But you could put us and the bodies ashore in a couple of lifeboats, then turn about and make for one of the banana republics on the mainland—one which doesn't have an extradition treaty—"

Roussos cut him short. "No chance! Thanks, but I ain't running and skulking in South America for the rest of my life."

Before Webster could reply, Irene raised her hand. "Quiet a minute."

They all listened. Through the open windows there came to their ears a distant buzzing sound.

Orchard said, "Sounds like a motor-boat."

Karin stood up, went outside and scanned the sea. "It is—a speedboat," she called. "It seems to be coming straight towards us."

The others, apart from Mrs. van Duren, joined her on deck. The boat, small and white, was approaching at high speed, the note of its engine getting ever louder.

Roussos said, "Where's it come from? There's no land for about five hundred miles in that direction."

Very soon they could see that there were two men in the boat, and then that they were dressed identically in white seamen's uniforms, caps and dark glasses.

The boat continued in a dead straight line until it was a mere forty yards away. At this point it reduced speed, turned sharply to starboard and took up a course parallel to the *Angel's* and at the same speed. Neither of the occupants of it waved, called or made any attempt to communicate.

"This is damned odd," Roussos muttered.

Karin said, "They're rather sinister, aren't they—just ignoring us. Like men from *Invasion of the Body Snatchers.*"

"There's no name on her—nor any marking at all," Webster said, shielding his eyes and staring at the boat.

At that moment a voice called from their left, "Mr. Roussos." Webster glanced sideways and saw one of the crew approaching.

"Yes?" Roussos looked round and took a step or two towards the man, while Webster turned his attention back to the speedboat.

Irene said, "You know, I don't like this. I—"

A shot rang out.

For one second Webster froze, uncomprehending. Then he spun towards the sound.

Five yards away Roussos was standing quite still, his back to them. Facing him, equally motionless, was the crewman. His arm was outstretched and in his hand was a revolver.

For two seconds the scene was like a photograph. But the next moment it became a movie. Roussos buckled at the knees and slumped slowly onto the deck. At the same moment the sailor dropped his gun, ran to the rail, climbed onto it and dived. He hit the sea cleanly and vanished beneath the surface. Then he reappeared—swimming madly towards the speedboat.

Irene screamed "Dad!" and rushed towards her father.

Webster stepped back from the rail, put one hand on it and vaulted straight over it. He dropped feet first into the water. It closed over his head and he felt himself sinking like a stone. Then he was rising again and a moment later broke surface. He dashed the water from his eyes, blinked round, trying to get his bearings, then struck out strongly towards the bobbing speedboat.

Behind Webster, the *Angel* began to slow sharply as Haller, in the wheelhouse, signalled "full astern." On the deck, Irene had fallen on her knees beside her father. Orchard and Mrs. van Duren had also hurried up, and crew members began to approach from all directions. Karin could do nothing to help and she remained glued to the side, watching the race going on in the water.

The sailor had had a start, but he was splashing a lot and clearly was not a good swimmer. Already Webster was gaining. Then, as Karin watched, the speedboat turned inwards and accelerated. Within seconds it was less than twenty yards from the first swimmer, and Karin realized Webster wasn't going to make it. She gripped the rail, almost jumping up and down with frustration. She looked round, desperately seeking somebody or something that could help. Her eyes alighted on the sailor's revolver, still lying on the deck. She raced to it, fell on her knees by it and snatched it up. She'd never fired a gun in her life, but years of movie-going now stood her in good stead. Still kneeling, she straightened her arm, raised the revolver to eye level, took aim at the speedboat and squeezed the trigger.

The gun jumped in her hand and the shot missed. But the bullet went close enough to make both men in the boat jerk their heads up and stare at the *Angel* in obvious alarm. One, who had been leaning over the side, arm outstretched towards the man in the water, threw himself down below the gunwhale, out of sight. Karin levelled the revolver again and fired a second shot. This time she had the thrill of seeing the white of the speedboat's hull suddenly scarred black. Then the boat's engine roared, the craft swung round and tore away, leaving a frothy, milk-like wake churning behind it. Even above the motor, Karin heard the cry of rage and despair from the sailor in the water. The next moment Webster was on him and the two men became indistinguishable in a wild threshing of arms and legs.

Karin jumped to her feet and spun round. The deck now seemed to be crowded with people—bending over Roussos, surrounding Karin herself or watching the struggle in the water. Among the former was Captain Haller, who had hurriedly left the wheelhouse. She ran to him, grabbed his arm and pointed frantically towards Webster. "A boat!" she yelled. "Lower a boat! Help him!"

Haller gave a crisp nod and shouted an order.

Three minutes later an exhausted Webster and a half-drowned sailor were being rowed back towards the yacht.

## 18

Webster, in dry clothes, followed Dimitri wearily along the passageway and up the stairs to the main deck. He was aching in every limb and his left arm was throbbing unbearably. The knife wound had opened up again while he was swimming and a lot of salt water had got into it. A steward had just re-bandaged it, but that hadn't stopped the pain and it would obviously have to be stitched.

Dimitri, tears running down his cheeks, led the way to the main saloon, pushed through the cluster of crew members waiting outside and went in, Webster at his heels. Roussos, a blanket covering all but his face, and a pillow under his head, was lying outstretched on the big settee. His face was a sickly grey and his eyes were closed. Irene was kneeling on the floor beside him, gripping his hand. Emily van Duren was standing near, and the only other person present was Hilary Orchard, waiting near the door.

Webster whispered to him, "Still alive?"

"Barely. He's just put a confession to the murders on tape. Did Dimitri tell you he's been asking for you?"

"Yes, that's why I'm here."

Webster went quietly across to the settee. Irene glanced up, then put her mouth close to Roussos's face and said softly, "Alec's here."

As if with a great effort, Roussos forced his eyes open. "Alec. You—you got him?" The words were barely audible.

Webster nodded. "Under lock and key."

"Who—who sent him? Was it the—the . . . ?" He tailed off.

"The backers? Yes. That sailor was planted on board to keep an eye on things. He had a transmitter in his cabin and he was reporting regularly to another ship that's been shadowing us. When we changed course, we threw them off and they dropped out of range of his radio. They must have caught up, because this morning he was able to get through and report the six deaths. Later they radioed back and promised him twenty-five thousand dollars if he would wait until he heard the speedboat which would pick him up—and then shoot you."

Roussos managed a weak nod. He whispered, "Thought so. Believed Maria really about those friends. Couldn't admit it. Did he say who—who they . . . ?"

"Who they are? No; he swears he doesn't know. Says he's never met them
—that his instructions before we sailed were given by letter and phone. I
believe him."

The next words came in a croak and Webster had to bend down to hear
them properly. "You find them. Track them down. Irene?"

Irene bent lower. "Yes?"

"You inherit everything. Hire Alec—full time—salary—expenses—everything he wants—assistants—access all my papers—nothing spared—to find
those backers. Promise?"

"Yes, of course, I promise."

"Alec—you'll do it?"

"I'll try. I won't kill them. But I will do my utmost to identify them, get
evidence against them, and hand them over to the police."

An expression of intense satisfaction spread over Roussos's face.
"Thanks."

"No—it's for me to thank you."

For half a minute Roussos lay silent, his eyes closed, seemingly gathering
his last remaining strength. Then his eyelids slid back again and he looked at
Irene. "You'll be one—richest girls in world. Not just seven—seventeenth
richest, eh?"

"That's right."

"Get rid of the *Angel*. Bad memories. Buy your own yacht."

"I'll do that."

"Keep on Haller—Dimitri—anyone who wants job."

"Of course."

"Call her something different."

"Shall I call her the *Helen?* Would you like that?"

"Yeah—yeah—good. Emily?"

"Yes, George?" Mrs. van Duren came closer.

"You been praying for me?"

"Of course."

"I gotta be all right then, ain't I? All leave now, please—'cept Irene."

Silently the others trooped onto the deck. Karin was outside. She said,
"How is he?"

"Dying," Webster said.

"I couldn't come in."

"No reason why you should."

Four minutes passed. Then Irene emerged. Her eyes were moist. "He's
gone."

"I'm very sorry," Webster said.

"I—I was never fond of him. But I suppose he wasn't too bad, really."

"No," Webster said, "he wasn't too bad at all."

"You know something?" Karin said in the dining-room later, when they were all finishing a final meal before reaching port. "I wouldn't live through all that again for a dozen Oscars—but I don't regret having lived through it once."

"What makes you say that?" Webster asked.

"I think it's done me good. I'd become so smug lately—young and healthy and successful and everybody saying I was beautiful and talented. It all seemed so permanent and important. After last night I'll never think that again. I suppose you could say I've got things more into perspective."

Irene said, "Well, at the very end I did get to know my father for the first time in my life. Maybe if he'd lived I wouldn't have liked him any better. But I had stopped hating him. So I guess it was a good thing I came too."

"I was certainly given a sharp reminder of what being a parson's all about," Orchard said. "And shown what a poor specimen of one I've been. I'm going to have to rethink my career priorities very carefully." He looked at Emily van Duren. "Thank you for being such an effective object-lesson."

"And so brave," Karin added. "She was by far the calmest one of us last night."

Unexpectedly Mrs. van Duren gave a sudden loud chortle. "Brave? Calm? I was absolutely terrified!"

They all stared at her. Karin exclaimed, "You? Terrified?"

"Utterly. All the time I was praying the words 'Take me. Spare somebody else and take me.' But my heart was saying, 'Not yet. Just give me a few more years.' "

Orchard said, "But your faith seemed so strong."

"Oh, it was. That's the trouble. I can't understand why a secularist should be frightened of death. But I know Who I'm going to meet when I die, and I can't think of anything more daunting than that. However, I think I may have conquered that fear last night. When my time does come, perhaps I'll really be able to face it calmly."

Webster asked, "How on earth did you manage to keep up such a bold front?"

"Why, Mr. Webster, you as an Englishman surely know all about the principle of not letting the side down."

Webster smiled. "I think that makes your performance even more impressive."

"Good. If I've made just one atheist think a little—"

"I'm not an atheist."

"Oh, a fence-sitter, eh? Got to get down sometime, you know—one side or the other."

"I think perhaps I'm a good bit closer to getting down your side than I was fifteen hours ago."

"Then grant me a favour. I suppose now that you're going to be working for my granddaughter, you'll be visiting Boston from time to time to report progress?"

"Very probably."

"Then will you come to church with me and give thanks for your deliverance?"

"Honoured, ma'am."

"Good. That's a date. If, of course, I'm still alive when you come, which must be doubtful."

"Grandmother," Irene said, "don't be a humbug. Anyone with a weak heart who survived last night is obviously capable of living to be well over a hundred. Besides, you've just got to be present at the opening of the best school in the world."

Webster raised his eyebrows. "Oh? So the project is on, is it?"

She nodded firmly. "Though not right away, of course. First I'm going to university, and after that get myself some practical teaching experience. So you see, Grandmother, you can't possibly die for years yet."

"Well," Mrs. van Duren drew her backbone one degree straighter. "I must admit that I haven't felt quite so well in a very long time as I do now. I daresay anything's possible."

A minute or so later they went to their rooms to make final preparations for going ashore. When he'd finished, Webster made his way back up to the main deck to watch the approach to St. Croix. Here, a minute or so later, he was joined by Karin.

"By the way," he said, "I didn't thank you properly for your help earlier on. That was great shooting. Congratulations."

"Oh, they don't call me the Swedish Annie Oakley for nothing."

They stood in silence for a minute, side by side, leaning on the rail, gazing at the sea. For some reason, Webster felt oddly constrained.

Eventually, Karin said, "Well, that's it. My first cruise on a private yacht. I must say, it wasn't exactly as I'd anticipated."

"No; still, no doubt there'll be plenty of others," he said stiltedly.

She said, "I suppose things will be pretty hectic for a while after we reach port—police, lawyers, court hearings, reporters and so on."

"Inevitable, I'm afraid."

"So I don't expect we'll have much chance to talk again."

"Probably not."

"And as soon as the formalities are over, you'll be off on this manhunt."

"Yes, at the earliest possible moment."

"I'm sure you'll catch them."

"Thanks."

He wanted badly to say more to her—a lot more. But he couldn't.

"Well," she said, "think of me sometimes, slaving over a hot film set."

Ironically, it was as if she were deliberately giving him the opportunity to say what he wanted. The temptation to do so was very strong. But he resisted it. It wouldn't be fair. All he allowed himself to say was: "You can rely on it."

She was silent, almost compelling him to continue. He forced himself to say, "And you can be sure I'll never miss another of your pictures."

"There'll probably only be two," she said. "That's all I'm contracted for."

"There'll be another contract, though, that's for sure."

"But I may not sign it."

He stared at her. "Why not?"

"I'm seriously thinking of quitting the business."

He gaped. "You can't mean it!"

She nodded. "I'm getting rather tired of making pictures. I've been disenchanted by seeing what goes on. Of course, I'd always been told that the film business wasn't a glamorous life at all—just toil and tears and so on. But I suppose that deep down I never really believed it. Then I went into moviemaking in Sweden and I saw that what they said was true. I must have told myself subconsciously that things would be different in Hollywood. But of course, they're not. And it's changing me—for the worst. I don't enjoy watching films so much, either. Basically, I'm really just a film fan who somehow got the wrong side of the camera. I was happier the other side. I might feel different if I knew I could get the sort of parts I want. But I never will be able to. They're not written any more. So when I've fulfilled my contract—in about twelve months or so—I really think I'll pack it in. And imagine retiring, not at the peak of my fame, but before I'd ever reached it! I'd out-Garbo Greta. I might become a legend."

Webster's brain was racing as fast as when he'd been facing Barrault's knife. Would she really do it? And if so, did it make a difference? If she stopped being a celebrity, stopped earning ten times more than he could ever hope to . . . Yes, it would make a difference. But not a big enough one.

"It'll take an awful lot of guts to do it," he said, "though I know for a fact that's something you don't lack. But what will you do instead?"

"Perhaps just settle down as a housewife. Unless you could do with a girl assistant, of course. How about it? We might end up like William Powell and Myrna Loy in *The Thin Man.*"

Why did she keep saying things like that? Was she just joking, or was she really trying to tell him something? He had to know. Somehow keeping his voice casual, he said, "Sounds great. But how do you mean 'end up'?"

"Well . . ." She hesitated. "You know."

Suddenly, to his own surprise as much as hers, he took her by the shoulders and swung her round to face him. "Listen," he said loudly, "this is ridiculous. Forget it."

"Forget *The Thin Man*?"

"You know perfectly well what I mean."

The next moment, to his amazement, there were tears in her eyes. "But, Alec, how can you be like this—after last night? Oh, I know there was nothing said, still less anything done. I don't think you even touched me. But I really thought we'd found something—that if we both came through all right—"

He interrupted. "Last night was exceptional. Nothing like it has ever happened to either of us before, and I sincerely hope it never will again. We were thrown together in a very terrifying crisis. You'd just lost Philippe. You needed someone to lean on, someone to look after you."

"And I still do."

"Now—at this moment—maybe. But not for long. Last night I was the only person available. But soon you'll be back in Hollywood. You'll meet boys of your own age and way of life. You'll soon find someone to replace Philippe —someone more worthwhile than he was. Now, let's leave things like that— it's the only sane thing to do."

"Trouble is, I've never been much of a one for doing the sane thing."

"Trouble is, I have."

There was quite a long pause. Then she smiled moistily. "That's quite a brush-off. OK, I get the message. I'll go off and make my movies. You go off and catch your crooks." She turned away.

Relief and misery fought within him. "I'll certainly try," he said.

"Are you looking forward to it?" She was making small-talk.

"Yes—in one sense. But I'm not underestimating the size of the job."

"Nervous?"

"Not exactly. Apprehensive, perhaps."

Her voice bright and cheerful again now, she asked, "How long do you think it'll take?"

"Impossible to say. But if I haven't done it in twelve months, I never will."

"So it looks as if we might both be at a loose end at about the same time." And with these words the brightness faded from her voice. She looked as well as sounded utterly forlorn.

Webster felt a sharp pang of remorse. *He'd* done this to her—and after what she'd been through in the past twenty-four hours. He'd been behaving like a rat. He had to undo the damage—quickly.

Suddenly the idea struck him. Twelve months. There couldn't be any question of taking advantage of her after all that time. Of course, she'd almost certainly have found somebody else by then. But it might cheer her up now. And it would give him something to dream about, too. Then, if by some miracle, she still felt the same in a year—well, was anything really impossible?

Quickly, before he had time to change his mind again, he said, "If you like, perhaps we could get together then—just to compare notes, and so on."

She looked up at him, her eyes big. She seemed to think the suggestion over, and he held his breath. Then her face lit up and excitedly she said, "You mean, fix the exact time and place now—like Charles Boyer and Irene Dunn in *Love Affair?*"

"Sure. Why not?"

"Oh, that's a super idea!"

"But you mustn't feel under any obligation to keep the date, if you don't want to. Just drop me a line—I won't hold it against you at all."

"I'll keep it, all right. You'd better, too—or else. When?"

"Twelve noon a year from today."

"Right. Where?"

"I'll leave that to you."

"Well, not the Empire State Building. Irene Dunn was crippled on her way there. We could meet under the clock at the Astor, like Judy Garland and—"

He interrupted with a grin. "Look—I'll pick you up, all right? Just be waiting for me at noon."

"But where?"

"Wherever you happen to be."

"But I'll have been filming. I could be anywhere. You're not to get in touch with me in advance—that would spoil everything. So how will you know where to find me?"

"I'm a detective, aren't I?" said Webster.

James Anderson is the author of nine other crime novels, six of which have been published in both England and the United States—and have been translated into German, Italian, Portuguese, Dutch, Swedish, Norwegian, and Japanese. He has written three Jessica Fletcher "Murder, She Wrote" novelizations. *Angel of Death* is Mr. Anderson's third novel for the Crime Club. His first, *Assault and Matrimony,* was a recent made-for-TV movie starring Jill Eikenberry and Michael Tucker.